Beauty and the Beast

Other **BEAUTY AND THE BEAST** *Novels*
from Avon Books

BEAUTY AND THE BEAST
by Barbara Hambly

Coming Soon

SONG OF ORPHEUS
by Barbara Hambly

Beauty and the Beast

MASQUES

A Novel by
RU EMERSON

Based on the series created by
RON KOSLOW

AVON BOOKS ◆ NEW YORK

AVON BOOKS
A division of
The Hearst Corporation
105 Madison Avenue
New York, New York 10016

First Avon Books Printing: September 1990

For my mother
and for Doug

But mostly,
for Linus

One

AFTER so many years in London, she had forgotten how cool it could be in New York after dark, this time of year. After the airless theater, after exacting hours of *Swan Lake* for a packed house, and then the overheated, richly rose- and carnation-scented warmth of her dressing room, the night air hit her face like an icy blow. Lisa Campbell pulled the collar of her dark winter coat against the back of her neck under dark, shining hair, snugged the red scarf close and stood still, studying the passageway before her. This was Manhattan—Lincoln Center, not the Bronx, she reminded herself firmly. But after so many years, it was unfamiliar territory, and so, threatening. The narrow alley that led from the stage door out to the side street was an eerie pale blue under mercury streetlights. Light reflected from windows in the buildings that flanked the passage, reflected from corrugated metal, from the wet pavement. The street was out there, only a few paces away and down half a dozen concrete steps. She couldn't see it from where she stood.

There were piles of things everywhere, remnants of ballets and plays past stacked along the walls to her right and left. Hiding places for the small and large hunters that plague a city, she thought. But they were not her concern at the moment; and she had a more skilled hunter to evade than anything New York might offer.

Lisa leaned back against the heavy metal door, letting only her eyes move at first, taking in her immediate surroundings. No one and nothing by the door itself, no sound of anyone on its other side, following her. Just now, that was all she cared about. *No one must know. Collin Hemmings in particular must never know.*

The air was almost too cold to breathe; still, it was cleaner than what she'd breathed the past hour. Reminder of that hour was both a pleasure and misery: the stream of admirers coming backstage to stammer at her and blush, to compliment her dancing, the ballet, to speak knowledgeably of *Swan Lake* and compare her favorably with other women who had danced the White and Black Swans. That was always wonderful; like the applause, she lived for it. But so many of them came this tour to remind her how many years it had been since she'd last appeared in New York, how many years since the first time they had seen her perform the Blue Bird in *The Sleeping Beauty*—as if she needed reminder of how many years it was since she'd first done a solo, how the years were slipping up behind her! And all the while Collin Hemmings, her husband's cold-eyed bodyguard, slouched in the doorway in a travesty of ease that fooled no one. He watched everyone with those ice-blue eyes, listening with suspicion to every word anyone said to her, every word she said, so he could report back to Alain, as he did every single night.

She had not wanted Collin with her; she could scarcely bear to share an entire city with Collin Hemmings, let alone the same theater or the same hotel; to have him in the same room made her skin crawl. But Alain was incapable of understanding that. And he had flatly insisted. "For your protection, my angel." She'd seen then it was the U.S. tour with Collin—or no touring company at all. No ballet at all . . .

Stop it! she ordered herself. Think of the applause, of the ballet itself, she ordered herself. Of the music that could still catch her unawares and make her weep, this wonderful opportunity to again appear with a company worthy of her, to dance in major cities and houses, in major roles: to return to New York. Of *Giselle* tomorrow night—ah, there was a role—and even better, the closing night of *Romeo & Juliet*. Think of the balcony scene; she could bring tears from an audience with her young Juliet in love, they would see her in that and know her ageless, know her for the artiste she truly still was. Like Fonteyn, who had danced it at fifty and beyond. They would see—

Think of an hour from now, think of midnight tonight, when she could lay her troubles before the one in all the world she could talk to. But go, quickly, before Collin found her missing from her dressing room, and discovered which way she had gone. Before he could catch her with that incriminating envelope.

It had rained, lightly, since she'd come to the theater; the pavement glistened. The least wisps of fog hovered over puddles, swirled and eddied as she hurried down the stairs, down to the street. Uneven and treacherous as the pavement was, she moved silently, with a dancer's ease, the high heels of her boots barely touching concrete, the narrow tweed coat no impediment to her long-legged pace.

Not far from the foot of the steps, she found what she wanted: steam rose from the metal grate above one of the city's maze of subway tunnels. She could hear a distant roar of machinery as she knelt beside it and drew the envelope from inside her coat. Machinery? Or perhaps the sound of pipes, someone beating out messages . . . ?

That was foolish, of course; there would never be such sounds so near the surface, where no one came except the men who worked for the city. Where anyone could hear such sounds and become curious. And besides, the sound of trains and the machinery that ran them would drown the hollow clangor of metal on pipe. But—there would be someone down in that tunnel to find her note and deliver it, she would dare believe nothing else. The single name, written much more neatly than her usual scrawl, centered on the front of the envelope: *Vincent*. In an hour, she'd see Vincent . . .

As she bent over the grate, the updraft touched her nostrils. The rich mixture of scent wrapped around her—comprised of warmth, motor oil, exhaust, an indefinable blending of odor that said home to her. *Home*. The band of muscle that had cramped so tightly across her chest for so long relaxed all at once, and she could have laughed or cried, perhaps both. She was smiling rather shakily as she turned the envelope over to kiss the seal before she let it slip through the metal bars of the grate.

She was still smiling when she ran back up the steps and into the alleyway, back to the theater and her dressing room. An hour; enough time to return to the Plaza, to Alain's suite, to slip out and into the park. She shook her hair loose from the upturned coat collar and her step became lighter, swifter. So many years since I left the tunnels, she thought. I've changed so much, done the things I promised I would do. I've become someone— someone important. He'll be so proud of me, they all will be. The night air was revitalizing her, bringing her alive.

She had turned away to watch her shadow pass light-footed and slender along the wall, and almost ran into Collin, who stood motionless and silent in the center of the passageway. For one agonizing moment, her heart stopped, then began beating wildly. She was suddenly cold all through. How long had he been standing there? Had he watched her bending over that grate, had he seen—?

She gazed up into his cold, smoothly pale face; it gave her no clue. But then, hers surely gave no clue of her utter hatred of him, the fear she always felt in his presence. Blond hair, blue eyes, broad shoulders under an elegantly tailored dark suit; he should have been hand-

4

some. But there was an aura about him that reminded her of mercenaries, of terrorists from the nightly news—of Nazis in the old black-and-white news films Alain liked. And his eyes were the coldest Lisa had ever seen. Colder even than Alain's had become these past years, when she had found herself less a wife, less an object of love and desire, more another of Alain's possessions. Something to be held closely, to be guarded, watched constantly. Even before she discovered—

No. She would *not* think of Alain!

Years of hiding her true self from Alain and from men like Collin automatically protected her; she uttered one surprised little gasp but somehow managed not to shrink from him. She even uttered a careless little laugh that sounded almost normal, and met his eyes. "It's a magical night, isn't it Collin?" she asked breathlessly. He didn't understand, of course. His face remained expressionless. No imagination at all! she thought in irritation. "Or maybe it's just cold," she went on, and some of the vexation edged her voice. His eyebrows drew together, his eyes narrowed in that suspicious stare she hated so much. She took his collar in both hands, felt the least edge of satisfaction as he recoiled in surprise at her touch, and pulled the cloth together across his chest. "You really should button up," she murmured sweetly, and walked around him. The buoyancy was gone from her step but she kept her back straight, her shoulders straight, and her step set her coat hems to swaying around the slouched boots. "Let him see nothing," she whispered to herself. Whether he knew what she'd done or not, he suspected her, always. As Alain did. No escape . . . Not tonight, anyway. Collin would keep her under his eye, she wouldn't get away from him again tonight. Despair tightened her throat. "Oh, Vincent—" What would he think?

Perhaps he'd never even see her note. Or even if he got it, he might not come. Why should he?

She could feel Collin's tight, distrustful gaze all the way back to the stage door.

* * *

5

The rectangle of envelope lay beside a curved track, well in shadow. A train passed, heading north, sending it fluttering away. When the last car was past, it slid slowly down the concrete wall.

A boy—perhaps a very small ten-year-old, or a larger but too thin boy of eight—came out of shadow across the tracks; squatted there and looked up at the square of tight-woven metal bars high above. City folk dumping trash again, he thought sourly—forgetting that until a year before, he, Julian, had been one of those folk from Above. He eyed the thing contemplatively, head tilted to one side on a neck too long and skinny for the look of his head. Short black curls bounced, he stroked a bare chin in an unconscious copied gesture. Finally got back to his feet and jumped across the tracks to pick up the envelope, to carry it to where there was a worker's light. "Vincent," he whispered.

Julian frowned. The paper was good, expensive stuff, nothing Woolworth, and when he sniffed cautiously, there was a faint floral scent to it. All the same, who except that Catherine woman knew about Vincent? Who from Above?

He stared at it a few more moments, shook his head and slid it into the waistband of his heavy shirt. Another train coming—he could feel the vibration in the ground under his bare feet. Not a place to be; Father had warned him about being seen. And it was none of his business where this letter came from; he'd see it got down where it belonged.

There was a workmen's door on a ledge several steps back; he pushed it open, letting it shut behind him just as light from the tunnel beyond touched the tracks and the roar grew deafening. The little machinery room was dark except for a small orange light plugged into a wall socket; just past this was a metal cabinet holding wire and tools. And behind this—Julian got down onto hands and knees, pushed the cabinet aside far enough for him to ease behind it, pulled the handle that pulled the cabinet back into place and concealed the hidden opening.

It was a different world here already: tunnel, dimly

lit by wide-spaced trouble lights, stretched in both directions. He turned left and ran. Workers didn't come underground at night unless there was an emergency, but it wasn't a good idea to hang around near the surface, even in an unmarked tunnel like this one; the kids passed around too many spooky stories about other kids who'd gotten caught up here and sent Above. He didn't want to find out if they were hokey or not.

The tunnel ended in a concrete tube that went down into darkness, marked by an aged ladder of solid metal tubing, green-brown with age. Julian descended this two rungs at a time, jumped onto a narrow spit of dirt and ducked under a low, broken lip in the tube. Here there were lights—lanterns or hurricane lamps with candles. Pipes ran along the upper curve of the right-hand wall, ten of them in various sizes, bundled together every ten feet or so in a wide metal band. Several of them dripped condensation. There was a marked odor here, a compounding of dirt, damp dirt, the scent of kerosene and candle wax, mixed, a more distant smell of wood fire and something that might have been cooking apples. Julian jumped as one of the pipes above his head began ringing, a high-pitched pattern. Silence, then it was repeated some distance away. Messages. He knew some of the ways to encode a very basic message, but hadn't learned many phrases yet. He hadn't understood any of this one.

He followed a left branch, came into an area that was all concrete piping, seven feet or more in diameter. It went off in a maze of directions; he went left again, right, right. Left, and then descended another ladder—a short one—jumped across the deep stream in its cement bed. Not far now.

Two levels farther down, he came into the area where most of the Underground people lived—kids like himself, unwanted and with no chance of growing up whole in the world Above. Grown people with almost as many reasons for turning their back on the so-called civilization of New York as there were people here. Men like Father—Julian slowed his steps as he passed Father's chamber, stopped and turned back. A little frown creased his young forehead. Men like Father, who had begun this sanctuary. This—second chance, Father had called it the other day. Julian had liked that.

And men like Vincent, so different in his looks from other men that he would never have stood a chance up there. Julian looked over his shoulder, the way he'd been going. Vincent's chamber was down there, not far. Julian had only met Vincent a few months before, even though he'd been Underground the better part of a year, and he was still a little shy around him. To have such a face, such hands—and still to be so kind. Julian wasn't used to kind men. A man such as Vincent—with such a face, such hands, such strength—Vincent surely could hurt anyone he liked with those enormously strong arms and hands, with the long and deadly teeth he seldom exposed even in a smile. Just to look upon that face might frighten many. Vincent chose understanding, gentleness and love instead—Julian was abashed by that.

Perhaps he could take the message to Father to give to Vincent. He nodded once and his brow cleared. He'd do just that.

Father had finally located the promised book of the early twentieth century German poems for him. It was a wonderful old gold-edged and gold-stamped leather volume. Vincent glanced up once to see the candle nearest his elbow had burned down nearly an inch since he'd sat down and begun to read. He resettled his shoulders against the back of his chair.

There is a world pooled beyond my doorway,
Deeply blue air, a mixture of cobalt and smoke,
And it draws me—
my tired soul awakens—
and I step, with renewed heart, into its shadow.
Letting the dark warmth surround me, fill me,
I welcome the night, and it calls me home.

He sighed and let the book lay flat on his lap, still open. His deep-set blue eyes were fixed, unseeing, on the far wall. Candlelight cast deep shadows under them, along the planes of his cheeks, turned his mane ruddy gold. "I welcome the night," he whispered again, and felt the inner satisfaction that came when another's words touched his own deeper feelings and rang true.

A scrape of foot against the floor outside roused him. He laid the book on the table, still open, as Father came into his room. "Vincent; there you are." Vincent looked up, brows furrowed: something was wrong; Father's dark face was strained and his eyes worried. The short, grizzled hair looked as though he'd run his hands through it; his cloak was pulled awry, as though he'd thrown it on and not bothered to get it on straight. "What is it, Father?" If it was Catherine—but no, she was well, he *knew* that. Trouble—? There had been a cave-in along one of the deeper passageways well to the east but they said it was under control; north of the park, someone reported a problem at one of the hidden entrances not long ago. Had those young toughs found a way in after all?

"A message arrived for you tonight. From Above."

Vincent looked at him. Father brought a sealed and slightly worn-looking envelope from inside his woolen waistcoat and held it out, rather as though it might go off in his fingers. Vincent looked at it in surprise, looked up at the older man, took it and turned it over. His name on the front of the envelope . . . and he knew that writing.

So did Father.

Something scratched at the back of his mind; it might have been the least whisper of an ancient, long-forgotten dread. His throat was suddenly dry. He abruptly broke the seal and withdrew the single sheet of ivory-laid bond paper. Her name at the top, embossed in Gothic letters: Lisa Campbell. And under that, in her swift, sprawling hand: *Come and see me at midnight. Our special place. Lisa.*

"Lisa," he said. The name felt foreign in his mouth. He could feel Father's eyes on him, could feel Father's tension, his uncertainty. Perhaps Father had good reason to fear. That had been—had been a bad time. Vincent had put it aside so many years before; he hadn't thought about Lisa in some time. But he could see himself so clearly as he had been then: young and all height, too tall for the weight he carried. Could still feel the shattering grief that had tightened like a bar across his chest, the guilt that had threatened to overwhelm a youth who had known love only as something fragile and beautiful, until then.

His own voice echoed in his mind across the years, cracking into an upper register, shaking with unshed tears that left a salt taste in his throat. "I must see her, Father. Please let me, please!"

And Father's gentle reply: "She's gone. She went Above."

It had hurt, terribly. It still hurt. Looking back, he knew it must have hurt Father at least as terribly. "It's because of me." The words had barely made any sound through his miserably tight throat. The older man's hand was warm on his shoulder, then warm around his shoulders. But for the first time, Vincent had taken no comfort from Father's embrace, or from his words.

"You've done nothing wrong, Vincent," he had said finally, forcefully—a man, Vincent thought now, trying to assure himself that neither of them had. "Nothing."

But if I did nothing wrong, Vincent thought unhappily as he found himself back in the present and staring down at Lisa's expensive notepaper, *then who did? And what went so wrong?* He had no answers.

Lisa . . . Something was amiss; he sensed that much. Lisa needed him. He looked up to find the worry in Father's eyes intensified. "I must go," he said simply.

He half-expected argument; Father simply bowed his head and left the chamber. Vincent refolded the note with care and put it back in the envelope, laid it on the table and laid the volume of Rilke's poems atop it. "I have faith in nights," he whispered. But his last memory of Lisa was a vision of light.

It wasn't far, less than a mile from his chamber along

well-frequented tunnels to the place Lisa called their special place. The narrow, circular well with its iron ladder was just through the first arch. He glanced at it, then turned away.

How many years had it been? It seemed forever, just now: but he remembered the long climb up that ladder, with Lisa before him; he'd scarcely noticed how far they'd gone, with her small feet even with his chest, her long, flowing skirts moving around her calves and brushing softly against his throat and his cheek—with the overture to Tchaikovsky's *Swan Lake* all around them, filling the dark. It was silent up there now; too late for ballet or opera or whatever else played on that stage this night.

He paced to the second arch where she would surely come momentarily, back down the other way. Back again.

So long; so many years. Had the years been kind to her? What would he feel when he saw her?

He'd walked back and forth for hours; it was now well past midnight. She wasn't coming. He turned toward the tunnel that would take him back to his chamber, his volume of poems. Hesitated, turned back. She might yet come; there was an underlying something in that short message that worried him. He'd wait . . .

Another hour, then two. He stopped pacing, leaned against the wall of the tunnel and gazed toward the ladder and the stage high above without actually seeing any of it. She wasn't coming after all. Perhaps his concern had been created of whole cloth and his own feelings; perhaps it had been a whim on her part to see him, forgotten or set aside for something she found more important. Or perhaps she'd been delayed through no fault of her own. It frustrated him. He closed his eyes briefly, drew a deep breath and then another, to clear his mind. Frustration and worry overlaid with a mire of old pain were no use to him and no help to Lisa. There was one thing, however, that might be. One person.

Catherine. Her name sang through him, warming his face, warming his blood, momentarily soothing. He would ask Catherine to help him.

Her apartment was dark when he arrived, a little short of breath; she must not have been deeply asleep because he heard her voice almost at once after he tapped lightly on the glass French doors that led from tiny living room to the small balcony. "Vincent?"

"Catherine, it is I."

"I'll be right there." He turned, looked down onto the park, out across the myriad lights of Manhattan. And then she was there, a thick robe pulled snugly around her, her usually smooth dark blond hair tousled from the pillow, her eyes still warm and heavy with sleep. He looked at her and she smiled back, sharing his quiet pleasure. She listened without comment as he told her about Lisa's note, about his wait.

Catherine blinked sleep from her eyes, shoved the spill of fine hair back from her forehead and considered. Lisa Campbell—she connected the name he'd told her with a person, and looked at him in surprise. "She is from the tunnels?" Vincent nodded once, abruptly. "You know her—knew her?" Another nod. She waited, but he didn't say anything. "You're upset by this," she said gently. "Why?"

He turned away to look out over the park, shrugged faintly. "It was—a message in the night, and it said so little, but I—when I saw it, I could feel the urgency that caused her to write it. Her need."

A faint line creased Cathy's forehead. She knew Vincent could truly sense such things; it was another facet of his differentness. "But she never came."

He shook his head. "No. It's almost as if I imagined it. As if I imagined she was—here again," he added in a barely audible whisper.

His distress was almost palpable; it hurt her to see him so unsettled. She shook herself free of that so she could find a practical solution to his immediate problem: locate Lisa Campbell. "There's a touring company here now. She might be with them." He turned back to look at her, and she added gently, "Your memories of her must be strong."

His eyes touched hers, moved away; he looked out across the city lights and she knew he saw none of them. "She left us so many years ago, but we heard of her successes. Helpers would bring us news."

"I saw her dance once." Cathy smiled as she remembered. Cinderella—the Prokofiev music still reminded her of Lisa Campbell. "It was truly inspired."

For some reason, that seemed to deepen Vincent's odd, unsettled mood. "Yes," he murmured; his eyes brooded now on the stone lip of her terrace, on the street far below. One finger absently traced patterns in the dew on her small patio table.

"Vincent," she whispered. No response. She hugged herself to ward off a sudden chill that had nothing to do with outside temperature. "What is it, Vincent?"

He must have sensed her concern; he looked at her and truly saw her. He swallowed. "Please. If you find her. Please tell her—" He swallowed again. "Please tell her that she has a place. And—that I'm here."

Riddles and forebodings—they worried her, and she had never seen Vincent so dreadfully unhappy. She ached for him. "I will." He seemed to relax all at once, as though she'd taken a heavy burden from him. Who is Lisa and what is she to Vincent? she wondered uneasily. There was something wrong in all this, and worse, Vincent was bottling that wrong up within him.

But perhaps it was simply something to do with the Underground, something he was not allowed to tell her. "Did—did she leave the tunnels so she could dance?" she asked finally.

Silence. For one terrible moment, she thought he would not answer her at all. He had gone back to tracing and retracing lines on the tabletop, his eyes followed the movement of his finger. "That is not why she left," he said in a quiet, flat voice. "Although it might have been a reason in time."

"Why did she leave?"

Vincent brought his head up and looked at her. There was a deep pain in his eyes and the words that came out scarcely sounded like his at all. "Because I loved her," he said. She looked up at him with wide, puzzled eyes; he looked back at her for what might have been a minute or an hour, then turned and vanished into the night. Catherine gazed after him with darkly troubled eyes and an ache in her heart that was mostly for him, but partly—suddenly—for herself.

Two

I⊤ was actually quite easy for Catherine to locate Lisa Campbell: there was an enormous ad in the *Times*, a prestigious London touring company was performing at Lincoln Center for four more nights. In a small box— white against the black of the ad, edged in Victorian frills—*Featuring Guest Artist Lisa Campbell*. There was a review on the same page, praising the previous night's *Swan Lake* and particularly Lisa's brilliant portrayal of the White and Black Swans.

She tried two of the better hotels near Lincoln Center; neither had a Lisa Campbell. Catherine set the phone back in its cradle and thought, finally shook her head. There were so many hotels, the woman might be staying with friends, or under another name, or she might have simply told her hotel not to say she was staying there. Well, there was another way to find Lisa Campbell, and it would be a treat for her to attend the ballet. These days, she didn't get to many cultural events like that, not with her workload what it was. Tickets could be a problem, though—she called the box office. If she went alone or didn't mind sitting alone, there were all of four seats left for that night's performance.

She had to make several more calls before she found someone who could get her backstage afterward; her father would have been able to do it, but he was out of town negotiating a contract for one of his corporate clients. She finally tracked down a friend of his who knew one of the big shots in the Lincoln Center office. She glanced at her watch as she set the phone down, hastily swallowed the dregs of cold coffee, grimaced and gathered up papers from her desk. There was too much going on at work just now for one lower-echelon deputy district attorney to be late. Particularly if she wanted to leave in time to change for the performance. And—she pulled the apartment door closed behind her, locked the deadbolt and rang for the elevator—it would be nice to eat a decent dinner first. They had been few and far between this week.

Perhaps it would have been better to wait until the weekend: she really would prefer to see *Romeo and Juliet*, and it would put less stress on an already crammed day. But memory of Vincent's face, his eyes when he spoke of Lisa— No, Catherine thought as she reached street level and walked out into morning rush hour. She didn't know why Vincent was so worried, but he clearly was. She'd sort things out somehow.

She thought about him all the way downtown and in the short, crowded trip up the elevator to her floor. After that, there wasn't time to think about anything but the tasks at hand.

In the end she didn't get a proper dinner, just a sandwich thrown together in her kitchen and eaten while she changed from the pleated wool skirt and jacket to royal blue silk and dark heels. There wasn't even time to do her hair up; in the end she simply brushed it smooth and let it fall in a dark gold spill over the blue dress. The theater lights were just beginning to go down as she slid into her seat. The hall was filled with Adam's sprightly music, the curtain went up on the first scene of *Giselle*.

When Lisa came on stage, there was a riot of applause; during her solos, absolute silence. She was wonderful, Catherine thought when Lisa first began to dance. And then she was caught up in the story and found herself no longer aware of Lisa Campbell, only of Giselle, a peasant girl in love with life and dancing, of her subsequent betrayal by Prince Albrecht, madness and death. The second act was all moonlight and white, gauzy gowns, a young peasant man driven to his death by the ghosts of betrayed young women, Prince Albrecht nearly driven to his but saved by Giselle. A plot that could be and often was hammily overdramatic; Lisa Campbell gave it a touching reality.

Catherine blinked herself back to reality as the ballet ended, applauded and finally stood with the rest of the audience as the company took encore after encore. Lisa came out half a dozen times by herself and with the young man who danced the Prince. The audience cheered and threw flowers, program confetti and tiny bouquets.

It took Catherine time to find her way through the crowded auditorium and the lobby to reach the office. Her father's friend's friend chatted with her for a few minutes, then put a card with his name and hers in her hand and pointed her in the right direction to get backstage.

There were still dancers everywhere behind the curtains: members of the corps standing in little clutches, cooling down, gossiping, arguing with the costume mistress, dodging the crew members who were trying to strike the last-act sets and get the stage readied for the next night's performance, so they could go home. Catherine stood and watched it for some moments, trying to get her bearings. She finally caught hold of the costume mistress as she hurried by. The woman peered over a high pouf of white gauzy skirts and little glittery wings that nearly blocked her vision and totally filled her arms.

"Excuse me. Can you tell me where Lisa Campbell's dressing room is?"

The woman freed a hand with difficulty, shifted her weight as skirts slid sideways and pointed across the stage. "Sure, honey," she said cheerfully, a little breathless, a dry edge to her words. "She's holding court right over there, at the foot of the stairs."

Cathy looked; there might have been a door over there. She started across the stage, her ears picking up odd bits of conversation as she passed dancers and crew. She smiled back at two young girls in corps costumes who were flirting with a young man half in and half out of his royal courtier costume. The stairs seemed to be down a short, dark corridor. It was overly warm and slightly stuffy after the open stage, and she had to watch her footing: there were bits of scenery everywhere— leaning against the wall, scattered outward along the floor.

Lisa's door was open, and Lisa herself seated at the dressing table. Her hair was still dressed for the last act, she still wore the heavy—and at this distance extremely exotic—stage makeup, but even the dramatic eyeliner and dark color on lips and cheeks couldn't conceal the fine bone structure, the wonderful wide-set eyes, the famous triangular smile. Her costume had been replaced by a pink silk flowered kimono and she was smiling warmly at a white-haired man who was practically stuttering his praises. Catherine stopped just outside, leaned against the jamb. The smell of roses, tuberoses and carnations was nearly as intense as in a florist's, the table against the far wall couldn't be seen for the flowers.

"I've seen you every time you've danced here." The man's coloring had gone high, his cheeks were nearly as pink now as Lisa's.

"Every time?" Lisa asked, and there was the least hint of gentle flirtatiousness in the simple question. He nodded, momentarily speechless. "And which performance was your favorite?"

"Without question, it was *Giselle*," he said ardently. "December twenty-third, nineteen seventy-eight."

She raised one eyebrow, tilted her head and laughed. "Why, I scarcely could walk back then!"

She was charming him, Catherine thought, and doing it very sweetly. Her elderly admirer would have something else pleasant to remember Lisa Campbell by. She turned so she could look back out at the stage, at the dancers still there. "May I say, Miss Campbell, you're even more beautiful now."

"Lisa. Please."

"Lisa."

"And thank you for the flowers." There was a very delicate suggestion of dismissal in Lisa Campbell's voice; her visitor took the hint and as Catherine turned back, he bowed over Lisa's fingers, not quite daring to kiss them.

"Thank *you*, Miss Campbell." His color went very high as he saw Catherine waiting behind him, and he hurried past her. Lisa had turned back to the dressing table and was removing her slippers.

"Miss Campbell? May I come in?"

Lisa glanced over her shoulder, saw her next visitor and smiled at her. "Please." Catherine took three steps into the small room and stopped. Now that she was here, she wasn't exactly certain where to start.

"You danced wonderfully tonight," she said finally.

Lisa inclined her head, a gracious acceptance of the compliment that somehow managed to appear humble at the same time. There was no sign of the famous Campbell arrogance. Of course, that had been years before, Lisa's last New York appearances . . .

"Do you come to the ballet often?" Lisa asked as she turned back to attack a knot in her slipper ties.

Catherine nodded. "As often as I can." She drew a steadying breath. "Actually, I'm here for a friend. A friend of both of ours."

Lisa looked up again, fingers still worrying the knot. "Oh?"

"Vincent." She spoke his name quietly, but it seemed to echo in the small, flower-laden dressing room. Lisa gazed into the small makeup mirror on her table; her fingers were frozen on the ballet slipper and the smile had vanished; her whole body might have turned instantly to stone. Her eyes met Catherine's in the mirror; hers were suddenly wary. "You left a message," Catherine said softly. "He waited for you. He was concerned."

Lisa still had not moved; Catherine watched her and wondered. She was afraid—but of what? Lisa brought her hands up to her lap, straightened slowly and turned away from the table to meet the other woman's eyes directly. "Who are you?" she demanded.

Catherine found herself speaking quietly, soothingly—as though Lisa might be a small frightened animal, ready to run at the least sharp word or sudden movement. "My name is Cathy Chandler. I told Vincent I would try to find you." She paused. Lisa still looked at her with those great brown eyes, the intense ballet makeup accenting their size and the thick, dark eyelashes. "To make sure everything was all right," she finished awkwardly.

Lisa absorbed this briefly, then smiled. But now the wonderful triangular smile went no higher than her lips. "Well!" she said lightly. "Everything is fine!"

It was such an obvious, deliberate lie, Catherine could momentarily find nothing to say. Lisa flashed her another of those meaningless, brilliant smiles and finished untying her shoes, concentrated on knotting them together by the long ribbons. "Vincent cares about you very much. I suppose he wanted me to remind you of that. In case you had forgotten."

Lisa came to her feet in one smooth dancer's motion and closed the slight distance between them. The fingers that touched Cathy's forearm trembled.

"Will you see him?" she asked in a low, urgent voice. Catherine nodded. But she never learned what Lisa would have said next. The woman's eyes slid past her to fix on the open door and her fingers were momentarily bruising. Before Cathy could protest at the sudden pain, before she could even form a question or turn to look, Lisa changed again—alarmingly. The smile was back, radiant and empty, her hands shifted to lightly clasp Catherine's shoulders, and her voice when she spoke was light, cheerful, warm and false as the smile. "Cathy, thank you for coming backstage." Her gaze shifted to the door and she went on in a heavily ironic tone: "Please! Come in, Collin."

Catherine turned. The man who lounged against the door frame was elegantly clad in a dark custom-made suit, a discreet tie; his pale blond hair had been well cut. His face chilled her all the way to the bone. He smiled in her direction; a mere turning of his pale, thin lips, but his eyes remained fixed on Lisa.

"Mr. Taggert is expecting your call." He had an accent—English, possibly; maybe Australian. It clipped his words but she couldn't think the man would ever sound friendly.

"Tell Alain I'm visiting with an old and dear friend," Lisa replied sweetly. "Collin, this is Cathy Chandler. We went to school together. Cathy," she added, and her words once again became crisply sarcastic, "this is Collin Hemmings. My ever-faithful and fearless watchdog."

It was an effort to meet those ice-cold blue eyes and smile. Catherine managed it somehow. "How do you do." She was glad she hadn't held out a hand; he didn't even return her smile, just stood there in the doorway, arms still folded, looking at her the way a Doberman or a pit bull might. Chill, suspicious . . .

Lisa had moved away to hang up her slippers; she sighed as she turned back. "Oh, Collin, you mustn't look so stern!" she snapped irritably. "It doesn't become you." He ignored her; Cathy somehow wasn't surprised. No wonder the woman had been so on edge; the man affected *her* that way, and after only a few moments. He watched Catherine through narrowed, unblinking eyes.

"Which school was that?" he demanded abruptly.

"Brookhill," Lisa put in smoothly, and smiled at Cathy. "Good old Brookhill, of course. School of the Arts."

21

Cathy smiled back, hoping Lisa would know she meant it as thanks for rescuing her. There were currents and undercurrents in this small room; they were thicker than the overpowering scent of flowers. She glanced at Collin, who was still watching her in that single-minded, fixed fashion. Trying to sort out the next question to fire at her, no doubt. She wasn't certain she could continue the facade any longer; she knew she didn't want much more of the situation she was presently in. "Well," she said briskly. "You probably have plans, and I don't want to keep you. I've got to be going anyway."

Lisa came close and took her shoulders. Cathy hugged her and exchanged a friend's kiss on the cheek. The other woman's fingers were tense with the effort of not clinging to her, but the smile stayed in place as Lisa leaned back and looked at her. "Call me. We can have lunch before I go."

Catherine nodded. "That would be great. We can catch up." Lisa let her hands drop and she turned to meet Collin's eyes—now apparently blandly disinterested in her. "Nice to meet you, Mr. Hemmings," she said. He replied with the least of nods and stood aside to let her leave. She walked into the corridor, took several steps back toward the stage and stopped; she would have sworn she could feel the man's eyes boring into her back. But as she turned, she could see him closing the distance between himself and Lisa Campbell; the door swung around with the force he'd put behind it and slammed behind him. It was very quiet on the stage; quiet back the way she'd come.

She gazed at the closed door for one long, troubled moment. This was unpleasant, not at all what she'd expected. There was something very ugly in Lisa Campbell's world.

She ate a carton of yogurt and a handful of crackers at her desk the next day while she finished a long-overdue report; she then spent her lunch hour at the library, in front of a microfilm reader, running down everything she could find on Lisa Campbell. The newspaper and magazine articles spanned ten or more years: Lisa Campbell at the White House, at Lincoln Center, at the Dorothy Chandler in Los Angeles, in San Francisco with the American Ballet Theater . . . The early reviews carried pictures, were spread over several columns, were thickly sprinkled with adjectives like "wonderful," "ethereal," "enchanting." Later reviews were smaller and less effusive; some spoke of disappointing performances, made mention of her skyrocket entrance into the world of dance, hinted at the possibility of an equally precipitous descent.

She'd left the United States not long after a performance in Dallas that had been—by the accounts Catherine could find—an absolute disaster. She'd performed with the Royal Ballet for two seasons as a guest artist and had regained some of her reputation for style and flair, but actual performances were widely spaced. Sometime after that, she was with the still honorable but slightly less prestigious London Ballet Theater.

The last article in the file Catherine had showed Lisa smiling into the face of a well-dressed man. The caption read *Campbell Quits London Ballet Theater for Financier*. Catherine enlarged the article and read it, then studied the grainy picture. Alain Taggert—had she heard that name before? British financier . . . That rang no bells. A financier could be anyone who dealt in large quantities of money or products, of course; it was one of those generic terms that covered a lot of ground on all sides of the law. It was hard to tell anything from a newspaper photograph, but what she could see of his face had a still, watchful look to it. A little like the man Collin's, she thought, and shivered. "Imagine a butterfly like Lisa married to a—a—" She didn't want to imagine. But she thought there might be an explanation of sorts for Collin now. A highly unpleasant one: some men treated their wives like they were possessions, and some wealthy men carried that to extremes only they could afford—surrounding their women with guards, with watchers and spies among their servants.

Poor Lisa Campbell.

She would have to work it out a little better, if she could, before she talked to Vincent again. He'd been deeply disturbed by what she had told him the previous night, by the undercurrents she had sensed in that dressing room. But, Catherine thought unhappily, as she turned the machine off and returned the microfiche to its place in the box, he's not the only one who's worried. I've never seen him so distant—not just from me, from everything. That's so unlike the Vincent I know.

What had distressed him so, and what was Lisa's part in it all? And—most of all—why would he not tell her?

Lisa was extremely pleased with herself and with life in general this particular Friday night. The Aurora had been even better than her Giselle; the auditorium had been filled to capacity and they'd adored her from the moment she came onto the stage. Lisa had sailed through the evening in a glorious daze, and even Collin's inevitable presence at her shoulder during the little party afterward failed to dim her mood. Carlos Palmieri, one of the patrons of the tour, had kept the gathering small and elite. There were so few parties for her anymore. Lisa had enjoyed this one thoroughly, accepting accolades with a dazzling smile and a gracious nod.

She had warned Collin to behave himself, and oddly, he had actually done so, not cross-examining her in front of everyone or asking rude questions of the others present the way he'd treated that nice young Chandler woman in her dressing room. Not attempting to drag her away from the party before she had finished her first glass of wine, as he so often did, or to get between her and any man who acted halfway nice toward her. Alain must have warned him, Alain must have listened for once when she asked him to talk to Collin. Of course, Palmieri was extremely wealthy; so were most of the others at this party—aside from the members of the dance company, of course. Alain was invariably polite when dealing with other men of means.

He'd look upon it as one hand washing the other, she thought sourly. Not that Alain was quite on the same clean footing with his finances as Carlos Palmieri or any other man at this party, but that thought flitted through her mind and was banished almost as instantly as it surfaced.

She began easing herself out of the crowd before Collin could become restless, thanked Palmieri and the others around him before Collin started casting obvious glances at his watch. Not that she wanted to leave yet, of course, but this way she might be on Collin's good side. Supposing he had one.

She let him lay the deeply fringed shawl over the shimmering white bodice, covering her bared shoulders. Fringe and long skirt swirled together around delicate high-heeled sandals as she walked toward the door; Collin waited with at least the outward semblance of politeness and only the least tightness around his eyes while she worked her way through the last of the guests. Everyone seemed to want to compliment her once more, to say good night to her, to get in one last word.

They walked the short distance to the Plaza Hotel in their usual silence: Collin never made light conversation; seldom spoke to her at all unless it was absolutely necessary. It was overcast, unexpectedly warm despite the hour, even warmer in the lobby of the hotel. Collin opened the door to Alain's suite for her with the second key—she was never able to convince Alain that she didn't want Collin having a key to her room. To her surprise, he didn't come in with her. She walked into the large sitting room, turning on lights as she went, poured herself a glass of white wine and leaned against the mantel, sipping it.

She tensed and relaxed her calves, feeling the muscles move, rolled her shoulders one at a time. They weren't as tight as she might have expected them to be. Aurora was a demanding role, particularly danced one night after Giselle, and that after *Swan Lake*. "But Fonteyn danced all of them at fifty," she whispered, and raised her glass in toast to the great square of mirror over the fireplace, to the reflection of a woman still young—a woman young and beautiful enough to wear her hair

pulled severely back from her face. "At fifty and beyond—and I am far short of that." She smiled at her
reflection again and let her thoughts drift. This tour
would put her back where she belonged, on top. A
dancer was only as good as her last reviews, but with
this Lincoln Center stop, she had it in her grasp once
more, the only thing she had ever truly wanted. The
thing she'd thrown away in the name of security, when
she'd married Alain.

But—to be once more surrounded by the music, the
lights picking her out from all the others—to dance and
feel the joy or the despair of the part she danced, to live
the part! No one knew better than Lisa Campbell how
much hard work and training and rehearsal went into
making a ballet the finished product the public saw. But
when she was on stage, that no longer existed: there
was only the music, the lights, the story and the other
dancers to help her tell it. Sometimes the audience took
her by surprise when they broke into applause.

If only Collin hadn't caught her after she'd dropped
that message for Vincent— No! She brought herself up
short. "Don't think about Collin," she whispered urgently. "Juliet—" Her trick of not remembering was so
practiced it was no effort at all to dismiss the misery
she'd felt, to replace it with more pleasant things. She
was again deep in such thoughts when she heard the
door click open; she turned and set her wine on the
mantel as Collin came in. Unasked, she thought angrily.
I doubt he even thought to knock!

She went very still inside then: Collin was smiling.
Collin never smiled unless he had found a way to get
at her; a way through the wall she'd built to hold him
at a distance. He knew the wall was there, he knew how
she hated him. He had his own ways of getting back.

But she had her ways, too, and enough practice at
them. She brought up a smile that at least appeared real;
a sidelong glance at the mirror assured her of that. He
sat on the edge of the overstuffed chair, looked up at
her and waited. "Yes, Collin? What is it?"

The smile widened. "A change of plans. We're leaving

26

for London tonight." And he waited again.

She laughed. "Don't be silly. I have three more performances yet."

"They've been canceled."

Her heart lurched painfully. "What are you talking about?" Her voice was dry, too high. She brought it back down, made it flat, emotionless. "I didn't cancel anything!"

"I suggest you take it up with Mr. Taggert when we get back to London."

He sounded like one of those horrid London street kids, and she was suddenly furious with him. Her hand gripped the mantel, hard; it was curling with the desire to slap that snotty-boy smirk off his face. "What did you say to him?" she demanded.

"You overestimate me," he said loftily, and now he sounded like Alain.

"Do I?" If anything, she'd underestimated him, badly.

The smile slipped and he regarded her coldly. "Look, I just do what I'm told. I suggest you do the same." He stood, bent down to take a chocolate from the open box on the little table next to the armchair. He was smirking again as he popped it in his mouth, rolled his tongue over it, savoring the taste, and he was watching her, avid for some sign of the pain he knew she must be feeling.

She had to turn away from him then. He knows he caught me this time, she thought furiously. But he thinks I am afraid to return; that it's because Alain is afraid I'll tell the world what I've learned about him these last horrible years! That— She didn't want to know about those things, she never thought about them, wouldn't let herself. Ugly things like how Alain made the fortune she once thought would be her security, back when she was still an innocent . . .

It didn't matter, it was nothing against what he'd done. Collin couldn't possibly understand the extent of the damage he had caused. Her career lay shattered all around her. What company, what theater, what backer would ever trust her again, with this on top of her record those last years before she had married Alain? And now she'd canceled three performances for no reason at all, with no advance warning? *She* had canceled. It stuck in her throat, a sharp-edged agony that wouldn't swallow. Even if she dared tell anyone—presuming Alain freed her to dance again—who would ever believe that her husband had done the canceling, that he had stopped her dancing because it was something he could not possess, because he wanted her under his thumb once more? Because it was the one thing she wanted?

She brought herself back to the moment with an almost physical wrench, set the wineglass gently on the mantel; she wanted to smash it. When she turned to face her husband's man once more, she was smiling, her voice was light and almost cheerful. "Well! If I am not going to dance, I suppose I might as well go back." Silence. "It will be good to get home."

He stood up and walked slowly toward her. "I'm glad you feel like that." He obviously didn't believe a word of it.

She tightened her grip on the mantel to keep from retreating; he made her feel unclean when he looked at her like that. He made her uncomfortably aware of the thinness of the fabric covering her body, that her shoulders were bare. It's only his way of intimidation, she reminded herself. It doesn't mean—that. She took another swallow of her wine. "You *will* give me time to change and pack, won't you?" She gestured, indicating the long chiffon skirt, bare shoulders—a dress totally impractical for a transatlantic flight.

He ran a pale tongue over pale lips. He still stood too near; it took everything she had in her and her hard grip on the mantel to keep from backing away. If he had touched her or even taken another step toward her, she would have clawed at him and screamed. But he merely said, "Of course," and added meaningfully, "I'll be right outside the door." He turned and left; the latch clicked shut behind him.

She stood utterly still, not even breathing until the click of the latch released her; she sprang away from the fireplace and ran into the little hall. She considered for one mad moment sliding the little brass chain into place, but at once knew that wouldn't do. He'd hear her, he'd open the door with his key, break the chain with no effort at all. This way she had a little time . . .

Time—? Time to do what? She couldn't *think*, the world was closing in around her, the walls were suffocating her, no way out, trapped in these rooms and then in a cab, in a plane with Collin between her and the aisle, trapped with Alain forever in that house, surrounded by cold-eyed men . . . She ran across the room, her breath coming in sharp little pants, feeling her vision begin to tunnel as her panic spiraled. Collin's voice, muffled by the wood of the door, spurred her to action. "Five minutes, Lisa!"

"Yes, I know, Collin!" she shouted back, and leaped for the window. *Out!* She had to get out, now!

The window was the old-fashioned sash kind; it was heavy. She yanked at it frantically, forced it up, digging in, lifting with strong dancer's legs. It abruptly gave and slid all the way up. Curtains blew across her face. She brushed them aside, cast one terrified glance over her shoulder, another at the horribly narrow steel mesh walkway and the street visible through it far below; she knelt without the least hesitation to remove her heels, scrambled out onto the metal bars, shoes clasped tightly in one hand.

She was ordinarily frightened half to death of even the least height; tonight she had eyes only for the fire escape at the corner of the building. Fire escape. Escape. Out! Panic tightened her chest and shortened her breath even more; it was coming into her throat in tiny sobs as she scuttled on hands and knees over the narrow walkway. There were bars at its end, between her and the ladder that went from this floor to the next; there were stairs after it. She wrenched at the bars, sending hot shockwaves of pain through her shoulders and bruising her hands. They gave just a little, and there was enough room—just—for her to turn sideways and slide between them. *He* could not follow her this way. But he was stronger than she, more determined . . .

Lisa cast one frightened look back at the still-empty window and another straight down; the ground blurred, receded and sprang back up at her. Her stomach twisted. She clutched at the bars, reeled back and yanked her eyes away from that appalling drop before fear could freeze her in place, then caught up the dangerously long skirt between clenched teeth and backed onto the ladder. She went down it in a blur, slowed on the landing only long enough to put her shoes back on—and to dimly wonder she'd retained the wit to remember them—before she started down the open metal stairs of the fire escape.

She looked up at the first turn to see Collin's blond head reflected in the room's light for the least moment before he vanished; sight of him lent wings to her feet. He'd follow her, he'd catch her, she could never outrun Collin . . .

Out, out, out! The word was pounding through her brain with every clattering step, racing with her thudding heart. She could almost feel his fury, coming down that fire escape after her like a black cloud or a blanket to wrap her and entrap her, could almost hear his feet clattering down the stairs inside the hotel, as he raced to intercept her, to capture her. Her whole body jarred with the sudden change from metal to the concrete of the walkways behind the hotel. She looked up and wildly all around her, caught hold of the door just beside her and yanked frantically on the handle, seeing in it only a way into a dark, safe place. It took her a moment to realize it was locked, to realize it led back into the hotel, that it might lead directly to . . . *No!* She turned, caught up her skirts again and fled, down a short flight of steps to the service ramp that came up from the underground parking, and flew over the sidewalk, dodging foot traffic there, cars on the street. She leaped onto the far curb and vanished into the dark of Central Park. A couple walking an enormous black standard poodle turned to stare after her and then at each other in surprise; the doorman looked up from handing a woman into a taxi and gazed in concern at the flash of white dress rapidly vanishing between the trees.

And back at the front of the fire escape, Collin burst from the door Lisa had just tried to open. He caught himself on the handle before he fell down the concrete steps, looked up to see bare metal and a high brick wall, curtains billowing in an open window a long way away. He whirled around, and he momentarily looked as wildly upset as Lisa had. She was gone and he had no notion which direction she had gone, of where she might run.

Mr. Taggert would kill him if he'd lost her. Literally. He tore his hair and began to swear furiously.

Lisa had taken a straight line between the Plaza and the concrete drainpipe halfway across the Park that was the nearest way to reach the dwellers Underground. She was beyond thinking of that, however. Instinct took her to that entrance because it led to Vincent, to their special place. She was forced to stop when her lungs could no longer sustain the pace her legs set. She sagged against an enormous maple tree, eyes darting in all directions, searching the darkness for Collin. He would follow her, he would find her before she could find Vincent, he would take her away, return her to London, to Alain. . . .

She slid around the tree, fingers clutching bark for balance, trying to breathe deeply through a wind-burned, aching throat, to gain enough strength to go on before Collin could come. And as she moved around the far side of the tree, the slender rill of running water and the enormous concrete drainage pipe that fed it were simply there. She had run farther than she thought. The knowledge gave her one last burst of strength; she pushed herself away from the rough trunk and staggered on.

She scraped her hands on the lip of the concrete, plunged one foot past her ankle in the water; pain, cold and the nasty feel of a squelchy, wet shoe brought her back to herself, a little. She made herself slow down enough so she could watch her footing; she was still panting—but not painfully—when she fetched up against the iron bars and the locked gate that separated her from the Underground.

Locked. The panic was rising in her once more: she beat on unyielding metal with clenched fists, then caught at them to hold herself up when her knees would have given way. "Please, oh, please, please be here." She was almost ready to let go, to fall to the packed dirt and weep when a deep voice spoke behind her and she sensed a presence at her back.

"I am here."

She whirled around and saw a tall figure, a spill of golden mane, a long black cloak. "Vincent. Vincent!" Tears blurred everything else as she threw her arms around his neck and hugged him desperately.

Vincent looked down at the shining, shaken woman, inhaled the delicate scent of her. *Lisa.* He let the name wash through him with no particular thought attached to it, then gently wrapped his arms around her shoulders and held her close.

Three

It wasn't until her breathing eased a little that Lisa realized the changes in him—more change than the size of him, though he'd grown since she'd seen him last. Her embrace went higher to reach around his neck, her hands felt hard muscle where there'd been the straight lines of long, thin adolescent arms.

But though he held her closely, protectively, his touch seemed impersonal, like that of the man who had danced opposite her earlier tonight. She stepped back to take him in, gazed at him in delight and astonishment.

He had been a wonder to behold, his lanky boy's build and the leonine face somehow not incongruous. Lisa could barely remember the time she had not known him; she had accepted him as her dearest and best friend from the first, but she had lost her sense of wonder, never taken his appearance for granted. The last times she remembered with him, Vincent had been young and eager, always ready to do whatever she wanted—her willing slave, some of the other girls said. He had never been still, at least not when they were together; he had

33

been lighthearted as she when they ran and played together, later when they explored the tunnels—talking, constantly talking. He had been unexpectedly graceful, at least until the growth spurt that gave him so much height had caught him off balance. Even then he'd not been as clumsy and wrong-footed as some of the other boys.

Now she sensed the balance and grace of him with a dancer's eye. He had grown into the height. His face was—not older, no. More mature. His brows were heavier, his face leaner; low lights from down the side tunnel touched him and made hollows under high cheekbones. His mane was darker, she thought; thicker.

The inner balance and the strength that would give him a dancer's beauty in motion—that was more than simply physical. There was an inner stillness to him, an emotional repose; and that, too, was new.

Or maybe it had been she who had talked constantly, Vincent who had listened to everything she said. On the rare occasions she ever looked back, she had never been able to remember the things that Vincent said to her.

She wasn't certain how long she stood there, simply gazing at him. He looked back at her with those deep-set wonderfully azure eyes, waiting. She managed to shake the last remnants of terror from her mind and laughed in delight. "Vincent! Let me look at you!"

"Lisa." His voice was deep, resonant. Warm. The chill that was Collin vanished as though it had never been.

"You've changed," she said and threw her arms around him, this time in delight. "You're my most special memory in all the world." She looked up at him; he was simply watching her, but she couldn't read the expression in his eyes. Her smile froze in place, uneasily. "I'd forgotten how quiet you are." She had, until now. It *had* been her, once, chattering like a magpie while Vincent listened. He still didn't move, made no attempt to come to her, to touch her. "You're angry because I didn't come the other night." He shook his head. Had she really intended to tell him the truth? How could she have ever thought it? But even if he'd been the Vincent she'd known then, she suddenly realized the truth wouldn't come. She simply couldn't put so much ugliness into words.

She couldn't let anyone think of her that way—not the way it really was.

She laughed lightly, turned away to run a finger along the bars blocking the tunnel and became suddenly very voluble. "I would have come if I could. I tried to. But, you see, Mr. Palmieri—" She drew a quick breath, turned back to face him. "Mr. Palmieri is a patron of the ballet, and he invited me to dinner. He first saw me dance when I was twenty-two." The lie was coming easier; she gave him her best smile. "And, well, he's underwritten the touring company for the season—" The smile faded momentarily, taking the words, the implied excuse—the lie—with them. He simply stood there, watching her.

Vincent looked at her and tried not to let the unhappiness show. He had forgotten so much about Lisa. She had frustrated him so often back then, acting the fool when she should have been serious—being silly and flirting when the time was wrong. As though she had no sense at all; as though there was nothing but Lisa, her beauty, her clothing—what Lisa wanted. But then, he had encouraged her at that, hadn't he? So many of them had. Like the lies she had never outgrown. He wondered if she still thought no one knew she was lying. He glanced down the dark tunnel that led to the concrete culvert and the outside world. Too near by half, and Lisa had just come that way as though pursued by all the evils in the world.

She saw the way his eyes moved and the long years of conditioning came back, after all those years Above. This place was not to be exposed, no one from Above must know of it. Too many lives depended on the secret—just now, her own among them. He was concerned for Underground, afraid she might have somehow compromised them. "Don't worry. I was in New York. I just—" She drew a deep breath. "I just wanted to see you again. And Father. And everyone."

"You never came before." He hadn't meant it to sound like an accusation; he thought she might have taken it as one. Her face went momentarily utterly still, all expression wiped from it.

"No," she said softly, and now he couldn't tell what she might be thinking. "You must think of me as a profligate sister," she replied, making a dry little speech of it. "Long-lost. Abandoned. Who's finally found her way home for a visit."

How could she pretend? Or had she truly forgotten all those years they had together? "You were more than a sister to me."

Lisa's eyes went very soft indeed, and the smile that touched her lips was unexpectedly gentle. She came close, and for a moment he thought she might fling her arms around him again; she stood looking into his eyes and her own seemed troubled. At last, she reached out, tentatively, to lay her hand against his throat. As if to say, *I know*.

He gestured toward the tunnel. "Come," he said. Her relief flooded his senses as she came to his side and walked with him.

Down a long, dirt-packed floor, down a metal ladder. Lisa caught her skirts up between her teeth and preceded him. She led along the narrow concrete ledge next to the deep stream, nose wrinkling at the smell of kerosene in the lanterns there, let him lead down narrow circular steps. He took her hand where the way was dark; it lay almost impersonally in his. She was utterly silent all the way to the inhabited area.

He was not certain what she was thinking. He did not know she was thinking exactly that—that she no longer knew what he was thinking.

Once they came past the Great Hall, though, there were people—a few, a few more. Children. Two young girls who stopped and gazed in rapt wonder at her rich, shimmering gown, and then in stunned awe at her face. Lisa smiled at them, tugged her hand free of Vincent's

and turned back to talk to them. Someone came up then
who had known her. When Vincent led her on again,
she had grown a tail like a comet's, and the babble of
happy reunion and excited young girls temporarily
drowned out the echoing sound of tapping pipes, the
distant rattle of subway trains passing far overhead.

Lisa went completely still and expressionless again
when Father stepped out of his chamber to see what the
fuss was. The smile was back in place immediately and
she ran to throw her arms around him. "Oh, Father, I'm
so glad to see you again." She stood back from him,
hands still on his shoulders, eyes wet. "And look! I
remember so many of your one-armed hugs, because
the other hand held a book!" She took hold of his wrist
and brought it up. "*Wuthering Heights*—gracious!" Father smiled—at least, his lips did.

"It is good to see you again, Lisa. And looking so
well." She nodded and smiled back as though she did
not see the reservations, the wariness in his eyes. As
though those final moments between herself and Father
years ago had never been. But she would not ruin this
moment with such a memory. "Come in, talk to us,"
he added.

It was a large chamber made small by the sheer volume
of books: shelves climbed every wall, books lined it ceiling to floor. Books lay in piles everywhere, crazy zigzag-
ging stacks that were leather-bound volumes piled on
contemporary novels still in their paper dust-covers, pa-
perbacks, heavy encyclopedias, enormous picture books
of the coffee-table variety. Father set his open volume on
a table already littered with open and closed books, began lighting more candles. By the time the chamber was
fully lit, Lisa had found herself a vantage point for holding court, and was surrounded by wide-eyed, admiring
girls, abashed young men, dozens of others.

Father settled down in his favorite chair, leaned back
with his feet propped against the edge of the desk and
looked around for Vincent. Vincent had taken a place
partly in shadow; he was leaning against the wall, arms

folded across his chest, his face expressionless, thoughtful eyes fixed on the shining center of all the attention.

It worried him; Vincent had not spoken of Lisa in all the years she had been gone—not since the day after Father had taken matters into his own hands and sent her away. Not until that note had arrived. He was not certain how Vincent had worked the whole thing out; it was not his business to ask, only his place to be there if Vincent wanted that. But Lisa, returned—he feared for the effect of such a stunning, charming woman, not simply on Vincent, but on Andrew—young Andy who was gazing down at her as though he'd just found a rare and precious gem. Or little Samantha, still a child and so impressionable, who hung on Lisa's words raptly.

Surely she would not wish to return to this! The girl Lisa had eventually no longer belonged; the woman she had become would never be happy here! But if she wished to come back, if she had to for some reason . . . He didn't like it; he didn't like what it might mean. A burst of laughter brought him back to the moment. Lisa was entertaining them with stories.

"And then, when I went to Russia to dance—"

Samantha gasped. "Russia?" In spite of his concern, Father smiled. Samantha clearly envisioned Lisa dancing in the winter palace for a czar, like her picture books showed, nothing less.

Lisa nodded and bestowed a wonderful smile on the child. "With the Kirov Ballet Company." She clasped her hands together over her breast and closed her eyes. "Oh! You should see that theater! Just to set foot on that stage . . . I've never seen anything so wonderful! It was like dancing in a cathedral."

The Russian company had been so pleased to have her, the Russians had adored her; she had felt like a fairy-tale princess in that company. The memory warmed her; the warmth stayed in her eyes as she looked down at the girl. . . . Samantha, she remembered. Samantha was leaning toward her eagerly, hanging on her least word. They all were. But why wouldn't they?

It was what she had wanted, their admiration for what she had done, for what she had become.

"Did you really grow up in the tunnels?" Samantha's eyes and her voice showed she couldn't believe it. Lisa smiled, uttered a little, warm laugh and leaned toward the child.

"I did. And do you know how many people have asked me where I was born, or where I learned to dance?" Samantha was beyond speech; she shook her head, wide-eyed. "That's something you should always remember, Samantha," Lisa added lightly. "Eighty percent of a woman's charm is in her mystery."

Samantha's eyes were still wide; she nodded in solemn promise. "I'll remember."

"In fact," Lisa went on, her warm eyes taking them all in now, "without this place, I might never have danced at all." The memory touched her briefly; her smile almost faltered. Life before this place, without this place . . . She pressed it aside, sought Father with her eyes. His were hooded, unreadable in shadow as he slouched behind his desk. "Father found me a teacher," she said, and her eyes moved on, fastened on Vincent; softened with one of her best memories. She could see an answering warmth in his own eyes, even across the candlelit chamber. He remembered, too. "And Vincent—why, it was Vincent who took me to see my very first ballet."

Vincent had retreated across the room, content to watch her from a distance, remembering how she had best loved to perform for an audience—charming everyone in sight with her fragile, almost unearthly beauty, her grace, her light laugh and dark, warm eyes. Once, it seemed to him, he had loved to see her playing to a crowd as she was now. Now it saddened him a little. For he could see that was exactly what she was doing: playing. But now there was an edge to her smile, a nervous quickness to her movement—graceful still, but a vulnerable, high-strung quickness instead of the lightness. Something up there, something in the world

Above had singed her butterfly's wings, something dark shadowed her lightness.

Her first ballet. He'd been so young, then, so light-hearted, so impossibly innocent. And she—she had been a creature of enchantment, beautiful almost beyond words. She had come young to the tunnels, and he thought she had no memory of life before them; her earliest and favorite companion was himself. Her dearest friend, her slave. Later, he'd recited Byron to her eyes: "She walks in beauty, like the night..." She had laughed when he'd said that, had laughed so sweetly and said, "Do I really, Vincent? Am I, really?" and touched his face with gentle fingers.

She'd loved poetry, and romances—he'd learned vast portions of Tennyson's *Idylls of the King* for her when she'd fallen in love with Lancelot, and she'd wept for poor Jane Eyre and her shattered wedding. Music and dance had meant the most, though, even while she was still tiny. By the time she was a half-grown girl, it was becoming an obsession; she'd absorbed what dance they had at Winterfest and other celebrations, any dance—bits of ballet and modern mixed—anyone could teach her. She'd tried to teach herself ballet exercises out of a book, convinced one of the men to construct a barre for her and some of the other girls in one corner of the Long Hall. She'd been the only one to religiously use it, and after a while the only one to use it at all.

But he, Vincent, had taken her to her first ballet. He remembered bringing her down a long, darkened passage, merely shaking his head in anticipation at her questions, her teasing attempts to wheedle their destination from him, escorting her with a champion's flourish. She had been like a small child awaiting Christmas, all wide eyes. He stopped in a small open area; dimly tunnels went in four directions, branching up and down from where they stood. A fifth was a totally black opening. She smoothed her skirts with a graceful motion—her grace, fingers held the way the line drawings in the book had showed her a ballerina's fingers should go, and he warmed at that. She was so young, so earnest—

so radiant. She looked up at him, a little anxiously: "Is my dress all right? How do I look?"

Always her first concern. The answer had come without effort. "You're lovely." She followed him into darkness, the long skirt whispering as it slithered against her legs and against itself. He had stopped; she had stopped with him. It was dimly lit here, a low-burning lantern he'd left earlier to guide them. There was an opening almost at their feet leading to a terrible depth, but there was a ladder within the well, leading up from below, going on above. Vincent had looked up; Lisa followed his gaze as a rumble floated down from up there, somewhere. Applause echoed.

Lisa had touched his arm, had drawn her breath raggedly, as though her throat was tight. "Vincent, listen," she whispered. It *was* applause. As it died away, they could hear the music: *Swan Lake*. Her favorite. He had felt her trembling. "You found a way."

He had smiled for her excitement. "We must hurry." He took her hand, guided her onto the ladder, let her get several rungs up before he followed her.

They had come out behind an air vent that gave onto the stage: metal grating covered it. He didn't believe she had seen the grate; she had barely been aware of him behind her, his body braced behind hers to keep from falling. But at that first moment, the first touch of his hand on her arm, she had turned to give him the most wonderful smile she had ever given anyone.

He would have had to be made of stone not to love her. Even if he had not loved her before, with all his young heart.

She had turned back to the grating then, her heart in her eyes, devouring everything she saw. I watched the dance, I must have, he thought. But all I remember is that music, that glorious blending of joy and tragedy— and Lisa's face.

She hadn't even seemed to breathe, all the way through the end, through the many curtain calls, the cheering and shouting of "Bravo!" and "Brava!", the flowers that fell to the stage. As the curtain had closed

41

for the last time, she'd begun to speak, eyes still fixed on the stage and the dancers—the mundane lights, men and women talking, hurrying offstage or talking to each other as though no miracle had just occurred out there. "One day," she said in a low, fiercely intense voice, and she almost vibrated on that high, uncertain perch, "I will be out there too, Vincent. I will dance for all the world. I will dance for kings." She turned her head to look at him, and her eyes softened; she smiled gently and touched his shoulder lightly. "But I will be dancing only for you."

And I was so young, so innocent, I believed her. He considered this thoughtfully, rejected it finally. Lisa had meant exactly that, every word of it. She had been as innocent and young as he, then. There was nothing at that moment to warn either of them; he could not have known—he wouldn't have believed if he had been able to see into the future. Not his fault, not hers. He smiled a little for the memory and set it aside. That one, at least, could never cause him pain.

He was suddenly aware of his surroundings once more, of the smell of Father's books, candles and Father's prized green-and-white Tiffany lamp casting light over half a dozen open volumes on his desk. That lamp—Vincent smiled. Father's greatest personal indulgence was proper light to read by; the lovely old wrought bronze base had been rewired to hold a handful of flashlight batteries, and Father went through them. Fortunately, one of their Helpers understood how important the older man's books were to him, and sent down rechargeable batteries as often as necessary.

He tested the air gingerly: faintly—exotically in this location—Lisa's perfume. Lisa's voice reached him, continuing as though he'd lost nothing at all of her conversation. Perhaps he had not; memory had time of its own, nothing to do with the real world.

" . . . and that's when I knew," she finished. Her eyes were tender, soft with memory as she looked down at the girls around her feet. "So you see, dreams begin right where you are, right now." She lifted weightlessly to her feet and sketched them a dancer's bow.

The girls absorbed this in silence. Samantha shifted nervously and finally managed to whisper, "Will you show me how to dance, sometime?"

Lisa nodded. "Why, of course I will." She paused, glanced up swiftly to see Father's eyes on her. She wouldn't actually meet them, and she was looking at the girls again as she went on. "Assuming Father allows me to stay for a while."

He gazed at her thoughtfully. "You're welcome to, for as long as you wish." He considered this; he hadn't sounded genuinely pleased to have her, but then, he hadn't felt that way, either. "But what about your performances?"

He'd struck a nerve; he wasn't certain what. She went still for a very long moment, finally shook her head and gave him a rueful smile. She turned away then, rather too casually. "Well!" she said lightly, and he knew for certain she was creating a lie—for both of them. "The show's closed. I was told yesterday evening at dinner."

He didn't like it; he wasn't quite certain what to do about it. Tell her no—and then find she'd had a genuine, desperate reason to flee the world above? No, he decided. Let her keep her lies and her illusions for now. "Well, in that case, please stay," was all he said.

But Lisa had already turned her attention back to her circle of young adoring fans.

Four

CATHERINE woke with a start from a terrible dream: Vincent in peril? At first that was all she could remember of it, until she lay back and closed her eyes, let it slip back into her thoughts. He had been on one side of a pond, she on the other, he had held out one hand. He had said nothing, but she had realized his intense need. She had been panic-stricken, suddenly; in the dream, she had sensed urgency. But she could not take her eyes from him, could not even move to find a way around the pond, to help him in any way. And then wings, white wings everywhere, sending buffets of wind against her face, blowing her hair back, blowing droplets of pond water across her cheeks. Vincent had vanished behind them; somehow, she knew if the wings went away, he would no longer be there.

No wonder I was panicked, she thought. But the scene, closely examined, was no longer so frightening: it had been purest *Swan Lake*. And white wings. She lay still, eyes closed, and smiled at the imagery her sub-conscious had conjured up. Why not black wings? she thought dryly. Black wings—and Lisa Campbell's face among them?

The smile faded. She sighed, opened her eyes, shifted under the comforter so she could look at the alarm clock. Three-thirty. I can't afford to be awake like this with a Friday staring me in the face. She sighed. It didn't seem to matter, though; she'd been awake a goodly part of the previous night, too—what little had been left of it— after Vincent had gone away.

She rolled back over, resettled the pillow under her head and gazed up at the ceiling. It was all so worrying; most worrying of all, of course, Vincent's visible distress since Lisa's note had reached him. And her growing sense of a distance, as though he were shutting her out of part of his life. He had never—*they* had never done that, not in all the time they had known each other.

"What are you worried about, Chandler?" she demanded softly of the ceiling. Because if she was totally honest with herself, she *was* worried. If he never came again—! "No," she said aloud firmly, and she knew that was true. Now that the thought was fully formed, it seemed utterly foolish to fear anyone or anything could make any difference in Vincent's feelings for her. "Because nothing that happens to me, no one who comes into my life, could ever change my love for Vincent." She considered this, smiled faintly. "Whatever he did, whatever happened. It doesn't matter, that can't ever change."

Putting her own feelings aside, though: she felt so helpless, so frustrated in her helplessness! Vincent's uncertainty, his pain had been almost palpable the last time she saw him; she could have wept for his pain. But she could do nothing to ease his pain unless he asked it of her. Unless he told her what its cause was.

Lisa Campbell was the cipher to the entire matter. "I found out what I could about her," Catherine murmured. "It didn't really explain anything, though." Lisa had been enough of a mystery the night she had been holding court in that dressing room. And Lisa Campbell was still bothering her when she noticed it had grown light enough out that she could see across her bedroom. She sighed, groaned and threw the comforter aside, padded into the kitchen to dump dark coffee beans in her little grinder, to start the coffee dripping, and then into the bathroom for a shower. There was such a backlog of work on her desk; if she couldn't sleep, she might as well be awake for a useful reason.

She completed research on one case for Joe, went over several depositions in another to compare testimony and found several glaring inconsistencies that would be useful to someone else. By ten, she had enough of the small, niggling things cleared from her desk that she was able to sneak away for coffee when Edie came looking for her. The rest of the morning was almost bearable, thankfully; she was feeling the two nights of short sleep all of a sudden, despite the double dose of caffeine. Joe sent her off to court in his place in the afternoon, where she spent hours sitting on a hard bench and trying to stay awake, waiting for his cases to come up; trying not to think about the height of the stack that people would be adding to while she was away, that would be waiting for her back in her cubbyhole.

She got back after dark and just as most of the clerical staff was leaving. The stack was almost as bad as she had thought it would be; three things were flagged "Urgent," "Immediate" and "Give this priority, it's more urgent and immediate than the urgent and immediate stuff. Joe." Well, at least she'd had the foresight to bring a sandwich and a bottle of apple juice back with her.

She was hard at it some time later, a stack of loose papers balanced precariously on her lap, the file in her hands, when she heard voices and heavy footsteps; the door to Joe's office opening and closing. Funny; she hadn't even realized he was still in there. She scooped papers off her lap, squared the corners on the one bare spot on her desk, slipped them back into the file, made a note on the oversized and lined yellow stickie attached to her typewriter. The footsteps came down the hall, and one of the two men went on. Joe came around the corner and stopped just inside the pool of light cast by her desk lamp. He smiled and nodded as she looked up.

"That's what I like to see," he said approvingly. "Taxpayers' money hard at work."

Cathy grinned up at him impudently, closed the file with a slap and stood up. "I never thought of that! I pay my own salary."

He shook his head. "Don't get any ideas."

She was still grinning as she sat back down and pulled the file open again. "Night, Joe," she said, and watched him go. Funny, she thought as he vanished back into the corridor. For the longest time she would never have *dared* kid around with Joe like that. Not with any of them. "I must be growing into it," she mused aloud.

She heard his footsteps again, marked her place in the file with a finger and looked up as he came back into sight, coat now slung over his shoulders. "Hey," he said. "Were you the one who asked me about that English guy? Alain Taggert?"

She nodded. "Yeah."

He leaned against the corner of her desk, snatched his hand back as the loose papers under it shifted alarmingly. "Right. I knew the name sounded familiar. Buddy of mine over at the U.S. Attorney's mentioned him." He was frowning slightly.

"Yeah?" Cathy prompted.

"Oh. He's some kind of international arms broker. Kind of guy who plays golf with Ollie North on the weekends. He's been dealing weapons to terrorist countries." His frown deepened; Catherine felt ice trickle down her spine. "From what I hear," Joe went on, "he's about to be indicted." He eyed her in speculation, a mild touch of suspicion. "Why'd you want to know about someone like that?"

She shrugged, managed to bring up a smile she scarcely felt. Don't get him worried, she reminded herself. Joe had a growing tendency to try and wrap her in cotton wool, to protect her from any and everything. It was almost funny, considering this was the man who'd sent her out into the worst possible New York streets and situations her first months here. "Heard the name," she said carelessly. "I was curious."

She wasn't certain he'd bought it. Wasn't certain what she'd tell him if he pushed; it wasn't anything she could talk about. Joe looked at her sidelong, grinning as if to say, *Oh, yeah?* But all he said was, "Okay. See you in the morning."

She freed a hand from the awkward, thick file to wiggle her fingers at him. "Bye." She caught the cardboard before it could slip to the floor; her smile vanished as Joe walked off and as she heard the door shut behind him. She set the file on the floor by her feet, shoved with both elbows to clear space for them, rested her chin on the back of her hand and examined what she knew in light of what she'd just learned.

It explained too many things too neatly: Lisa's high-strung nervousness; the man Collin. If Taggert was the kind of guy who played golf with Ollie North, as Joe so neatly phrased it, where would that put Collin? She shivered. In the field, the man who exchanged semiautomatic rifles for money? Or one of those who silenced nervous men who wanted out of the bargain?

He looked the type who would do that and never consider the danger or the consequences. But that was speculation, just as it wasn't fact, only her own observation, that told her she had seen faces like his before— on men who killed, horridly, and never lost sleep over what they'd done.

And Alain Taggert—was he simply a smothering, jealous husband? Did that kind of love, so-called, motivate him? Or was it fear of exposure, a little of both?

One thing was certain: Taggert could not have known about the indictment beforehand or he surely would never have allowed his wife to join that touring company. Catherine shifted her chin from one hand to the other and gazed unseeing over the ugly stacks of yellow pads, depositions, files, faxes and notebooks. Of course, it was possible that Lisa Campbell had no idea how her husband earned his money.

But how long could a man keep such a secret from his wife? How long could a wife surrounded by men like Collin Hemmings be deceived by innocent explanation for great wealth?

It still left more questions than it gave her answers, that tidbit of information. And she had to know, for Vincent's sake. For her own. And even for Lisa's. The fear Catherine had sensed in that dressing room—whatever she had done in her life Underground, whatever she had done to cause Vincent such distress, she did not deserve to live in such terror.

Catherine glanced at her watch, sighed and reopened the file. One more hour, just one. And then she'd call it quits, see if she couldn't get home in time to eat something hot before she went to bed. Maybe tonight she'd be able to sleep.

Lisa had told her best stories first; she was still talking, but not as animatedly, after the children were packed off to bed. A few people who had known her as a young girl remained for a little while, but she had lost some of her vivacity with Samantha no longer there to look up at her in such rapt adoration. She looked tired, all at once—tired, frightened, drawn. At last there was only Father, who was fingering his book, clearly longing to open it, herself and Vincent. She let Vincent hand her to her feet and gave Father a rather subdued good night. "I'm rather tired, suddenly."

Father smiled faintly. "Good night, Lisa," was all he said. Lisa cast a glance over her shoulder as she and Vincent moved into the tunnel; Father already had the volume open, placed flat on the table, and was to all appearances deeply engrossed.

She truly *was* tired; her legs wanted to tremble and it seemed nearly too much effort to breathe. Small wonder, she thought. A rehearsal this morning, photographs and an interview before that for *People* magazine and then the performance itself. Aurora wore on her these days more than it had in 1978; she could hardly bear to admit that to herself. But it wasn't age, it was conditioning. So much of the muscles' edge was lost in the first three days; after a few weeks it was a terrible uphill climb to get back into shape. And that was for the young ones, the twenty-five-year-olds with their elastic-band tendons and springy muscles. I've been away from it too often, she thought in despair. Too long these past years since I married Alain.

Alain, who had been pleased when she gave up dance to marry him—she had called it a temporary hiatus, and he'd agreed. He'd said so often he would never argue if she was invited to perform with Nureyev's company in Paris, to dance for some special occasion. The few times she had brought it up, though, there had always been a prior commitment, travel on the Mediterranean once, a week in Bermuda another time—always some excellent reason why Alain must be away, why his beautiful wife must accompany him.

Some excellent-sounding excuse. He'd been preoccupied with some business dealings, some problem or other when the New York tour came up, or he'd have doubtless created another obstacle for her. Instead he'd made her promise to telephone him every night—and he'd sent Collin to "protect" her.

She let her eyelids sag as she gazed down the long, rough-hewn tunnel, the scent of smoke and candle wax wrinkling her nose. Collin: hanging mistrustfully over her shoulder, making the *People* reporter nervous, firing questions at Cathy Chandler, the look on his face in Alain's suite . . . But no, she would not think of them. Not Alain, not Collin. Not now, not ever again.

She had escaped them both; whatever else life held for her, they were over and done with.

She became fully, properly aware of Vincent at her shoulder, though she'd never really lost the sense of him to her right side and a little behind her—near enough to touch, not quite touching. They were past his chamber, past a dozen openings she remembered with startling clarity, considering how many years it had been since she'd last walked through them. They were half-way to the guest chamber and he still had not said a word. She spoke abruptly, and the despair in her voice surprised her. "Father hates me."

She felt his eyes on her; dark, grave, considering. She kept her own on the passageway, on the mixture of candles in wrought-iron footed sconces, in chipped glass hurricanes, in shining drinking glasses—set into the rock wall, placed along the smoothed stone floor. "He doesn't hate you," he said finally. The depth of his voice, the resonance of it still surprised her; there was no particular inflection to his reply. She had no idea what he might be thinking, and that made her uneasy. Once he had been an open book, every thought clear on his face, in his gestures, his words. Now . . .

"He hates me," she said with low-voiced passion. "Or why does he insult me with his politeness?" Welcome to stay as long as you like, she thought bitterly, and every line of his face, his body giving graciously spoken words the lie, his eyes and the hard set of his mouth making it clear he wished she had not come back at all! "He blames me," she added, and bit her lip.

Vincent looked down at her tense, bared shoulders, at the stiff line of her proudly carried head. He could not see her face just now. "Perhaps a part of him does," he agreed softly. If she would only say something, if they could go back to it long enough to understand each other! For a moment, he thought she might.

But she shook her head and said, "Let's not talk about it."

Yes, that was so like Lisa, he thought sadly. Poor Lisa, who wanted no dark places in her light world. Lisa, who thought that denying the dark would make it vanish. Catherine had never done that. Catherine . . . He wanted to see her now, at once. To touch her. To touch her, to feel her unreserved love, her strength . . .

"Lisa," he said suddenly, tentatively. "There are things you don't know of."

She shook her head again, looked up at him with a little smile on her lips. "Vincent, please."

"A time in my life after you left—"

She touched his hand lightly and turned away to

throw her arms wide, embracing everything. "I want to remember the pleasant moments." He simply could not reach her. Had he ever reached her, he wondered, and the thought was almost unbearably saddening. She was laughing now, and when she turned back her eyes were soft and unfocused. "I remember running through the tunnels as a girl. So dark, so fast. And I always ran toward the light, the blinding light." Her face was rapt with childhood memories. "Do the children still swim naked in the pool beneath the falls?"

He hadn't thought of that in some time. "I believe they still do."

"And the cliffs, do you remember the cliffs?"

He smiled, nodded. "I remember."

Lisa laughed quietly. "Diving where the water was deepest, staying down as long as we could..." She sighed, fell silent, but he could almost feel her thoughts moving from one pleasant moment to another.

"You were happy here," he said finally.

There was a look of surprise on her face. "I *was* happy, wasn't I?"

"I think you were."

The smile slipped as she turned away. I was happy, she thought. Here as a child, and then when I found dance; dancing here, dancing Up There. If I have lost that, forever, what is left for me? She could feel the chill settling over her bones, feel the breath stop in her throat, almost as though she had just died. Perhaps a part of her had. Never again to dance... She came across the tunnel and let him take her hand. They walked on in silence for some moments. "I'm suddenly tired," she said, and withdrew her hand.

Vincent looked at her uncertainly as she turned away and started down the tunnel. "The guest chamber is near," he said.

"I can find my way," she replied. "You needn't walk me any further." She brought up one of those brilliant smiles that left her eyes haunted. "I remember the way."

He stepped back from her, uncertain whether she feared to have him with her, if that was only his thought, his own ancient guilt, his worry. She had already turned to walk away from him, and now she moved lightly and quickly. At the far end, she was almost running.

He watched her go. "Sleep well," he whispered. She walked—she even ran as though there should be music for her, always. Perhaps she heard it. Just now, he heard music, but it was in his mind.

He turned abruptly and walked back the way he had just come, until he was near enough his own chamber and Father's that he could see the particular, familiar stone outcropping that marked the entrance to Father's chamber. He went on past the Long Hall, went down the Great Stair and turned to the right, walked a short way down a narrower passage; descended a clattering flight of metal steps that circled a deep, black pit. His boots kicked small stones into the depths, and far below he could hear the echoing, whispery splash as they hit water. A low tunnel, branching off to one side, and then another; it was behind a spill of rock and some ancient timbers, hard to find unless you knew what to look for. Once beyond the rock, he had to stoop to keep from hitting his head, and the way was almost totally dark at first. "It has indeed been a long time," he murmured, and his words fell dead in the little passage. He could not remember having to duck before.

It was a short tunnel, a shortcut used by the children who came to swim. Water splashed as he came into the open; droplets touched his face and sparkled in his hair. There was a wide ledge here, a pool shallow nearest the entry, quite deep under the falls. Water dropped in a wide, frothing stream from high above, and by tilting his head back he could see the edge of the cliff where it began, where the braver children climbed to dive alongside the falls into deep water so far below. There was a lantern up there; a flickering one set in a niche to his left. Two on the far side of the pond, where children had apparently left them, something brightly green by them. He picked his way across the damp concrete and gravel surface, squatted and picked up a nearly new

T-shirt. He turned it over, smiled faintly at the "New York Jets" logo there.

So, Billy had come swimming, and forgotten his precious shirt. Vincent would return the garment, put it across the foot of the boy's bed while he slept, so he would find it in the morning.

He folded and refolded it with deft-fingered hands, gazed out across the empty pool.

He and Lisa; he could remember when she had first come, a skinny little thing—like young Billy—not more than five years old. She'd spent those first years in one of the projects with no father, a mother who had cared more about drugs and men than her daughter until both had killed her. Vincent's first memories of Lisa were those huge, dark eyes, a face that promised the beauty that came later, that wonderful smile when she had first learned she would not have to return to the projects, or go into some kind of home. Her eagerness, the way she had accepted him at once. He had been extremely sensitive in those days about meeting new children, even though Father and the others carefully prepared them for Vincent and his—differences.

Lisa hadn't cared. "She liked me for myself," Vincent told the falls. It had been more than that, of course, though he hadn't wanted to admit it for a long time. "And also, because I did whatever she wanted."

But many of the other children, and later many of the boys also were her willing slaves. She had given more of her free time to Vincent than to anyone else.

He remembered his irritation in those first days at the stories—the truly astonishing lies she made up about who her father was, who her mother was; stories about the wicked woman who had stolen her away from a life of privilege and carried her off to the projects. Father had explained as best he could. "She hasn't anything pleasant to remember, Vincent. And she has no belief in herself yet. Once we give her belief in herself and we can convince her that she has worth, she will no longer cling to such fantasies."

Worth and belief in herself. Vincent shifted and gazed

down at the folded green T-shirt. Thanks to Father, *he* had that. Young Billy was developing it, losing his fear, shedding the armor that kept people away. Lisa—had she ever believed in all their love? Or had she accepted it and still believed herself unworthy? And whose fault was it, if that was the truth about Lisa? Was it anyone's?

He got to his feet, taking one of the lanterns and the T-shirt with him. It was a long way back, and he was accomplishing nothing here, save to remind himself of things he could remember anywhere.

As he left the low passage and started back up the circle of metal steps, he could see it all so clearly: candles everywhere. The Great Hall was not so brilliantly lit as when all the denizens of the tunnels came together there to celebrate, but enough to drive back the darkness, to cast circles of brightness upon the ceiling, to show where the walls were. And he heard music, her favorite music. Lisa, her long, waving spill of dark hair pulled back from a slender, oval face of utterly enchanting beauty. She had worn a ballerina's costume to surprise him, a sleeve-less bodice held up by slender straps that left her shoulders and much of her back bare, a long, sheer skirt that swirled around her legs as she danced or fluttered and fell to stillness as she paused.

And the best surprise of all—at least she had called it that as she brought the skirts up in a two-handed dancer's gesture to show him pink toe slippers. She had taken hold of his shoulders and pulled him with her so he was in the very center of the great open door. "You just stand here, Vincent." He could hear the metal stairs, the echo of his footsteps as he climbed in the here and now; at the same time could hear Lisa's high young voice echoing in the half-lit Great Hall. It was light, flirta-tious—slightly bossy, filled with the certainty he'd do just what she wanted.

Had he protested? He couldn't remember what he had said when he realized what she wanted, only her words as she moved away to begin her dance again. "Stand very still, Vincent; you needn't do anything but just be there. You'll be my Prince."

She had danced around him, for him—with him, surrounding him with the vision of her loveliness, her grace and the wonderful dancer's costume that accented her beauty and grace; the music, her joy as the sequence of steps and turns and leaps went as she wished, as that gave her confidence.

He could almost feel what that young Vincent had felt even as his feet trod the passages and moved along a concrete catwalk and a train thundered overhead, somewhere nearby. For one precious moment, he had entered Lisa's world, where music and movement played off each other.

And then a sudden, horrible change: a nightmare of pain and anger and loss, his own roar echoing in his ears—and Father's voice hauling him back from that beast-fury, back from inner darkness.

Vincent stopped and leaned against the wall, arms folded across his chest, brought himself back to the present with an effort. There was more; the little he had recalled just now left him writhing inwardly with the knowledge of the rest of it. "I wish I could not remember," he whispered. "Or that it had never happened, or that I had been someone else, or she had. But that is Lisa's way, not mine." His eyes were troubled, his thoughts deeply distressed. The time had come to bring it all out; to face what had happened so long ago, to resolve the feelings that tortured him.

If he could.

"Why did I push him aside?" Lisa asked herself as she dropped onto the guest bed and stared at the distant wall. "I'm not afraid of him, of being near him." She wasn't certain if that was honest or not; it was too easy anymore to believe her own words, even when she knew they weren't true. She was too tired to even care just now if she was being honest with herself. Only happy memories, she had told him; that, at least, was completely true.

"But I can't alienate Vincent, he's the only—" She swallowed, let her eyes close and ran a weary hand over her hair, pulled the chiffon flowers off the chignon and shook her hair loose. As loose as she could; it was stiff with spray and her fingers snagged here and there as she tried to work them through it. Vincent was *not* the only one she had left; there were others who loved her, who would help her and protect her.

But of all those who loved her, only Vincent was Underground, that was a brutal truth. To find anyone else, she would have to venture back into Alain's world, Collin's world—she wasn't sure she'd ever again be able to go Above. If only Vincent would not keep trying to remind her of ancient, unpleasant moments! There was no profit in her remembering Father's face that last evening; the things he'd said—so careful to assure her he did not blame her even as the look in his eyes convinced her he did exactly that.

She had more things to deal with just now than unpleasant memory, anyway: there were blisters on her toes from running so far in high heels that had only been intended for the limited amount of walking a woman might do at a party. She drew her stockings off carefully, massaged her toes, the arches of her feet.

She wondered what Collin would do when he could not find her, how long it would be before he called Alain to admit he'd lost her. She smiled grimly and rather triumphantly. Collin would learn that Alain could lose his temper at others besides his wife! He had it coming, nasty, horrible man!

She finally gave up on her hair—it would have to be washed, but not tonight. She did not want to venture out of the guest room again tonight in search of water and soap for it, had no desire to wash standing folded in half over a basin, her scalp and fingers trying to retreat from the chill of tepid water. But she was beyond tired at this point; she was utterly spent.

At least she could sleep safe. However uncertain her welcome.

Tomorrow she could begin to plan what she would do.

She laid the party dress gently over a chair, smoothing

the skirts with her hand. The hems were damp; miraculously, she hadn't snagged them in that headlong flight. She was grateful for that; it was one of her favorite dresses of this season.

A thick shirt with long sleeves had been laid out across the foot of the bed. How long, she wondered with sudden amusement, has it been since I slept in a garment that belonged to someone else, or several someone elses? *Used* and *hand-me-down* were words that hadn't been in Lisa Campbell's vocabulary for more than a decade. But the shirt was warm and soft; it smelled like childhood and home. She slid into it and hugged it close as she walked barefoot around the room, extinguishing candles until there was only the single light on the wobbly stand beside the bed. She climbed under the patchwork pile of covers before she blew that one out.

At first the darkness was total; she had forgotten how complete it was in the moments between turning out the last of the lights and when her eyes adjusted. She could see faint light from the corridor now, a little high above and off to one side where there was a chink in the vaulted ceiling. She let her eyes close then and let once-familiar sounds lull her to sleep.

On the top floor of the Plaza, Collin Hemmings lay in Lisa Campbell's bed and listened to the sound of late Friday night New York through the open window. She might still come sneaking back in tonight. If that was her plan, she'd expect to greet him in the morning with an arrogant look on her face and some wild, easy lie on her neatly polished lips.

It would be like her; he hoped she did exactly that. Because he'd like to see the look on her face when she came sliding in here and found him waiting in the dark for her.

Vengeance aside, he really did hope she acted according to her usual style. He had no more than twenty-four hours to find her, before Mr. Taggert expected them. She would have to be found, somehow hustled onto the private jet and out of the city in that time, or

he'd have to call London. He ran down a mental check-
list of people she knew, places she might have gone.
He'd wait until daybreak for her, then begin a systematic
search.

She wouldn't go to the police. What would she tell
them? "Please, Officer, my husband wants me to come
home and I don't want to go"? New York police had
more to worry about than one overly dramatic ballet
dancer, and Collin knew Lisa would never deliberately
make a fool of herself that way.

No, she'd be with a friend, or one of those ballet
people from the Center. He could start in the morning
by calling that man Palmieri. Or, better yet, he'd get
hold of one of the local men, have someone's wife or
girlfriend call around posing as a girlfriend, looking for
her. He and Lisa were supposed to be on their way to
London already and besides, Palmieri hadn't liked him.
Maybe he'd get nervous, even go to the cops if he
thought Lisa had gone missing.

Strategy set, he let himself sleep. He'd hear her if she
came in, however quietly she moved on those famous
little twinkle-toes of hers.

Five

CATHERINE woke Saturday morning early, refreshed after a full night's sleep, full of happy anticipation. For the first time in weeks, she had the day all to herself and she was making the most of it: it was going to be like one of the old days—a constant whirl of events, socializing. Something she seldom wanted anymore, and all the more enjoyable when she let such a day happen. And like one of the best days she could remember from back then, she could see a brilliantly blue sky out her windows. So rare, that kind of October day. She threw on a light-weight kimono and stepped onto her terrace to gaze out and around her in delight.

It wasn't exactly warm, but there was no real hint of the chill that had reddened her cheeks the night before, when she'd left work. There wasn't a cloud anywhere; only yellow and red leaves on the elm and maple down in the park, leaves covering the grass and walks, to remind her it wasn't late spring.

"An enchanted day," Cathy told herself, and hurried back inside to change. A silk dress—the red one that went with the wide-brimmed panama with the silk rose in a black-and-white striped band. Suitable for a posh gallery opening; her old friend Eileen Clancy had vanished from her life for years after Radcliffe, until the neat little embossed announcement of her opening came in the mail—an announcement marred by one inky fingerprint and Eileen's messy scrawl on the back, *Hey, Chandler, wanna come see me before I get too famous to know you any more?*

After the opening—and, she hoped, a little time to drag Eileen away, at least into a corner, so they could catch up with each other's lives—she had promised her father lunch. Or, as Charles would no doubt say, he'd bribed her to suffer with his presence in exchange for a decent meal—after which patently untrue statement, they'd both laugh.

She deftly applied makeup, brushed out her hair until it gleamed and fixed the hat at a rakish angle. She made a face at her reflection, caught up a jacket in case the weather suddenly turned cool and went out to catch the elevator. She thought about her father while she waited—nice Saturday mornings and her building elevator didn't mix, she should have allowed for half the tenants going out for breakfast. Charles had spent most of the summer out on Long Island, as he usually did, and she'd been almost too busy to see him. She'd had a couple of days off in September but he'd been in Germany with Kim, taking a castle- and art-lovers' cruise down the Danube. Two—no, three phone calls since he'd come back, and somehow they hadn't been able to get together.

"I have to spend more time with him, somehow," Cathy murmured as the elevator stopped, groaning, and the doors reluctantly opened. Well, she would see him today, anyway, and for at least a couple of hours, they could talk and kid around with each other over excellently prepared food and a cup of cappuccino.

There was a party later, just a cocktail hour get-together and something she ordinarily passed on anymore, but this one was an informal congratulations and farewell combined for Jenine Van Hulden, a friend from law school, who had just landed the position she'd wanted so badly in Los Angeles. Cathy had heard some of the guys were chipping in to buy her a surfboard. She came out of the elevator grinning at the thought of the extremely unathletic and uncoordinated Van Hulden trying the thing out. Better yet, trying to squeeze it into her suitcase . . .

She was still grinning as she stepped out into the street and hailed a cab.

She would have known Eileen anywhere, even without the ink stains all over her fingers and the fingernails that were clipped short and more or less polished with chipped sparkly stuff. She'd caught so much flak for those hands, all the way through school. She was even, Cathy suspected, wearing one of the same shirts she had owned back then. She was very much the same, cheerful Eileen, exuberantly glad to see Catherine, and her showing of pen and ink sketches was brilliant. "It's my second—first in New York, of course," she chattered happily. "The *Times* is supposed to send someone out to talk to me later on—maybe it was one of the other papers," she added doubtfully, and ran an inky hand through short, tousled hair. There hadn't been as much time as either one wanted, but they'd talked. "We can get together later, right?" Eileen insisted as Catherine took another look at her watch; there was just enough time to meet her father in front of the restaurant and be on time, if she had luck with cabs. "Or are we going to be like the jokes with the yuppie chicks who can't find matching blank pages in their diaries?"

Catherine laughed at that, hugged her friend hard. "We'll manage somehow. Call me, you have my number. I'll call you if I don't hear, all right? I'm so proud of you, Clancy!"

"Yeah, well." Eileen hugged back. "I'm proud of me, too." She pulled back, studied Cathy's face for some moments. "I'm proud of you, too, Chandler. What I'm doing only takes determination; what you're doing takes guts. I don't know if I'd have them."

Catherine grinned. "You have a *Times* art reviewer coming down here and you don't think you have nerve? I'd be scared to death, and look at you!" She could still hear Eileen laughing as she went out the door and onto the street.

She reached the sidewalk in front of the restaurant scant moments before her father did; he was smiling as he came away from the curb and took hold of her arm. "Just exactly on time, weren't you?"

She tilted her head so she could look at him from under the broad-brimmed hat and smiled back. "Fashionably late isn't in my vocabulary anymore, remember?"

They talked mostly about the Danube, the Rhine, the castles. "Next time I think I'd like to do Stuttgart—the Mozart festival."

"What," Cathy inquired dryly, "you're planning on going back four years from now? I hear the wait for tickets is that long."

"Well, but not for everything," he said and as the waiter brought coffee, he took her hand. "It was a wonderful trip, Cathy. I wish you could have been there."

"I know," she said softly.

"I kept seeing things and telling Kim that Cathy should see that, or—" He paused, shrugged and released her fingers and concentrated on stirring a lump of sugar into his coffee.

"You had your hands full with Kim," Cathy said in mock accusation. Charles laughed over the rim of his cup but his eyes ruefully acknowledged the truth of that. "Two of us would have driven you crazy, trying to keep track of us."

"You'll have to come out soon, see all the pictures. Kim should have purchased Kodak stock before we went."

"Your fault for buying her that neat little camera," Cathy retorted cheerfully. "I will come out, though; next time I get an entire day to myself, like this."

There was a little silence; unlike some of those in earlier times, it was a comfortable silence. Charles Chandler still couldn't understand what drove his daughter to leave his lucrative corporate practice—the corporate firm she'd have one day inherited, if things had gone as he'd hoped—but she seemed happier these days than she had when she was still Charlie's girl, and the heir apparent. He still worried that she worked too hard, didn't eat enough, that she was under too much stress. That she ventured into poor neighborhoods, into apartments and houses in places he would never drive through in a locked car.

But that was a father, worrying; any father worth his salt worried about his child, even when there was no cause for it—or when the child was so capable of taking care of herself. She was happy; she was doing what she wanted to do, and doing it well. That was the thing that counted.

He waited until the waiter slid the check onto the table and moved discreetly away before he sprang his surprise. "How'd you like a date for Halloween night?"

"Halloween night—what day is that?"

"Don't know. Does it matter? I'd like to take you to a costume party."

"Oh." She considered this momentarily. "How fun! I can't remember the last time I did that. Where?"

"That's the other part of it. Remember John Brennan?"

"Of course I do."

"Well, the party's partly because of Halloween—if you remember Brennan you remember how he likes fancy dress parties." She nodded. "But it's mostly on behalf of Brigit O'Donnell."

Catherine clapped her hands together and stared at her father over her fingers. "Oh! You mean, she'll *be* there?"

He laughed and nodded, delighted by the reaction he'd provoked. "I talked to John last week and he mentioned this party, and I knew a lot of your old crowd would be coming. But when he said Brigit O'Donnell was going to be there—I remembered you telling me about her books, how much you thought of her." He watched her; watched in slight puzzlement as her smile faded. "Cathy? It's all right, isn't it?"

She shook herself and the smile came back to life. "Oh, it's wonderful, Dad. I—was just thinking about the friend who first introduced me to Brigit's work." She hadn't thought of Vincent in hours, she realized, and she felt vaguely guilty. But she would have done him no service by staying in her apartment and moping; he wouldn't have thanked her for that, either.

It was just a pity he would not be able to meet Brigit O'Donnell.

She became aware Charles was watching her, with that look on his face that was a father trying not to butt into a daughter's personal life. She brought herself back to the moment. "I'd have been honored to be your date even without Brigit," she said softly, and squeezed his fingers briefly. "Thanks, Dad." She sorted out the day, the date. "I thought I was going to do my laundry after I left you this afternoon, I think I'd better get a costume reserved instead. Should we match?"

"You feel like playing Scarlett? Kim got me a Robert E. Lee costume for that cruise we took last spring, I can't see just wearing it the once, can you?" He left her at the corner—she decided to walk since the costumers she remembered best was only a few blocks and her heels weren't really *that* high. She waved as he turned around in the back seat of the cab.

No Scarlett, she decided firmly as she entered the shop—more like a barn, really, with garments lining the windows, on racks, hanging from the ceiling—everywhere. No seventeen-inch waists and seventy-inch hoop skirts. And—and let's see how quickly I can get in and out of here, she thought after she glanced at her watch. The afternoon was going rapidly, there was still Jenine's party, a swing by her apartment first for something warmer to wear, a different pair of shoes, definitely a jacket—and the gift-wrapped box that contained the little gold bracelet with two charms—an apple and a palm tree. She hoped it would remind

Jenine of her once she was out in Lotus Land. At any
rate it would be a little more practical than a surfboard.

Monday was the usual hectic mess: Moreno was having fits because one of his witnesses against a Chinatown
protection gang had vanished without a trace—into the
East River, probably—and the other two witnesses had
decided maybe they hadn't seen anybody's face after all.
Three ADAs were gathered around one of the word
processors while a harassed typist tried to make sense
of three men talking at the same time. The papers she
was trying to finalize and print out had been due across
town on Friday; the new fax machine was on the blink
again and the woman who'd sworn she didn't believe
in anything that newfangled was the one hanging over
it anxiously, nearly in tears because she couldn't get
anything *out*. Cathy threaded her way through the chaos
but before she could reach her desk Joe popped out of
his office and motioned her in.

"Big time, Radcliffe. Wanna go play with the big boys
over at the federal courthouse?"

She perched on the arm of the client chair and did a
quick mental count on the code-three items on her desk.
"I'd like to. I have your Hollingwood thing, though,
and—"

"I'll shift Hollingwood if you aren't back in time. I've
got to be in front of Judge Beatty right at nine forty-five
and it may go all morning. Hell," he ran his hand
through his hair, throwing it into disarray. "You know
Beatty, it may go all day. It's Black Monday around here,
all right."

"It's Friday the Thirteenth come on a Monday," she
agreed with a smile. He considered this, gave a snort of
laughter.

"Hey, that's not bad. Anyway, federal court: it's the
Perez-Hech thing. I don't think they'll need much out
of you; you're going in mostly as an observer on the
preliminary hearing. I'll give you my notes—I got them
typed up, so you'll be able to read them. And you know
the bottom line."

She nodded. "We want them for murder, first degree."

"Aggravated murder," he corrected her. "And the AG thinks they should get precedent because those bozos smuggled in the planeload of cocaine that started the whole mess." He looked at her critically. "You'll do fine. Here, unload your junk, come back, I'll walk you downstairs and give you the notes and the rest of it. You don't mind?"

"It's fine. Stipulating Hollingwood," she added.

Joe laughed again. "High-falutin' talk, Chandler. Sound like a lawyer."

She didn't feel particularly confident about appearing in a federal courtroom; she'd had too little exposure in that particular arena. But this sounded like a good way to break in. And if there was a little spare time—a break somewhere that she didn't need to study Joe's notes or run through one of the myriad points of procedure he'd shoveled into her arms in the elevator—she intended to hunt up someone who could give her some information about the Alain Taggert indictment. If it had come down; if they could tell her; if they had a list of witnesses. Perhaps Lisa Campbell was already in protective custody; that alone would be worth knowing. Particularly after the news in the Saturday afternoon papers.

It hadn't made big headlines; mostly a one-inch article on an inside page of three different papers. The *Times* had it on the front page of the Sunday arts section, together with an article inside by the man who'd reviewed her *Swan Lake*.

Dancer Cancels Performances at Lincoln Center. No explanation had been given by the Center, the company —by anyone. Lisa Campbell hadn't been available for anyone to ask—including Catherine, who had called the theater between matinee and evening performance hours, and talked to the man who'd supplied her with the backstage pass. He'd been cautious; he hadn't been certain of much except that Lisa had attended a Friday night party and that seemed to be the last time anyone had seen her. The *Times* reviewer had praised the bal-

lerina hustled into Juliet's costume for Saturday night
and had delivered a series of stinging remarks at the
end of his column, directed to "a certain prima donna
who apparently finds a New York audience no longer
to her tastes."

If she'd been ill, the paper would have said so,
surely. And there would have been commiseration, not
anger, in the articles. No, it was more likely she had
simply vanished—possibly of her own free will, to
avoid being embroiled in this investigation. But Catherine found herself wondering where Collin Hemmings
was at present—and what he might have had to do
with it.

The day dragged; she had forgotten how exceedingly
slow federal court could be. Late in the afternoon, the
judge took the matter under advisement. Catherine
wasn't looking forward to telling Joe he wouldn't know
the outcome for somewhere between days and weeks—
depending on the judge's backlog of matters already
under advisement. She decided that breaking the bad
news could wait another few minutes, and went looking
for information.

She talked to the security guard at an information
desk, who sent her upstairs to a receptionist, who spent
several minutes on the phone and then turned her over
to a secretary in a vast room broken into a maze of gray
sound-insulating panels. The secretary took her through
corridors and past what seemed like hundreds of desks,
left her with a vaguely familiar man who occupied one
of the windowless cubbyholes along the far wall. He
stood, held out a hand. "Cathy Chandler, isn't it? We
met over a document production a couple of years ago.
David Brukowski," he added before she had to admit
she remembered his face but not his name.

"Right." She smiled and nodded. "I remember that
day and a half. I almost quit law right then." Back in
her corporate law days, when she was dissatisfied with
what she was doing anyway. She'd volunteered to take
over that document production, she remembered with

an inner shudder; guilt over her lack of enthusiasm for her dad's practice had prompted her to go overboard the other direction. Which had left her cooped up in a tiny room with this David Brukowski while they went through four deep boxes of paper one sheet at a time, coping with the noisy Xerox machine, the heat, terrible coffee.

"Me too," he said. "But I don't imagine you're here to recall the good old days, right?"

Cathy nodded again. "Alain Taggert." David Brukowski stopped smiling. "What can you tell me about him—what," she amended carefully, "are you allowed to tell me about him?"

He considered this. "Precious little. Except that we think we can reel him in. We have a pretty good case built up against him for selling weapons to terrorists; we think we can prove he was involved in the explosion in Madrid that killed American soldiers. If so, it won't matter that he isn't an American citizen himself. If it goes down the way we intend, we'll be able to get him extradited."

"Is his wife going to testify?"

He looked at her sharply. "Lisa Campbell? Why do you ask?"

"I—I'm a friend of hers," Cathy said. "She was here until a few days ago, but she's dropped out of sight. I thought perhaps—"

"That we had her? I wish we did," he said feelingly. "We have sources that say she knows enough to bury the man. But we haven't been able to get in touch with her." He shrugged. "We put the word out, via some of her dance friends in London and here, that we'd like to talk to her. She's had one of Taggert's men all over her since she stepped off the plane two weeks ago, no one's been able to even blink at her."

She let her eyes close briefly. "I know. I had the pleasure. You think she's run instead?"

He shrugged again. "We've heard everything: that she'd love to testify, that she's too afraid of Taggert to open her mouth, that she really doesn't know anything.

That she's trying to figure out how to reach us, that she's back in Taggert's hands—willing or otherwise. Hell." He sighed. "Listen, you're a friend of hers? You hear from her, tell her to at least talk to us. We'll keep it quiet, Taggert doesn't need to ever know."

Easier said than done, Cathy thought soberly. But she merely nodded and let the man walk her out of the rabbit warren of offices and into the hallway. It was nearly five and the corridor was full of people: attorneys, witnesses, clients—a motley blend of people all talking loudly, trying to be heard.

He stopped short of one of the courtrooms and held out a hand; Cathy turned back to take it. "Thanks for your help," she said. "I appreciate—" Her voice died away and she stared hard over his shoulder. Brukowski turned to follow her glance. "Nothing," she said. "Thought I saw someone I knew." Blond hair, broad shoulders in a dark blue jacket—but as soon as she'd seen that much, the head vanished behind two enormous men in federal marshal brown. The man coming down the hall after them, now she could see him clearly, had sleek yellow hair, a navy blazer, but his face was unfamiliar. She let go of David's hand. "Anyway, thanks. I'll pass on your message if I get a chance."

"Great." David pushed his way back into the crowd—rather like a salmon swimming upstream, she thought. She turned away and let the rush carry her out into the street.

Not far from where she'd been standing, Collin Hemmings stood with one of Alain Taggert's attorneys—a sleek, well-fed, white-haired man with a permanent look of satisfaction in the set of his mouth—and watched her go. "She's a—you said Catherine Chandler?" he murmured.

The attorney nodded. "I've gone against her father often enough to know her by sight. She used to be Charlie's heir apparent, works for the DA these days, though." He tilted his head to regard his taller companion thoughtfully. "Why?"

"Oh, nothing," Collin said carelessly. "Thought I recognized an old girlfriend. It wasn't her."

It was patently a lie; the attorney let it slide with the ease of a man who was used to hearing less than all the truth from his clients; a man who didn't want to know all the truth, most of the time. "Oh," he said, and dismissed it. "Well, look. I can try and get some more information for you, but I warn you, they're keeping the lid on this thing until they can convene the grand jury; my usual source can't pick up things the way she usually does."

"Do what you can," Collin said. "Mr. Taggert wants to know." He hesitated, finally said: "And his wife—?"

The attorney shook his head. "They don't have her; at least, I don't think they do." He looked up at his companion. "It would be better altogether if she did not come forward, her testimony would only confuse the issues. Mr. Taggert tells me she is high-strung and tends to imagine things."

Collin nodded. "I understand," he said flatly. The attorney shifted his grip on the briefcase.

"Ask Mr. Taggert to call me at the Long Island number tonight, will you?" Collin nodded. The attorney left him without further words.

Collin gazed after him, eyes narrowed, but it was not a broad little man in an expensive handmade suit he saw. It was a young woman with swinging, dark blonde hair and a flair for clothing. Catherine Chandler; she hadn't lied about that, at least, though he had already checked and found no record of her at Brookhill.

He'd tried everyone else, tried every possible place Lisa might have gone to ground. She had simply vanished into thin air, and Mr. Taggert was extremely displeased with him.

This Chandler woman was not his last lead, but she was his best at the moment. And the DA's office: perhaps they were cooperating with the feds to hide Taggert's wife. He'd known there was something suspect about her, right from the first. Lisa was an absolutely rotten liar.

He glanced at his watch. He'd lost her for now, but tomorrow—. All those elaborate ideas for finding this Chandler woman and she'd practically fallen into his arms. He smiled, and went to find a phone.

Six

SHE went home and changed into a thick wool skirt, and boots, a long coat and scarf, took gloves out of the pocket as she went across the street and into the park. It was almost dark—in two more weeks it would be fully dark at this early hour—but now she could still see some distance down the sidewalk, and there were bicyclers, a few runners. She smiled at a neighbor walking her dog and went on, striking off across open ground when she finally had the sidewalk momentarily all to herself. She reached the culvert a minute later; checked with inbuilt caution to make certain there was no one around her, that no one had followed her from the path. There was no one in sight. She could hear a couple of young boys a short distance away, apparently throwing a football back and forth.

It was cool inside the thick concrete pipe at first, then warmer. Several feet of darkness, a bend; light.

He had sensed her, of course; he always knew she was coming. And he was waiting at the first branching of the ways, as he so often did; waiting by the locked bars that separated the outside world from his world.

Catherine smiled, went to him and put her arms around him, let her cheek rest against the quilted shirt and the rough wool of his cape for a moment. But his touch was tentative; there was still that awkwardness between them. She moved back to lean against the wall. "Lisa," she said finally. He nodded. "I found out more—I learned things today I thought you should know."

"What things?" His voice was soft but she thought he spoke unwillingly; as if he was not certain if he *did* want to know.

"She's involved with a man—her husband," she corrected herself. Nothing less than the truth would do between her and Vincent, even in this. His gaze was bent upon her; his eyes were deep and she thought unfocused. "He sells weapons to terrorists. And he's about to be indicted for that. There's a good chance Lisa will be called to testify against him."

He nodded again, rather absently; when he finally did speak she barely could make out the words. "For Lisa to come back to us, I knew there were other reasons." He sounded so terribly unhappy.

"Her performances were canceled," she said. "She's probably gotten herself out of the country."

He looked at her for a very long, still moment. "Catherine," he said softly. "She's with us."

It hit her like a blow. For a moment she couldn't find any answer to that; her mouth felt very dry, suddenly. "Well," she said briskly, but her voice sounded stiff and unfamiliar to her ears, the attempted lightness ringing with horrible falsity. "At least we—know where she is."

"Yes," he replied softly. Thoughtfully.

She couldn't bear it any longer; if he would not or could not simply tell her what was so wrong, she must ask. "Vincent. What does this woman mean to you?" He looked at her with troubled eyes and she thought he wanted to speak. "Can you tell me?" she asked gently.

He couldn't make the words come; he still couldn't

bring himself to remember it all, to force himself past misery, pain, guilt. . . . The look on his Catherine's face, her growing unease for her own sake, her concern and love for him that pressed aside her personal fears. He could feel that even through his own unhappiness. He loved her so for her courage. But— If he brought out this ugly truth, if he set it before her; if she could not face it any more than he could—if she shrank from him and from the thing he had done?

But he might never know what Catherine would say or do; he simply could not make the words come. Finally he turned away, taking his eyes from her face and fixing them on the distance. It helped a little. At least, he could try. He would try. "There are moments," he said at last. "Images I remember so clearly, burning so deeply . . ." His voice was low and uneven, and finally faded away.

She didn't even hesitate, even though she could tell his thoughts were not pleasant. "Tell me about those times," she said softly.

He could almost hear the music quickening his blood, movement, the scent of candles . . . . "It was a time when I first felt the tremendous joy dreams can bring, the intoxication of sending your heart into the realm of hope," he said at last; that sickening inner twist of almost-memory touched him, drenching him in guilt and blotting out every last bit of the remembered beauty once more. "And it was at that same time I learned that—for me—dreams could bring more pain than I could ever bear. Enough pain to destroy me." He glanced at her, met her eyes only to shrink from her open concern and her love. He turned away once more. "To destroy those around me."

She had never seen him in such distress and it smote her heart. "How?" she whispered. He could not speak, could only shake his head. "What happened?" Silence. "You can tell me," she said, and there was fear in her voice now. "You can tell me anything."

"I once thought that." He could barely force the words out. "But there are things, things I had dreamt away—"

"Vincent," she said urgently. "We've never withheld the truth from each other, not ever." Her own voice was too high, her throat tight with dread.

He looked up, gazed at her longingly for what might have been a breath, a moment, an hour. "I know." He turned and walked down the tunnel, closing the iron bars and the heavy steel door behind him. He did not look back to see her standing there, frozen with his pain, and her own misery.

Vincent moved down the tunnel, along the fastest way that would take him back to the inhabited region; later, he could not remember at all how he had gone from ground level to his own chamber. How long he sat staring at the high arch of stained glass before he roused himself to go in search of Father. Lisa would not deliberately compromise them. But if she had been watched or followed the night she fled here, if men who sold death to other men knew where she had gone—Father must know.

But he stood in the near darkness of his chamber for several more long moments, eyes fixed on nothing, his thoughts probing at an old, half-buried memory the way a child might prod a bruise, or an aching tooth. And it did hurt. Everything within he thought of as good writhed at that memory. But his unhappiness bore a new layer, an extremely recent one. *Catherine; oh, Catherine, I am so truly sorry.* The look on her face when he left her just now. He had hurt her, and her pain was his. If he could not quell this thing that ate away at him, if he could not bring it to light, he might have irrevocably damaged something infinitely precious. "We have never lied to each other, she and I," he whispered. "We have always told each other everything, freely, knowing that to do otherwise is simply another kind of lie."

He thought of her for some time—hours, minutes, he was not certain. Catherine. It soothed him, and finally helped give him the courage he would need. Once he had given Father his warning he would face himself as he had so often in the past. He would discover the worst in himself, and bring it into the open. And he would conquer it.

Father was as angry as Vincent had known he would be. It was an anger less made of concern over discovery, though; more that Lisa had brought such upheaval with her. He wanted to have her brought to him at once, to send her away. Vincent shook his head. "We cannot, Father. We have a responsibility to her. She has no other place."

Father eyed him in exasperation and waved an arm to take in everything above them. "She has the world!"

"But this is her home."

"This *was* her home, you mean!" the older man retorted furiously. But when Vincent looked up at him, he shook his head in frustration and limped away. He leaned against the wall, fixed his eyes on his thick walking stick, as though he intended to end the matter right there.

Vincent watched him unhappily. "Why, Father?" His throat was trying to tighten once more, making the words hard to force out. But this much had to be settled and what better time than now? "Why do you persist in punishing Lisa for what happened?" He looked down at his hands. "For what *I* did?"

Father looked up at him angrily. "Don't ever say that," he said flatly.

Vincent sighed in exasperation. "*Nothing* has changed since you sent her away!"

"I never sent her away!" Father snapped.

"But you did!"

"No."

Vincent turned away so sharply the hair flew in a golden swirl around his head. "How can you deny it?" he demanded harshly.

He jumped; Father had slammed his stick against the floor with a loud crack. "Oh, for God's sake! Don't you understand? I had to protect you!" He was almost shouting. They stared at each other, aghast at the sudden burst of anger on both sides.

Protect—this was an almost devastating truth. "Protect me?" Vincent whispered; he sank into a chair and sat there, stunned as he considered matters in this new light. "From *her*?"

The older man shook his head. "From disappointment." He sighed, ran a hand through his hair and went back to a brooding study of his walking stick. "I watched you from the moment she came to us, watched you growing up beside Lisa. Knowing that one day she would leave the tunnels. That she would leave you." He ran the hand over his hair again, shielded his eyes with it and his shoulders sagged. "I tried to be fair in raising all of you. I made choices that had to be made. I—I don't know anymore whether what I did was right." He looked up; light reflected in shimmering refraction from damp lashes. "All I do know is that they were made with great love."

Vincent gazed at him, unhappily. So many layers to everything, and nothing that seemed simple ever was: what Lisa had done, what he had. What Father had done. It must have hurt the older man terribly, to be certain he could see what was coming, to not know how to deal with it. He was conscious of Father's eyes, watching him. Waiting. He met the older man's gaze. "And it is with love," he said finally, "that I make the choice I must now make." There wasn't anything else he could say just now; he touched Father's arm as he left, knowing the other would understand his love—just as he understood Father's.

Samantha came running up from the direction of the Spiral Staircase, catching him just outside his chamber. "Lisa is looking for you, Vincent, she said to tell you. She's at the pool."

"Thank you." He smiled down at the child, watched her pelt back up the hall, back stiffly straight and hands out in conscious imitation of a dancer's hands. The love in that little one's voice when she said Lisa's name, the naked worship. Did I sound like that, once? he wondered. He turned and went into his chamber.

Lisa would find him, in time. Or she would wait. He had something he must do—now, while he was braced for it.

Catherine returned to her apartment, still deeply shaken; the face reflected in her mirror was pale, the eyes too wide and all pupil. She went through the motions of preparing dinner and ate little of it; tried to work on some of the things straining the hinges of her briefcase and finally gave that up when she realized she'd been staring at the same piece of paper for almost an hour and still had no idea what it said. She turned the radio on and went through several stations, then snapped it off; put on a tape of Chopin and shut that off after a few moments. It was one of the nocturnes that had been incorporated into the ballet *Les Sylphides*. She didn't need to think about ballet, swans of any color—dancers of any description—just at present. She finally removed her makeup, brushed out her hair, took a quick shower and crawled into bed at what must have been an indecently early hour.

Sleep wouldn't come; she tossed and turned, wrapping the sheets and the comforter around her legs. The noise of the street halved; the faint sounds of other tenants faded away completely. She finally fell into an uneasy doze, dreamed herself and Lisa falling from the stage at Lincoln Center—a stage for some unexplained reason hundreds of feet above the auditorium floor. And Vincent standing down there, coming nearer and nearer as she fell, as Lisa fell, and such a look of dread and confusion on his face. He could not rescue them both, could not decide which of them he would catch, visibly could not move to save either woman. She woke with a sharp cry just before her body struck hard concrete.

Sometime during the night she slept deeply and without any more nightmares. Except that once, she thought, in a perfectly ordinary dream, Collin had been there, watching her from the midst of a vast crowd. She remembered the falling dream when she woke just before the alarm went off; the one with Collin, over her first cup of coffee. That one at least had a painless explanation: the man she'd seen at court the previous afternoon. She managed a smile. Funny—not the amusing sort—how things incorporated themselves into nightmares.

The other dream had its explanations, too, if they weren't as easy to face. She gathered up her purse, her briefcase and her coat. It had hurt her so deeply—the unexpectedness of his retreat, the misery in his voice before he left her. Shutting her out. She ached for him, but she'd been terrified that he might have shut her out of his life forever. A night's sleep had fortunately banished that fear: "Whatever he is, whatever he does, I will always love him," she whispered and smiled. That love was between them, his as well as hers and as immutable as stone, as life itself. It was no guarantee that things would be easy—there was no such guarantee for anything. It did mean obstacles were only that—and this obstacle could be overcome, somehow.

If she was there for him; if he knew she was there for him.

She glanced at her watch as she came out of her building; it was early enough she could catch the bus and still be at her desk on time.

It was a quiet day only compared to the day before; Joe had been predictably irked by the judge's refusal to rule on the spot, but this was Tuesday and he already had other things to take precedent over the Perez-Hech matter. But he bought her lunch as thanks for taking over for him—a hamburger at one of the little hole-in-the-wall places nearby that was nothing more than a counter with too many stools bolted to the floor in front of it, so people seated at the counter had to eat with elbows tucked into their sides. They managed to get one of the two tiny booths back in an airless and windowless corner.

He let her get most of the way through the meal in silence. "Everything going all right, Cathy?"

"Mmm?" She washed down hamburger with a swallow of syrupy coffee, grimacing at the battery-acid taste. "Oh, yeah. Going fine." She wondered if he was trying to worry about her again—when he fussed over office matters, asked if she were keeping up with her work load, he'd call her Chandler or even Radcliffe. He only called her Cathy when he started thinking of her as not only human but small, female and potentially vulnerable.

He looked at her for another moment, thoughtfully, and she wondered if he had heard about her talk with David Brukowski. But he merely nodded, drank coffee and finished his sandwich. "Great. Well, you gonna sit here all day or can we get back?"

She grinned, gave him an ostentatious sigh and drained her cup. "Just waiting on you."

They walked back to the office in silence. Neither one of them noticed the Jaguar that had been parked across the street from their building—that was still there. Or the two men sitting in the spacious front seat. The driver, a squarely built man in an ill-fitting gray suit, nodded to get Collin's attention. "Hey. She's back. Got that guy with her still."

"Fine." Collin didn't bother to say he'd seen her half a block earlier; John Farley had his limitations, but Mr. Taggert didn't hire the man for his intellect, his keen eyes or his brilliant conversation. He glanced at his watch. "We can't stay here. Damn New York street parking anyway. We'll come back—around quitting time, don't you think?"

Farley merely nodded, started the car and pulled away from the curb. Collin glanced at the building as they passed it. It was taking a chance, of course. She might have another hearing in the afternoon, might go straight home from there, be gone when they got back to grab her. Or she might leave with that man, or with someone else. With a crowd.

He didn't worry about it, though. He had a feeling his luck was turning.

It was about time.

It was still early afternoon Above; in the tunnels where Vincent walked, it was—as always—night. He moved rapidly, as if driven along deserted passages, hurrying through vaulted chambers, hallways, rough-hewn rock corridors. He paused only once, at the head of a long flight of wooden steps, a slender railing running down one side. He drew a deep breath, gazed down into the dimness of an enormous, vaulted chamber that must be presently lit up by no more than one or two lanterns. He finally shook himself, set foot on the top and began to descend into the Great Hall.

There was a small cluster of three candles in glass holders set on a table; they cast odd shadows on the wall, little shards and prisms of light on the ceiling. He looked down at them for one long moment, then turned away to pull a high-backed, ornately carved Victorian dining room chair away from the wall. He carried it past the table, set it down so the back shielded him from the candlelight, sank into it and let his hands fall onto the incised arms. His fingers explored the wood, briefly, then went still as he let his thoughts go back.

Back years.

The same room, overlaying the moment in which he sat here, but there were many candles lit: Lisa's doing. She had sent for him. "A surprise," she had told them—whoever it was that had come to find him. He couldn't remember; but that, at least, was unimportant.

It was like being back there once again. He could see himself standing four steps up from the floor, looking down at the slender young woman in the very middle of the Great Hall floor, candles illuminating her. For one moment, he scarcely recognized her: this was not the Lisa who played and laughed with him; Lisa who wore the curious collection of garments that immediately identified her as one of the Underground children. Not Lisa with her wild, loose hair falling all around her shoulders, half-hiding her radiant smile, falling over her wide, dark eyes to be pushed impatiently aside by a long, graceful white hand. This was a dancer—tall, slender, hair severely pulled away from her face and tied with a ribbon. She was dressed plainly: a snug bodice of palest pink and long, flowing skirts the same color. Her stance was the tall, straight grace of a dancer in repose.

He gazed at her for so long. And then she clapped her hands together in delight, Lisa's wonderful, bubbling laugh spilling over him, echoing in the empty chamber. He went down to her.

"You are beautiful," he whispered, and that pleased her as it always did. But he had never meant it as much as he did this time. She was so very lovely, it made his heart ache.

"Look at me!" She had turned, watching his face over first one shoulder and then the other as she turned. "Elizabeth got me the leotard and tights, they're *new*, and she made the rest." She turned back, gathered the skirts two-handed and lifted them daintily, to extend first one foot, then the other. "And look—!"

"Your toe shoes," he had said, and Lisa had laughed again, at him this time—but gently.

"No—they're pointe slippers, Vincent. They're for dancing on pointe. I finally earned them. But there's more—remember *Giselle*, remember the second act, all white dresses and the Wilis—the fairies who dance unfaithful men to their deaths?" He nodded; he wasn't certain he could place that out of all the dances he had seen with her. But he didn't think Lisa noticed, or cared. She was much too excited. "I can—oh, watch!" And she began to dance.

He watched in surprise and then delight. His world was bound more in words and music—Shakespeare and Byron; Chopin and Debussy. He cared for ballet because it mattered so much to Lisa; each time he followed her up that long ladder to peer through the grate at the vast stage, he watched her and enjoyed her pleasure more than he watched the dancers. But he *did* recognize what she was doing. "How wonderful." He barely whispered it, but she heard from halfway across the room and turned neatly on one toe to smile gloriously.

That was when she had come across to take him by both hands and tug at him. Until he at last followed her to the middle of the empty room. "You stand here," she said.

He tried to protest, to say he couldn't do any of that. "Lisa, no. I don't—" But she laid her fingers across his mouth and shook her head.

"No, Vincent, don't argue. Don't deny me this, you must. Please! You needn't dance, just stand there. Very still. Just—be there for me, I will do all the rest, you'll see." That silenced him. And then she added, "You can be my Prince," and he smiled at her and capitulated all at once, and did what she asked.

Seated in the high-backed, worn chair, he remembered music. Thinking now, he was not certain there had been music. Perhaps not. Perhaps Lisa's inner sense of the proper music had convinced him it was there. But he remembered music, just as he remembered the hall suddenly radiant with lights—as brilliantly lit as it was at celebration times. And Lisa—always Lisa.

She moved slowly at first, her eyes nearly closed, her shoulders tense and her face expressionless as she sought to recall the exact sequence of movement, to keep her ankles and knees properly positioned above the pink satin slippers, to move her arms and hands the right way. And then, suddenly, she executed a pirouette on one toe, the other leg bent at the knee behind her, a coquettish little turn he'd seen often on that stage; she'd done it every bit as beautifully as any of those dancers had. When she turned, she looked up and smiled at him. And from that moment, he was lost.

"You are so very beautiful," he had whispered once more, but this time she did not hear him; she was dancing—for herself, for him. Just as she had once promised. There was music, then—in his mind and hers, if nowhere else; Lisa moved away, nearly into shadow, back again in a series of whirling leaps that sent her hair flying across her shoulders, the sheer skirts swirling high above her knees, snug against her thighs. They settled back around her ankles as she balanced on one toe, in a long arabesque, and he felt his skin burn through his thin white shirt as she laid one slender hand on his shoulder to balance against him. The dancers on that stage had done the same thing—an arabesque, a sidelong glance, a turn that moved across his back, an arch look across his shoulder and into his eyes. He only vaguely remembered that: because it was Lisa who touched him, and it was as though she had never touched him before. She came around his left side, balanced one long moment against his forearm and danced lightly away from him. He was desolate, he reached for her the way the male dancer would, but his heart went with it. *Lisa.* She surrounded him, dazzled him; his eyes saw only her, a pale, fragile and utterly desirable creature of light and beauty; his ears heard music, or perhaps that was the beating of his heart. She was all he wanted, all he had ever wanted: she was grace, she was joy, she was—

She came near him again, her eyes mischievous, a gentle smile touching her lips; his feet would not obey him when he tried to move, to follow her. She was a blur of light, she was a butterfly brightness in shadow; she was a presence against his right arm, and then his left; he turned one way and then the other to watch her, his ordinarily expressionless face alight with his own delight. She went on pointe and she was nearly his height; she pivoted on his left shoulder, both hands touching his chest as she leaned forward to touch her lips to his right cheek, and to his left, and again, and again . . .

She had followed the choreography so well, he realized now. Even those fairy kisses, the least pressure of lips against his skin, had been part of the dance, she had added no single thing of her own—save herself. But he had been drawn into the moment too far to remember that. He was aware of himself as Vincent, he knew she was Lisa, that she danced a new sequence of steps, in a new dancer's costume and new slippers, and all for him. But that was the prosaic, real world underlying this froth of grace and beauty, and music that all made his face burn. He was giddy, his breath would not come properly: she was the beautiful creature she danced, she was perfection and joy and love. And she must be his. He simply could not resist her. When she leaned into him once more to kiss him, his arms went around her, to draw her against him.

For one moment, she went utterly still; he was not certain she even breathed. He could not remember that he had, though he remembered the scent of her in his arms, the feel of her dance-warmed bare arms and throat, her small breasts pressed against his chest—the thin white shirt he wore might not have been there at all. Her chin came up, her eyes met his and there was surprise—and fear—in them.

Had he seen that fear immediately? He could not remember; he honestly doubted he had. He had been trembling with the sudden overload to all his senses, and he could not bear to let her go, not even when she put both hands on his chest and tried to press herself away from him. Even when her voice, thin and high, rang against his ears: "Let go of me!"

But—the dance, her hands on his arm, on his shoulder, her face so near his, smiling at him from first one side and then the other, those sweet, soft kisses—! He must have that, he must have, must— She was fighting him now, panic-stricken, and he was fighting a panic of his own. He must hold her, must find the words, tell her! She must stay, she must stay close in his arms, her hair silken against his throat, she must touch his arm, his shoulder, his face, as she just did, she must not flee him! If he took his arms from around her, she would run from him, he would lose her, he could not bear that, she must not—! "Lisa, no!" Had he spoken that aloud? Or only thought it?

"No!" She twisted against his arms, unexpectedly supple. But he could not let her go! He must hold her until she understood, until she stopped trying to free herself! He must tell her—she must not fight him! The right words wouldn't come, and now her eyes were locked on his face—the face that she seemed to see for the first time as different. Not like hers. Not a Prince after all. Not—completely—human.

His fingers dug into her, and his nails—long, deadly nails—extended desperately to hold what he must *not* lose. They caught at the thin pink fabric, slicing through it as though it were paper, tearing through the skin beneath to leave four long red, bleeding lines across Lisa's shoulder.

He was panting, sweating, horrified at the feel of her skin parting, and the stickiness of blood against his fingertips. Lisa was somehow out of his arms, halfway across the chamber, her face paler than her torn bodice, her mouth sagging in shock, her body crouched, ready to flee as soon as she could decide which way to run.

"Lisa!" There was a world of horror and misery in that one word; her name echoed across the vaulted ceiling. She was backing away from him, looking at him in sick, stunned horror, as though he were a stranger, a monster, something unspeakably evil. His stomach twisted with guilt and revulsion at what he'd done; it was nearly doubling him over. He couldn't leave her looking at him like that! Almost without realizing, he had started toward her; someone caught hold of him, holding him in an iron grip.

No! Pain, fury and frustration, blended with the certainty that someone else knew his shame. He then flung himself around with a hellish roar, one massive hand coming back to strike a roundhouse blow, to kill . . .

Father's voice tore through the murderous rage, shouting his name over and over again until he came out of it, Father's hands cradled his head while he wept. When he was able to see once more, Lisa was gone. He had not seen her again, all those long years. Until she fled back Underground. Back into his life.

He became aware of himself once again. Of his fingers, his nails shredding the wood of the chair arms. He withdrew them, held them out before him and gazed at them thoughtfully. Small wonder he had not wanted to remember.

But he must think through it logically; must find the key to understanding why it had happened. Lisa had been dancing a role—acting the part of a young woman, recently dead, trying to save the life of her beloved. She had been copying—faithfully, if he recalled well enough—choreography she had seen. She had not, he told himself with painful honesty, been dancing out her love for him. Oh, she had been fond of him as a friend. She knew he worshiped her, of course; but he thought she was unaware of how deep his love went. He considered that gravely. But he himself had not been aware how deeply he had loved her, until he had taken her in his arms and she had fought to free herself.

Perhaps she had been as innocent as he in understanding real adult love. She had been only a girl of perhaps fifteen years, her entire life had been ballet: all her thoughts of love stories set to music. Where princesses were cursed and turned into swans or cast into enchanted sleep, to be saved by the pure love of a young prince. Where peasant girls went mad and died for true love, and then saved the lives of princes who hardly deserved it. There was little in Lisa's stories to prepare a girl for real love, for the real world. Vincent considered this. How much real love was there even now in Lisa's world?

And he, too, had been young. What he had known of love then came from books, from poetry. He hadn't known how desperate real love could feel, how painful it could be.

"But I was wrong," he whispered. "To try and possess another living being, to destroy love and innocence both in one moment. I did that. Hers, and mine too. But mostly hers. And—I—" He swallowed. Shook his head. He could see her in those last moments, as though she was engraved on his eyelids. Her blood welling from four deep parallel cuts running across her right shoulder; her blood, his violence against her—against his beloved Lisa. He couldn't make the words come, to say aloud even to himself what he had done. He wondered if he would ever be able to forgive himself.

Seven

He shifted, suddenly aware he'd been sitting for hours; that the chair—typically Victorian and therefore enormous—was still not large enough to comfortably hold him. His legs were a little numb. He smoothed the curved wood where his nails had made splinters; he hadn't done it much damage. He pushed it back as he stood.

Someone— He turned. Lisa stood four stairs up from the floor, looked down at him. Her face was nearly as expressionless as his. He'd been so deep in thought, he hadn't heard her come.

She was dressed tunnel-fashion, in a motley of clothing. But she'd contrived to put things together so they looked intended to go together; she resembled a member of the ballet in one of the peasant segments: long skirt that swirled around her ankles as she came to a halt, full-sleeved blouse and loose scarves fluttering about her throat. A great triangle of fringed paisley bound around her hip to snug the upper part of the skirt close.

Vincent waited. He wasn't certain he could speak, not

with that memory still scalding his thoughts. She tilted her head to one side, studied him. The silence stretched. She caught hold of the rail with both hands then, and slid under it. "What's the matter?" She sounded like a child playing mother; the cajoling note in her voice was out of place and at odds with the wary eyes. "You have such a strange expression on your face." She came closer, so near she might touch him. He suddenly couldn't bear to meet her eyes; he bowed his head, fixed his gaze on the floor. He felt her skirt brush over his leg, felt the air stir as she moved around behind him. "Something's the matter. But never mind," she said airily. "I'll just pretend I don't notice anything different about you at all."

It was horrible; he couldn't bear it. He brought his head up to gaze across the dim chamber. She had moved a few steps away from him, but as he found her, she came close again. Her eyes were still wary, but there was an underlying concern in them. She touched his arm gently, embracing it for one long moment, looked up into his face. "What on earth *are* you thinking of?" she asked.

His voice sounded as though he hadn't used it in years. "What happened here—in this hall."

She smiled at once, a determined smile, swirled away from him to spread her arms wide. "Winterfest! Candles, music—!"

"What happened between us." He still couldn't seem to speak above a whisper but the words silenced her at once. She swung back around to stare at him, the smile freezing to her lips. He forced himself to continue. "For so long, I couldn't forgive myself. For hurting you." He couldn't begin to guess what she was thinking—not from her expression, her eyes. But her hands were clasping and unclasping at her waist, and he doubted she was even aware of them. "For driving you away," he whispered.

She shook her head, extended the hands in a kind of helpless shrug. "Vincent," she said in an earnest, low voice. "I'm *going* to make a new life for myself." He could only stare at her in rising frustration mingled still with guilt and misery. Did she understand nothing? She came across the floor, until she was nearly touching him. She held his eyes, as if by that intense look she could convince him of the truth of her words. "You have too great a reverence for the past, Vincent," she said softly. "It was—" She shook her head helplessly. "It was nothing! It was child's play." She let her fingers trail across his shoulder and walked toward the stairs, ready to leave him.

He let his eyes close. Words, so many words, none of them meaning anything—no sense reaching from one person to the other. It made him feel very tired. "So, are we playing now?" he whispered.

"Now?" Softly as he'd spoken, she had heard him, and she stopped at the railing, turned back to face him.

She looked so—lost, standing there. So alone. If he could not find the words to make her understand, what must she feel? His anger at her games was gone as if it had never been, his frustration; nothing was left but the certainty that he must help her. That his love for her, if no longer the intense boy's infatuation he'd once felt, was still deep. He nodded. "Now that you are in danger, that you're afraid," he said softly, persuasively. "I know that you're afraid, Lisa. That you're hiding." She whirled away from him, as though hoping she might not hear him if she could no longer see him, and she went utterly still. "You—surround yourself with illusions, but illusions fade." He touched her arm, and something deep inside twisted painfully as she jumped convulsively, as she faced him just out of arm's reach, eyes wide and blank with remembered fear and pain. "Lisa," he whispered. "You must trust me. As you once did."

He thought she would speak, but her mouth moved soundlessly and after a moment she closed it. He wondered much later what he might have said or done then, if every nerve in his body had not exploded with sudden terror. Catherine? *Catherine!* Her voice echoing wildly, reverberating in his skull: "What is this?" He could feel her frantic attempt to pull free from an iron grip on her elbow, pressure of a gun against her ribs, superior strength that forced her across a darkened street. And then the interior of an automobile, moving into traffic, a horrible sensation of being trapped.

He was up the stairs before Lisa could even recoil from the terrifying change in him; before she could realize it had nothing to do with her. She stood at the foot of the steps, staring after him in blank astonishment long after she could no longer hear his footsteps.

Catherine had decided to finish summarizing one last short deposition before she went home; somehow one short deposition turned into that, two letters and a long phone call. It was properly dark when she pulled on her coat and wrapped the scarf around her neck. But at least the worst of the rush hour traffic was gone, always a good side to things. Her feet were tired enough that she wasn't certain she wanted to ride the bus; she wasn't sure about standing on the curb waiting for an empty taxi, either. But she could see one coming, half a block away, the vacant sign out. She started across the sidewalk, shifted her grip on her briefcase so she could wave it down.

The hand that came around her shoulders had the look of a lover's grasp; it and the arm behind it were as hard as an iron bar. Something hard pressed into her ribs and Collin's face loomed over her right shoulder. "What is this?" she demanded loudly. But there was no one close to hear her. The pressure against her ribs had to be a gun. The nasty little smile said it was. She tried to shift her weight so she could bring her high heel down on his instep, but he was ready for that; he gave her one hard jab with the gun barrel, taking her wind away, hustled her across the sidewalk.

Somehow she was at the curb, the back door of an enormous black Jag was open, the darkened leather interior all she could see as she fell, off balance. The wool of Collin's suit rubbed against her stockings; his weight was momentarily bruising as he threw himself into the car on top of her, yanked the door shut, and the car pulled away from the curb and into traffic. By the time she got herself away from him and upright in the seat, he was sitting in the corner, one ankle crossed over his knee, the gun casually balanced on his thigh. And his eyes were very, very alert to her least move.

Catherine shifted her weight, backing away from him until she had inched herself into the corner. Collin continued to smile; a glance assured her the door was locked from the driver's control, the window up by the same means. And that Collin might not kill her if she tried to force either door or window—but he'd enjoy stopping her.

She forced herself to go very still, to let her hands fall open, relaxed-looking, into her lap, to turn her gaze to the street outside. To wait her chance.

Below her and now some distance behind, the A train clattered through darkness, heading north. A dark form clung to the back of the last car, his mane and long black cloak whipping wildly in the wind.

She was looking out the window still, but somehow she'd lost direction entirely these last few minutes: the driver had gone into a web of narrow streets, tall warehouses, overhanging stone and brick walls, rough, cobbled alleys. She couldn't see any familiar landmarks from down here, only occasional pools of orange light, the bright lights inside an occasional guard station by gates in high fences. There were a few other cars, one or two large freight trucks. A very few furtive-looking men. They were doing this deliberately; driving back and forth, around in circles, hoping she'd lose her bearings. She let her eyes close momentarily and swallowed dread. *Vincent, please find me.* But she couldn't count upon him; she must be ready with what weapons she had—with her wits, with the street fighter's skills Isaac Stubbs had taught her.

Two men, at least one gun. But dark, deserted streets: a woman who appeared intimidated might get free of such men. A woman who—unexpectedly—wasn't frightened of dark, deserted streets might disable one of the men and outrun the other.... She watched the shadowy, damp streets roll by.

Vincent had leaped from the train as it slowed short of its station, had thrown himself back into the subway tunnel when the car suddenly began traveling east. It took him a few minutes to find an opening, to descend the two levels so he could go that direction himself. Her fear was not as intense as it had been in that first terrible moment. But that was her courage, not any change in the danger she was in. He quickened his pace; the heavy black cloak flared out behind him as he raced through the dark.

The Jag pulled through an open gate in a high chain-link fence; there was a deserted guard box just inside the gate, an air of nonuse to the parking lot. The car crunched over gravel to stop just short of a ramp lit by a blue-white mercury vapor lamp that swung loose from its stanchion. A rubble of broken windows and window frames littered the ramp; there were fallen bricks and strips of tarred roofing paper everywhere. The driver turned the key, killed the headlights and they sat for one dreadfully still moment. The door lock clicked at her side, but before she could move, the driver was there, both hands gripping her arm to yank her to her feet. Her head snapped back. Collin came around the car to take her other arm. The gun shone a dull silver in the uncertain yard light.

She would have tried then, but Collin must have read her intentions in her eyes, the tension of her arm. He smiled, shook his head, showed her the gun. They jerked her forward, sending heat coursing through her shoulders, and dragged her up the ramp. A double doorway gaped black at the far end. The driver freed one hand from her forearm and produced a small flashlight from his pocket.

The place hadn't been shut down for long, she thought. There were still large pieces of machinery dotted across the floor. Conveyors ran from machine to machine, but most of the chairs were gone. Drop cloths shrouded two enormous pieces. A glass- and wood-walled office worked into the middle of the floor stood like a box that had been shoved there by a giant foot, rather in the way. The door gaped. The driver hesitated, indicated it with a jerk of his head and a gesture of the flashlight. Collin shook his head and tugged at her arm.

There were skylights further back: just grubby, wire-covered boxes set high in the ceiling. A little light came through them, not enough to illuminate anything but a few more of the pale drop cloths, shrouding meaningless shapes. The flashlight touched a pile of unfinished, turned table legs, a line of backed wooden bar stools, shorter legs that must be for chairs. I'm in an old furniture factory, she thought dazedly. Fingers gripped her right biceps hard, dug into her left forearm. Collin and his unpleasant-looking friend didn't show any signs of letting go of her. She felt the chill of sudden dread run down her back and wondered if it showed on her face.

Vincent had had to retrace his steps when he came up against an unexpected fall of dirt. It wasn't far: twenty steps, a ladder's metal rungs set into the stone wall. But he could feel seconds ticking by with every step he took. His boots rang on the ladder, echoing in the tight space around him. Down, down again. He knew the next level well enough to make up the time he'd lost by his detour, the time he'd lose coming back to the surface.

He could feel where Catherine was: the car had stopped, she was moving on foot now. Nowhere near the subways; he'd do better to get above ground once he cleared this next tunnel. His mouth was dry with her rising fear as he tore down the stone-floored passageway, his footsteps echoing all around him, drowning out distant trains, the clang of pipes.

* * *

Collin was being picky; Catherine could sense the other man's rising irritation—John, Collin had called him. John's growing displeasure. Collin had a businesslike air about him she found unpleasant but this John— The way he looked at her—

The factory was perfect for a woman eluding two men, even with that gun in Collin's hand. He had to be able to see her to shoot her. If either one of them would only loosen that hold on her arms! "Here," Collin said abruptly. The moment she had planned for came and went before she could even draw breath: as John let her go, Collin brought the pistol up to her throat and caught her close. She tugged briefly, felt herself staggering away as he spun her around. He shoved hard against her chest and she fell into a chair.

Dust rose in a cloud, threatening to choke her. The flashlight was in her eyes, blinding, unwavering, and John's breath—licorice over stale tobacco—warm on her face. He leaned over her, one hand pinning her to the chair. "Lisa Campbell," Collin's voice came from behind him crisply. "I want to know where she is."

Catherine shook her head; John's hand cracked against the side of her face, hard, bringing an explosion of white lights behind her eyes; the backhand wrenched her neck and made her ear ring. She and the chair would have gone over if he hadn't been holding onto her coat. She forced herself to open her eyes, to look up at him; he was smiling.

"Lisa Campbell," Collin said again, exactly the same as he had before. "Tell me!"

"I don't know where she is," she began in a flat voice. John's open-hand blow silenced her.

"Tell me." Collin's disembodied, emotionless voice went oddly with John's looming, grinning, eager face. "Where is Lisa?"

"I don't know."

John smiled and she had to fight shuddering away from him, from what that smile promised. "Wrong answer," Collin said lightly, in counterpoint to the slashing openhanded slap and backhand that sent her head flying to one side and then the other. "Let's try again, shall we?"

Don't know, don't know, don't know, she told herself. She could never have handed Lisa Campbell over to this man—not to either of them. But it was not simply Lisa. Not my secret, she told herself. Mustn't— It wasn't good to even think that much. Don't know, she told herself numbly, told Collin in a dreary litany punctuated by hard pain. The sound of John's hard, square palm against her bruised face, her ears ringing so loudly now she could scarcely hear Collin's low, even voice asking the same question over and over. Don't know, don't know, don't know.

There was a little fog, the result of damp streets and a humid, cool night. Vincent's passage tore still pools of white froth into little eddies. Her fear, her pain—but she was near now. A stray dog yelped in surprise and set up a racket of barking as he raced past it, tore across the street and passed the deserted guard station. A high-walled, dark building loomed ahead of him. He scarcely slowed at all as he reached it, caught hold of the low roof above the main sales door and swung onto it. He climbed the wall steadily, leaped over the parapet onto a grubby, tarred roof and began to thread a path between pipes, exhaust vents, ventilator fans and skylights. There was a faint light, down in the far corner of the building, the least reflection of it against sooty glass. He made for it unerringly. She was there.

Catherine blinked rapidly, trying to clear her vision. Her head was far from clear; she couldn't think, and she could taste blood on her lower lip. She'd lost a moment, somehow; Collin now had a grip on her shoulder, holding her up by the coat, and then from behind, arm around her chin, flashlight fixed on John. The man's arm moved sharply—karate, perhaps. The sharp sound of dry wood cracking and splintering cut through the scree in her ears; part of the wall disintegrated into a pile of rubble. John was smiling—in anticipation, she thought dully. Collin tightened his arm around her throat, brought his face down next to hers, and whispered against her ear in a horrible travesty of a lover's gentle speech: "You see? It's just that easy with a human limb. Easier, really." He stroked her hair with his free hand. "John's done it a thousand times. And you wouldn't be the first woman."

She could only watch as John shifted his weight, as his smile broadened, as he started toward her. Collin moved, releasing her throat, catching hold of her arm so he could force it out straight— She fought him, shifting in his grip. Glass crunched under John's shoes. There was no other sound, except her too-rapid breathing.

The crash far overhead froze all of them. The pressure on her arm eased momentarily as Collin stared at the enormous, dark, cloaked form falling with the shattered skylight. *Vincent!* She wanted to scream out his name; she couldn't make the sound come. John screamed and threw his arms over his head to protect himself from the falling shards of glass; he shrieked mindlessly as a golden-maned, roaring fury leaped at him. The flashlight shone on impossibly long, pointed white teeth, on curved, needle-sharp claws that ripped across the man's body, on the enormous creature that pulled him off his feet, shook him like a rabbit and threw him across the room. John fell with a floor-jarring thud, already dead.

Collin dropped the flashlight, dragged her up against him and brought the pistol up, barrel cool against her bruised face. *No!* He wouldn't—! The strength flowed into her arms, her legs, and she fought him like a fury, trying to pull away from him. Her hands wrapped around the pistol, dragging at his fingers as Vincent swung around with a terrifying roar that exposed murderous-looking fangs. Collin was backing away, tiny step at a time; his index finger tightening on the trigger. He might have been terrified, that wouldn't matter; men like Collin knew only one answer for whatever danger faced them. She slid her middle finger through the trigger guard, jamming it hard against his, dropped and twisted, turning in the direction Collin would never expect: into him. She threw all her weight into him, forcing the gun down, away; for that one moment, he was too surprised to counter her, but almost at once he shifted his own weight, fought to bring the gun back up. It caught in his jacket pocket and went off.

Catherine was stunned into immobility by the roar of the gun and the smell of powder. For one long, timeless moment, she could see his eyes, wide, blank and already dead, staring into hers. She fought free of him, then, half-deafened and shaking, catching her breath on a sob. Vincent's arms were warm around her; his breath lifted the hair from her forehead.

She clung to him desperately and felt his arms tighten in reply. "I'm all right," she whispered. "I'm all right." She let out a little sigh and closed her eyes.

Eight

SHE felt so warm, so protected—so utterly safe. Vincent's arms around her, his face against her hair as she fought off the memory of that moment when Collin's gun went off in her hand; the blankly astonished look in his eyes and then only blankness as he fell heavily against her and slid to the floor.

He would have killed me; would have killed us both. She hoped she could live with that.

Catherine stirred after what seemed hours but could only have been moments; dust still hung heavy in the air where Collin's fall had disturbed it. "Vincent, we cannot stay here."

"No," he agreed softly, and took her hand to lead her from the building. She glanced over her shoulder just once but now there was nothing to see except shadow and shrouded machinery, an occasional grubby moonbeam forcing its way through grimed glass high above them.

She remembered only individual moments of their long return trip to Vincent's chambers: her hand beginning to throb where she'd scraped it; the scree in her ears gave way to a pounding headache. Forcing her knees not to fold under her as Vincent took her along a narrow tunnel and into one of the endless cement culverts. He carried her for some distance there, where the footing was sound and the way wide and high enough. She had to walk when they branched off and edged along a concrete retaining wall bounding an almost full drainage gutter. He had gone ahead of her when the ladder loomed up out of darkness, had kept his hand on her ankle the whole way down. Had talked continuously, saying she couldn't remember what, only the soothing warmth of his voice mattering. Once down, he swept her into his arms and carried her once more; she let her eyes close and leaned against him; tried not to think how dreadful her lip felt.

It could have been much worse, she reminded herself. She was away from Collin and his terrible friend John; those two would never hurt anyone else, ever again. She was safe; Vincent was safe.

She lost track of time and place for a while, then. Sometime later, he stopped and set her down; she opened her eyes to find herself on a red velvet chaise in his chamber, the familiar walls, books, the familiar scent of books, candle wax, dirt and damp stone all reassuring. Vincent tucked pillows behind her with swift, deft movements, touched her face with gentle concern and looked at her for one long moment. "You've been hurt. I'll bring Father."

She nodded, winced as the movement made pain knife from temple to temple. She brought her hand up to lie on his as he leaned toward her, his eyes dark with worry. "It's all right."

His eyes searched hers, but he finally nodded and stood. "Rest now."

"I will." The air currents shifted around her with his passing. She let her eyes close again and leaned cautiously back against the cushions.

Pipes clanged overhead in a short pattern that repeated twice nearby; she jumped when they began, tried to force herself to relax once more but the hand massaging her temples was trembling. She drew a deep breath, another; the tremors slowed and she ran the fingers lightly over her cheeks, touched her lips. The physical damage seemed less than her outraged nerve endings said it was.

Collin—what would she do about Collin? She could understand people who didn't like facing ugly realities, just now. Catherine thought she would give anything to be able to simply forget Collin, to never think of him again.

But that would never do: not in the real world. It would go against everything she thought of as right, not reporting a crime. It was no way for an attorney—a member of the district attorney's staff—to behave. Besides, she thought wearily, her fingerprints would be on that gun, on the interior of the Jag. She'd have to come up with a very good story, though, to keep Vincent entirely out of it.

She heard the rustle of fabric, the startled "Oh!" and turned her head cautiously, opened her eyes. At first they blurred; the dark-haired form in the middle of Vincent's chamber came clear as she blinked and Lisa was staring at her face in wide-eyed shock. "I'm sorry, I didn't mean to—disturb—you." Her voice fell away to nothing and she turned, would have fled but Cathy's voice stopped her.

Sitting up made her head throb almost as much as speaking did. "Lisa, wait!" She kept it soft, as much out of consideration for her headache as for Lisa: Lisa, who looked like a young doe caught in the glare of headlights, terrified, ready to bolt at the least loud sound.

Lisa turned back, made a complicated gesture with her hands, shrugged rather helplessly. "I was just—I was looking for Vincent," she said finally.

Catherine managed a faint smile. "He's coming." Lisa's eyes flinched away from bruised cheekbones and lips as she took another step into the light. She wore a designer dress Catherine knew for French, this season's, as outrageously expensive as it was simple. And there was a look about her—the look, Catherine realized with a sinking sensation, of a woman whose bags are packed, who is ready to move on.

Her face was elegantly, simply made up to highlight that soft, mobile mouth, the exotic cheekbones, the deep brown, wide-set eyes; her hair swung just short of her shoulders, framing her face, and Catherine realized she had never seen Lisa Campbell—in photographs or life—without the hair and makeup of the ballet. She is a beautiful woman, Cathy thought. She was also a frightened woman: the eyes were dark and too wide with fear; her teeth caught and held her lower lip in a gesture that had nothing of beauty to it—a gesture such a woman would never knowingly use. She swallowed. "What—what happened to you?"

Catherine managed a faint, rueful smile. "Your friend Collin was determined to find you," she said finally, and tried to make her words light, a little dry—to take the edge from them. To keep the worst of the ugliness at arm's length from them both. "He thought I might know where you were."

There hadn't been much color in Lisa's face to begin with, save what the candles gave it. That faded, leaving her cheeks ashen, the blush standing out as though she'd smeared it in place. "Collin?" She shook her head so hard the hair swirled, momentarily shrouding her face. "I don't believe it!"

That was so clearly a lie, there was no point in remarking on it. "Quite a few people are wondering where you are," Catherine said pointedly.

"Who?" Lisa's voice went up a notch. "Who is wondering?"

"The U.S. Attorney. A federal grand jury." She caught and held Lisa's frightened gaze. "They'd like to ask you some questions about Alain Taggert."

The name released her. Lisa turned away and when she spoke, her voice was light, her words of no consequence. "Well! That's—quite a statement." She cast one sidelong look at the bruised woman on the couch, looked hastily away. None of her doing, not that! And she would not think of Alain, nor Collin, she wouldn't—!

Catherine's soft voice penetrated the increasingly hysterical, familiar circle of thoughts. "I'm sure Mr. Taggert would like to get you out of the country before that happens. Or find some other way to keep you from incriminating him."

Oh, *God*. The thing that had hovered at the back of her worst nightmares, not daring to show itself even there. That Collin would never take her home; or that once within Alain's flat or his country estate, she'd never pass through the doors alive again. She had to try twice before the words would come; had to stuff her hands between folds of shimmering skirt. "I promise you, I don't know what any of this means." It sounded horribly false even to her, she could see disbelief in the set of Catherine's bruised lips, in her eyes. "But you've made a mistake."

Catherine folded her arms across her chest and walked toward her. "Now you're lying to me."

Lisa's color came back all at once. "Don't you dare say I'm lying!" she shouted.

"You've lied to Vincent," the soft voice went on inexorably.

"No! Never! Never to him!" But that truth was hovering just beneath the surface, unwilling to be shoved down any longer.

"You've caused him some deep pain," Catherine said unhappily, "which I cannot reach."

With a terrible effort, Lisa drew herself up majestically, straightened her shoulders, looked down her long, elegant nose at the woman facing her. "Well!" she said frostily. "If that's so, I'll leave! Immediately."

"But you have no place to go."

"Nonsense!" The laugh was brittle. Lisa smiled, but the muscles that held flawlessly glossed lips away from her teeth suddenly felt like chilled glass, ready to shatter at any moment. "I have a hundred places to go. Buenos Aires—I have wonderful friends there." Her voice gained strength as she finished; the smile hurt less.

"How long do you intend to keep hiding?" Cathy asked quietly.

"*I* intend to survive," Lisa snapped in reply and spun on her heel. She wanted to run, to escape—to close her ears. It was too late.

"What are you going to do, Lisa?" That soft voice cut through everything, froze her in place with her fingers digging into wood in the doorway, with her eyes fixed on the floor of the passageway. "What will you do when it's over? When the world no longer loves you?" Catherine had wanted to shake Lisa, to shout at her, to force the truth down her throat, to make her admit— But she couldn't find the anger, all at once. To have had everything: beauty, talent, grace—and know she had thrown it away in bad choices. To have hidden from that knowledge for so many years, only to face it for the first time as Lisa must be doing right now—. Lisa stood frozen in mid-flight; Catherine couldn't tell if she was weeping, listening, cursing, frantically searching for excuses, for any way to hide from the truth. She could have wept for Lisa. "Will you just cling to whoever will have you? Is that all you're worth?"

In the ensuing silence, they could both hear the faint laughter of children playing hide-and-seek down one of the side tunnels; distant trains and the drip of water nearby. The rustle of fabric as Lisa turned to study Catherine's face. Lisa took one uncertain step toward her. "You don't mean to be unkind—do you?"

"No," Cathy said gently. "Just realistic."

Lisa's eyes closed briefly; she walked past the other woman and sat heavily on the edge of the red velvet chaise. "Realistic," she said and laughed quietly, bitterly. She squared her shoulders and nodded once, sharply; the eyes that met Catherine's had intelligence in them for the first time. "Okay. It *is* over." Vincent came through the doorway, stopped as he saw her. Father, just behind him, slipped off to one side, into shadow. Lisa, eyes fixed somewhere between her hands and the floor, did not see them. After a moment, she looked up into Catherine's face once more, and seemed to take strength by what she saw there. "Over," she repeated, and swallowed. "Played out. You know what played out means to me?" Her eyes went blank, her voice trembled. "It's when the music stops." When the music stops. He took everything and left me nothing, she thought blankly. Not even the music. Not even the dance. What would she do—afterward?

For once she wanted to directly confront an unpleasant truth, and it evaded her.

Catherine got through the next week in a blur; somehow satisfying both District Attorney Moreno and Joe Maxwell that she hadn't deliberately stuck her neck out, at the same time assuring the feds that she hadn't done anything to compromise their case against Alain Taggert. Once she'd produced Lisa Campbell, the attorney general had more or less patted her on the head, taken deposition testimony, warned her she'd likely be called for oral testimony in the next month and left it at that. Moreno had thrown five separate fits over the whole knotted mess—at least until the feds cleared his young assistant DA of any wrongdoing in Collin Hemmings' death and of any possible role in that of John Farley, whose demise was put down to "massive damage caused by long-bladed knife, type unknown, not found on premises." He had enough of a record, enough of a reputation, that no one was likely to mourn his passing.

The following Monday morning was cool and bright—suit weather. Catherine wore a cream wool jacket and skirt, a new jade green blouse—clothing that would be visible, but wouldn't particularly call attention to her—and stood on the top step of the federal courthouse, looking down the long flight of marble stairs at a mob of reporters, TV cameramen, two recognizable news anchors. The usual crowd of curious sightseers. She had been waiting almost an hour; most of the media had been there when she arrived. Lisa Campbell was late; Catherine could hear snatches of conversation. "She's not coming." "She will." "She's late." "She'll be here." "Sez you. No one's seen her in days." And then someone caught sight of the shining black limousine pulling slowly around the corner. Approaching the curb. There was a concerted rush to surround it; policemen and federal marshals everywhere, clearing a space for the rear door to open, for a slight, dark-coated woman with shining brown, swinging hair and enormous sunglasses to be handed out; a lean man in a navy pin-striped suit, white shirt, burgundy tie—very obviously her attorney—put himself at her side, trying to shield her. Lisa lowered her head, let the uniformed men lead her across the sidewalk, up the stairs. She looked small, beleaguered, terribly vulnerable. Reporters shouted questions at her from all sides; her attorney shouted back half a dozen variations of "No comment!" and Lisa herself shook her head almost continuously but didn't even try to speak.

Something must have alerted her—peripheral vision, some inner sense, perhaps only hope. She brought her head up something short of the doors and saw Catherine standing to one side. She tugged at the sunglasses, met Catherine's eyes with pride in her own, as though to say, *I did it. I'm doing it.* And Cathy was smiling at her in approval. She really was there for me, Lisa thought in surprise. I hadn't expected anyone to be there for me. Her attorney took hold of her elbow and escorted her into the building, a comet-tail of media following them.

Catherine gazed after her. "Be brave, Lisa," she whispered. "You can do it." There was unexpected strength and determination in her—or perhaps, not unexpected in a woman who had climbed to the top of a difficult art with little formal training. And now no one in the world would blame her for those canceled performances. Even if she had to go into hiding once she'd testified against Taggert, she'd have that. She'd know the people who mattered knew her for a hero—not the dilettante who whimsically canceled performances.

Perhaps they already did; as she passed the few remaining reporters, she overheard one of them remark to another: "Know whose car that is? It's old man Palmieri's—you know, the ballet patron? Think there's a story in it?"

Cathy was smiling to herself as she walked back to her office.

Monday night was brilliant—sharp with mid-October, still. Fog pooled in the park, filling hollows, floating above dew-wet grass, shrouding the lake. Steam rose in clouds from the grates. But Catherine had come onto her darkened terrace to look up; for tonight there were stars: hard, bright points of light brighter than the competing city lights. She let her head fall back, gazed out across the park then, across the buildings on the East side. The flower-print dressing gown was not going to be warm enough for long; she could feel October touching her back, her sleeves, turning the silk to ice.

"Catherine."

She turned. Vincent stood in the southernmost corner of her terrace, looking as though one wrong look, one word too loudly spoken and he'd be gone. But he had come. And she thought she knew why. "I wonder," she said gently, "if I'll ever not be surprised to see you there."

He was silent so long, she began to wonder if he had heard her. And then he stirred uncertainly. "We've never withheld the truth from each other."

"No." She took a hesitant step toward him, then a second, until she could see his eyes in the light escaping from her living room. He would not look at her for more than a moment or two.

"Catherine," he said finally, and the words came from a dry throat. "There are things I must tell you." She stood utterly still. His mouth worked. "About who I am." He met her eyes, turned his away and down. As if—as if ashamed, she thought in surprise. "What I am."

"Vincent. To me, you are beautiful."

He swallowed hard and shook his head. "What I must tell you is not beautiful. It is terrifying and shameful." He blinked rapidly, looking at her, the terrace paving stones, the city, the sky—at her again. "But it—is the truth."

"Then I want to hear it." He could hear the uncertainty in her voice, but there was none in her eyes. He met them again, took strength from the trust and love in her gaze.

"You asked about Lisa." He was speaking almost in a whisper now. "About what she meant in my life."

"Yes."

He looked at her, then past her, into the night—into the past. "I would watch her dance," he said finally. "She would dance in the Great Hall. Alone, for herself. And for me." His mouth worked and he blinked rapidly. "There was nothing in the world then as beautiful as Lisa."

"And you desired her," Cathy said gently. He nodded, lowered his eyes; she could see tears beginning to slide down the side of his nose. "There is no shame in that." There was quiet certainty in her voice, but he was shaking his head miserably.

"For me there is."

"Why?"

He couldn't make the words come. And then they tumbled out, spilling out of him, scalding his throat, burning his eyes. He couldn't bring himself to look at her at all now. "Because I hurt her. Because, in my desire, I forgot who I was, who I am. As she moved closer, I wanted to hold her. She was dancing and—I felt her pull. It was pulling me to her." He shook his head in frustration and shame; the words weren't right, he couldn't explain it, it wasn't— But it came out anyway, spilling like water from a broken dam. "And I reached out for her." He looked up and his blurring eyes met Catherine's. Somehow, it was easier now, looking into her eyes, seeing the compassion in her level, unshrinking gaze. "Suddenly, in her eyes, I saw her fear. Of me. I saw—" he swallowed. "I saw myself. But I could not let go of her."

"Vincent," she whispered in sudden agony, and her

pain was his, was hers—as though she relived it with him.

He brought up his hands and held them between himself and her, palm up. Light touched the nails. He stared down at them, at brilliant little stars of light refracted by unshed tears. "These hands would not let go of her," he said softly, and caught his breath on a painful sob. "I hurt her. And—I knew that these hands were not meant to give love—" His voice failed him at last; he could not move, not even to wipe the tears away, nor to take his eyes from the ends of his fingers. Dreadful, horrible, murderous hands. Killing things . . .

Catherine caught hold of his fingers in a hard grip; she turned his hands over and brought them to rest against her throat. Startled, he looked up and into her eyes. Her lashes were beaded with tears. "These hands are beautiful," she whispered fiercely. And kissed first one, then the other. "These hands are *my* hands."

For one long moment, he stood utterly still. Then he bent over her, his mane fell forward to shroud his face and hers. He wept, but with a sense of release now; she could feel his hands relax in hers, his body no longer shrank from her touch. His breath was warm against her hair.

He would never forget, Catherine knew. She pressed his fingers to her face, kissed them once more. Her own tears dampened the thick golden fur that covered them. But surely he could let it go now. And she would see that Vincent never again thought of himself as incapable of giving love or unworthy to receive it. Not as long as she lived.

Nine

THE line of roofs was visible against deeply blue sky in the east when Vincent finally left her. They spoke little during the night hours, content simply to be together; by dawn it seemed to both of them as though the terrible void separating them had never been.

They had stood together for a very long time; Catherine was surprised to discover when Vincent finally swallowed a last time and stepped away from her to blot his face on the back of his hand, that the traffic noises in the street below were much fainter—very early morning sounds. But when he would have left her, she shook her head, reclaimed both of his hands, and tugged gently on them, leading him across the terrace to her table. He drew a chair close to hers, draped his heavy cloak around her shoulders, sharing his warmth with her.

For some time he was silent while she talked—quietly at first, with no seeming pattern. Mostly stories of her childhood, cherished memories from growing up. Her first sight of the Tower of London, the shiver it had given her. "Why?" he asked softly as she paused.

"I'm not certain." She thought about this. "I wanted to cry, and I'm not sure why I should have felt that way. All the terrible things that happened in there, I suppose. Or maybe the age of it. Some of it is so old, the stone steps are worn down in the centers."

He gazed out across the city. "I cannot imagine placing my feet on floors where men walked a thousand years ago. Or putting my hand on a wall and knowing that Richard the Third had touched the same wall."

Somehow, it was easier after that. He discovered she confused the poet Rilke with the novelist who wrote *All Quiet on the Western Front*, and he recited poetry for her. She found much of it too dark, and gave him back things she remembered from college—a verse of e.e. cummings, which still reminded her of happiness because of the boy who'd read it to her. Vincent argued it was sad, and countered that with Emily Dickinson's "I Heard a Fly Buzz," that she had forgotten entirely. She made him laugh, a little, with a line of doggerel from Ogden Nash.

He left while it was still dark, but not by much.

The next two weeks went quickly: she had to juggle a workload made even heavier by the flu that kept five people at home. And she was called back to federal court to testify before Alain Taggert's grand jury, and to give a formal deposition that took most of a day.

She was able to learn a little from David Brukowski, a little more from his boss after her deposition. They had already possessed some information—semiautomatic rifles taken in a terrorist raid in the Philippines that could be traced back; videotaped testimony by a man whose face and voice were both digitally blurred for his safety; the funds from one transaction that had been tracked from London to Morocco, Lebanon to India to Ceylon and then to El Salvador. But Lisa's testimony had been the most damaging of all: she had seen many of the men who came to visit Taggert—men who could be traced to specific groups in certain countries. She had seen enough papers, heard enough numbers over time to give the grand jury information that could be pieced together to locate bank accounts, paperwork.

And having testified, Lisa was gone. Cathy asked, as much concerned on her own behalf as on Vincent's. She found out the feds had offered her a new identity, full immunity. But Lisa hadn't wanted that; she'd told them flatly that she couldn't have her ballet if she was someone else, and if she couldn't have that, she didn't care what happened to her. Palmieri had been an emotional mainstay for her throughout the entire proceedings, though, and she had already rejoined his touring company, out in Chicago.

The attorney general did the one thing certain to guarantee her safety: he brought in the media when she came to testify and made sure the media knew they had her signed testimony. Alain Taggert was too practical a man to kill her out of spite. And he surely knew by now that if anything did happen to his wife—illness, accident, anything at all—he'd have Scotland Yard, Interpol and the Americans all over him, certain he had had her murdered.

When Vincent next came, she told him. He was silent for some time, eyes fixed on the distant lights of the Chrysler Building. Finally, he sighed quietly, deeply. "It is no guarantee of her safety, but it is safer than she has been in many years."

"I'm sure it must feel that way to her, too," Catherine said. "And—I think—this way she will be happy."

"If she has her music and her dance, then she will be happy. And if she is, then I am very happy for her." Vincent then turned away and took Catherine's hands in his. She only realized a long time later that he never spoke of Lisa again.

She told him about the party and about Brigit O'Donnell. "I wish I could take you there," she said wistfully.

He shook his head but he, too, looked wistful. "I would never dare. That is your world, not mine."

She hesitated. "You know, I thought about it. Since

117

it is Halloween. Everyone will be in costume, masked—" She hesitated again, uncertain whether he would find her suggestion offensive, or if it would simply be like entering her apartment—a line he had made for himself, a line he would not cross. If she would make him unhappy by the suggestion, offering what he wanted and could not have.

But when he shook his head there was only faint regret in his eyes. "No. I could not pass for someone used to such houses, such wealth. There would be too great a danger someone would find me out." All the same, there was not as much finality in his "no" as she might have expected. He looked at her for several long moments and gave her one of those small smiles that warmed her heart. "I do so envy you the opportunity," he said finally.

The last days of October were unexpectedly warm; the wind blew from the south, bringing air that felt like it had come straight from Jamaica. Catherine brought home her rental costume—an eighteenth-century ball gown that Dolley Madison might have worn. She tried on one of the powdered wigs at the costumers, decided it was hot and itchy and looked dreadful. She found the box high in the back of her closet that contained the curled ponytail switch that matched her hair, bought it new ribbons.

Locating just the right mask gave her problems: she didn't want a simple domino, but nothing elaborate seemed to work. The evening she picked up the gown, though, the woman proprietor pulled one out of a box she was unpacking—white feathers, a point of nose, long, white hackles above the eyebrows, and plain holes for the eyes. She waggled it so the hackles bounced wildly and held it out. "I ordered a few of these and didn't think they'd come in time; post office could drive you mad, couldn't it?"

"Sure could," Catherine agreed, and moved over to the counter mirror. "Oh, *yes!*" It hadn't made sense until she got it on: an owl's face looked back at her with her own eyes. It reminded her of one of those masks in the surreal ball scene in *Labyrinth*—the very thing she *had* wanted and had been unable to find. She took it off and set it down. "That finishes it off, just right."

The woman shoved the pre-printed contract across the counter; Cathy signed it, paid for the mask and went out the door with an enormous garment bag of the unexpectedly heavy silver and pink satin gown over her shoulder.

Halloween was unfortunately a Friday—unfortunately, because it meant her desk had been piling up most of the week, getting slowly ahead of her. And Monday was looming on the other side of the weekend as truly ugly. Cathy was sitting at her desk, staring at it gloomily; she could hear the rising volume that meant quitting time for the clerical staff—"What'cha doing this weekend?" conversations, chairs getting shoved back across uncarpeted floors, drawers slamming. And then less noise, less again.

She looked up as someone stopped in front of her desk. Joe Maxwell stood there, arms crossed, glowering down at her like a trench-coated Buddha. "You told me you have a party tonight, Chandler." She nodded. "Then get out of here." He unfolded his arms and flapped them at her. "Shoo!"

"I'm not going as a chicken, Joe," she laughed, but she reached across to turn off the desk light and got up.

He grinned suddenly. "Can't clean it off tonight anyway, so why frustrate yourself, huh? Have a good party."

"I will. Thanks, Joe."

It was late enough she decided to take a cab; she wanted a shower, wanted to wash the grit out of her hair the wind had deposited there during her lunch hour.

It was getting dark out; two little girls in fairy costumes with heavy coats thrown over their shoulders were already being shepherded between buildings by an abashed-looking man in a three-piece suit. Four boys—a pirate, a Ninja, two bums—who looked almost too old for trick-or-treating were standing in the light, talking; they had UNICEF cans and seemed to be waiting for their adult sponsor.

Children in the lobby—several she knew, belonging to other tenants. She got into the elevator with a cowboy—homemade chaps, she thought, and another little boy who wore one of those dreadful plastic bags with the picture embossed on the front, the pressed-out mask. His was some kind of turtle, she thought, a rather surreal one with swords and a blue bandana over the eyes. Curious.

They got off at the second floor, and she had the elevator to herself the rest of the way up.

Fortunately she'd shaken out her costume the night before, had hung it out before she left for work; the wrinkles that had set into the fabric when she brought it home were mostly gone. The hairpiece had properly taken curl and was tied with its new ribbons—white, to match the mask, attached to a padded hanger in her closet by two antique hat pins. The mask itself hung by its elastic band from her mirror, where it could contemplate her with its empty eyes and hooked beak. Even the dish of wrapped candies was right by the door, ready. Luckily, because she had children in the hall waiting when she came out of the elevator. A Zorro, a pirate, a little girl in another of the plastic bags stamped with a very busty pink dress and the name "Malibu Barbie"; instead of the costume mask she wore four shades of eyeshadow, false eyelashes and a long blonde wig. Cathy praised them all, wondered in irritation why a mother who would spend so much time on her child's face wouldn't simply dress her in one of her own dresses, and closed the door behind them.

"Quick shower," she told herself as she snapped the locks, kicked off her shoes and dumped everything else—jacket and skirt, coat, briefcase and purse—on the bed. Sandwich? A glance at her watch told her she'd better not; better count on food at the party. John Brennan had always used the same caterers for his parties, anyway; it would be a shame to get there and not have any room for exotic goodies.

The doorbell again: she dragged a robe around her and ran back into the living room to open the door on the two little fairies she'd seen in the street. They'd shed their coats and given them to the man in the suit— Daddy, by his resemblance to both girls. He stood back by the elevators, still looking like he'd rather not be doing this. Or maybe he was simply shy; the little girls certainly were. "Wonderful wings," Cathy told them, and both girls blushed, giggled behind their hands. She thought one of them whispered "Thank you" as they turned away; she doubted the other could have even managed that.

The doorbell was ringing again when she turned off the shower and bent over to wrap a towel around wet hair. She caught up a bath towel that went around her twice and covered her discreetly from shoulders to almost her ankles, hurried into the living room, peered around the edge of the door. The three children from the floor below stood waiting expectantly: a knight in aluminum-foil armor, and a prince or a king. Their little sister was the perfect foil for them in a homemade princess costume. Someone had spent some time with a sewing machine.

Cathy slipped the chains so she could open the door a little wider, took up a handful of candy and distributed it between the three bags. "You kids look terrific," she said enthusiastically. The boys glanced at each other, a little embarrassed; she didn't think they'd be out in costume this next year. Little Ellie looked into the bag, back up and smiled enchantingly.

"Thank you!" she said and went scampering off after her brothers. Catherine stepped back into her apartment and was about to close the door when the elevator stopped and a tall man in gray got out. Robert E. Lee in person, give or take the beard, she thought, and stepped out into the hall, holding the door for him.

He looked her dubiously up and down and finally

BEAUTY AND THE BEAST

laughed. "Am I early, are you late—or is *that* your costume?" he demanded.

She thought about assuring him it was but knew she'd never be able to manage it with a straight face—not for long. He'd never believe it anyway. She shut and locked the door behind him, leaned over to give him a kiss on a freshly-shaven cheek. "I'm late. Sorry, Dad. I lost track of time at the office."

He chuckled. "You never lost track of time when you worked for me."

"Sure I did," she retorted lightly. "Every morning. If you hold the trick-or-treaters at bay, I can get dressed. I think we'll be just in time to be fashionably late."

He shook his head. "Likely story! I figure an hour and a half."

She stood poised on one foot at her bedroom door, pulled the towel up to dry one shoulder. "That was the old Cathy. I'll be ready in fifteen minutes." He gave her a very old-fashioned look indeed as she grinned and went into the bedroom; and she could hear him trying to settle onto her couch. By the sound of things, that long cavalry officer's sword was going to give him trouble.

The south wind was causing disturbances, blowing paper and dirt along the streets, raising whitecaps in the Hudson River and the East; awnings along Broadway snapped like firecrackers in sudden gusts. Gritty, sooty particles rose in little whirlwind clouds on steps leading down to the subway platforms; scouring no-longer-white wall tiles and shining rails. Far below street level, below the deepest trains, air currents found their way, sending dust into the air and giving the appearance of a smog alert; candle flame blew sideways and fluttered noisily in the drafts, while lantern light was ruddy and sullen.

Father's chamber was barely lit and the air was thick, but to the Halloween-costumed children huddled together on his floor, this simply added to the atmosphere of the ghost story he was telling them. It was an old

122

story and sounded very Russian with its deep passions and its silent, snow-bound forests. But it was in fact Irish, for all its setting: there is no one who can tell a ghost story like the Irish. One of the older boys sat nodding, lips moving with Father's as he spun out the tale, a Plains Indian feather headdress sending queer shadows across the face of the girl next to him; she seemed not to notice at all, so rapt was she. Two smaller girls clung to each other, wide-eyed.

Father's voice was deeply reedy, like a bassoon—well-suited to such stories; better, he had a gift for the proper dramatic telling of them. Vincent, who leaned back against a chair near him, could almost see the blue-white snow, the black shadows of endless forest cast across the unbroken whiteness, the utter silence as the older man described them—almost chanting the words as a bard might once have. The younger man's dark eyes brooded in the shadow cast by his wildly loose hair; brooded on the unhappy young hero and his fate. ". . . And from that day on," Father said softly, "John kept a light burning in his window by night, so that Dierdre might find her way back to him. And in the deepest winter, when the snows lay thick against the walls of his cottage, and the cold wind came shrieking from the north, John would take down his bow and he would walk through the forests, calling her name until his voice grew hoarse and the tears froze hard on his face. But she never answered, and till his dying day, John never saw her again."

Dead silence. One of the older girls drew a ragged breath, then, breaking the spell. "Oh," she whispered. "Oh, that's *sad*." The boy in Indian garb clapped softly once with delight, the girl next to him turned to say something, then turned back to Father, her eyes alight.

"That was a good one!"

"Tell us another," the boy demanded. "About the Headless Horseman—"

"Yeah!" someone else chimed in. "Tell us that!"

Father smiled faintly and shook his head. "You've had enough ghosts for one night, go on, now. Mary says she needs help carving up more jack-o'-lanterns.''

They were reluctant to go, but most of them knew Father wouldn't be persuaded once he'd said ''No more.'' They got up and trooped out; some of the younger ones took off running as soon as they got into the passageway. Heading for the kitchens, and those pumpkins, no doubt. Father watched them go, gazed after them until he could no longer hear high, excited young voices and the fast clatter of young feet above the moan of wind through the tunnels and the rattle of a subway train directly overhead.

Vincent shook his head in wonder. ''Every year, they ask for the same stories. By now they must know them better than you do.''

Father laughed softly and spread his arms wide. ''Well, you know! Old stories are like old friends. Every so often, we must drop in on them once more, to see how they're doing.'' He looked up sidelong, smiling at his companion. ''Anyway, one little boy I can remember would never have let a mere jack-o'-lantern deny him a visit to Ichabod Crane.''

Vincent gave him one of those faint smiles that his facial structure allowed without exposing his teeth, and turned his attention to his sleeves.

He seldom dressed in such fine fashion these days; Father looked with approval at the narrow velvet pants tucked into his boots, at the long white shirt he wore loose above them, with its spill of throat and cuff lace, the wide belt that brought it close at his hips. It gave him height and unaccustomed slenderness, to dress in such a way. It made a romantic figure out of him, like a prince from one of those tales the children clamored for.

But this was not a tale, and Vincent was not a prince— not even an ordinary man costumed as a prince. Father's pleasure was gone in an instant, smothered in concern. Worry. ''You're determined to go, are you?'' he said abruptly. One hand found the slender volumes Vincent had brought two days before, when he'd proposed this mad venture. His fingers ran along the binding. He felt the gold-embossed letters, let his eyes fall to read what his hands felt: *Fables and Fantasies—Brigit O'Donnell*. He sensed rather than saw Vincent's nod. "I wish you would reconsider."

"Father." Vincent spread his hands helplessly, let them fall into his lap. They had already argued this, said everything that could be said on the subject. But to reassure a man so visibly upset—*for love of me,* Vincent knew—*and worry for us all, here.* If there was any chance of soothing this beloved man who had been his father all his days, he would willingly say it all one more time. "Surely on this night of all nights, I can walk among them in safety?"

Bad choice of words. Father's eyes darkened, his mouth set and he sat up sharply. "Safety? Vincent, there is no safety up there! Not for you or anyone!"

Vincent inclined his head. There was no denying the older man's fears were often nothing less than the truth. Tonight, with what he wanted so near to hand— "But sometimes we must leave our safe places, and walk empty-handed among our enemies."

The older man turned away abruptly. "Those are Brigit O'Donnell's words," he said angrily.

"Those are true words," Vincent corrected him gently. "Words that have opened doors for me and let some light in on the dark places." Silence. "You know what she has meant to me."

Father glanced at him; his mouth was still set in a narrow, furious line. "I do. And I also know the danger of confusing the magic with the magician." He turned away to consider what he'd said, to choose his next words with care. "Sometimes the person is smaller than the work. Weaker, more frightened—more human. I don't want you hurt. Disappointed."

Vincent shook his head. "She will not disappoint me," he said with quiet certainty. "Our lives have been so different, and yet, I know that we will understand each other." Another silence. "I will not lose this opportunity," he said firmly, and Father closed his eyes, knowing he'd lost the argument. "I must see her, talk to her."

125

The older man pushed to his feet and limped a few paces away. "Well, go then!" he snapped. "Obviously, there's nothing I can do to stop you." But as he heard Vincent's boots on the gritty floor, he turned abruptly. "Vincent!" Vincent stopped. Father drew a deep breath, tried to let some of the desperate fear out with it. "Be careful."

"Don't worry." Vincent came back across the room and wrapped one long arm around his neck, gave him a son's kiss on the cheek and left quickly. Father stood watching him go, surprised into silence: Vincent occasionally hugged him, but he seldom kissed him anymore. He understood it for what it was: love for the man, apology for ignoring his advice, equally mixed— and perhaps a means of silencing any further attempts at persuasion. When he was still a boy, Vincent had had a trick or two for getting his own way, and that had been one of them.

Father smiled ruefully at the memories that brought, but his eyes were dark with concern. Don't worry, indeed! he thought, and went back to his chair, tugging woolen garments more closely around him as he sat. One of the Helpers who'd come down this night had said the night breeze was warm Above; down here, it seemed to get into everything and to lower the temperature very uncomfortably. He adjusted the long fingerless gloves one of the older women had knit him, reached across the table to sort through the books there.

He was in no mood for fairy tales just now: he set *Fables and Fantasies* aside to pick up *Three Hundred Days* and rather thoughtfully began reading the front flap of the dust jacket.

Charles Chandler finally began to get the hang of standing and sitting without tangling up in his costume sword after four more sets of trick-or-treaters. There was a lull, then; dinnertime for the kiddies, most likely, he thought. Late. But he barely had time to glance at his watch once and wonder how late they would be for Brennan's party when the rustling of satin told him his daughter stood in the door to her bedroom. He slewed around on the couch and gazed up at her.

She was a beautiful young woman—not just his own prejudiced opinion, that—and the costume she had chosen emphasized that beauty: her hair was swept high and back, off her brow, and it was darker—one of those sprays, he thought, but the darker color made it the color of her mother's. Length that was surely a hairpiece lay in ringlets along her neck and over one shoulder; narrow ribbons twined in and out of it. The dress itself stood away from her throat and shoulders but was modestly cut for the historical period. Lace bodice, at the neckline, puffed sleeves that stopped at her elbows, dripping lace from bands there; a white, lace-edged scarf that ran across the backs of her shoulders to hang down on both sides. A pink fitted bodice with a long, slender bit of white stuff hanging down like an apron; pink skirts with rose-colored poufs at either hip. She looked like a young, sweet Marie Antoinette—or perhaps an older and wiser Miss Muffet. He liked it, very much.

He applauded and sketched her a bow. "Well! Hardly fifteen minutes, but well worth it!" She smiled enchantingly and gave him a deep curtsy, then turned so he could see the entire effect. "You don't know how happy I am you let me talk you into this," he went on. "Since you quit the firm, I hardly ever get to see you."

She smiled, settled the bodice lower on her waist. "I know. They keep me pretty busy. I've missed you too."

He shook a mildly admonishing finger at her. "Now. Don't you be shy about leaving me to fend for myself." She laughed and shook her head; long skirts swayed and whispered as she went to get her mask. "I'm not so old that I don't remember how romantic these affairs can be. A lot of your old friends will be there tonight."

Cathy cast him a smile over her shoulder as she stooped to check her hair in the mirror, tightened a hairpin. "I," she told him firmly, "am going to this party to be with you."

He snorted. "You're going to this party to meet Brigit O'Donnell, just like everyone else."

She held the mask up, gave her reflection one last approving look and came back across the room. "Well— that too," she admitted with a grin.

Charles looked down at her for one long moment. He shook his head. "Have I told you lately how beautiful you are?" he asked her. "Sometimes you remind me so much of your mother."

She touched his shoulder, nodded. "I know, Dad. I miss her too." Her eyes were soft, and his were overly bright.

"Someday," he said quietly, "you'll find someone you can love as much as I loved your mother. We were two of the lucky ones." His eyes had gone distant with memory. He sighed. "I have my memories—and I have you." She was deeply touched. It was seldom they could talk like this; very seldom of late he mentioned her mother. Cathy's fingers tightened on his shoulder and she stood on tiptoe to kiss his cheek.

Ten

THE streets were brightly lit; blue and gold street lamps, white headlights, the red and green of traffic lights, the buildings with their random patterns of single lit floors partway up their immensely high sides; highest of all, searchlights and headlights on passing helicopters, red blinking lights marking the very tops of skyscrapers—the distant, matching blink of planes. The streets were ablaze with the yellow of taxis at this hour; the sidewalks cluttered with a few children in costume, and many adults outrageously dressed and masked.

Somewhere above the racket of horns and engines, a clock bell tolled six. Inside a hole-in-the-wall storefront on a side street just off Madison, an elderly man took one final look at the clock he'd been watching the past half hour, compared that with his wristwatch and levered himself off the stool behind his counter. Small feet under an enormously round body pattered across the floor; he caught hold of the card sign that hung against his door over the gold-and-red lettered MOE'S MASQUERADE CITY—COSTUME RENTALS and turned it from YES,

WE'RE OPEN to THANK YOU, COME AGAIN. He sighed gustily. Such a week! There weren't three costumes left in the entire store, barring some that needed the attentions of his sister's sewing machine, one that was desperate for a cleaning. Well, now this rush was gone, maybe he could begin to tend to all that—get it caught up before New Year's Eve, which was nearly as mad as Halloween these days.

Moe sighed again. Not that he'd argue with something that paid his rent, but damned if he could understand grown men and women wanting to play dress-up for Halloween. Halloween was kid's stuff. He shook his head over the pack of foolish adults out there and reached for the doorknob, so he could push the snap lock in. It turned in his hand.

He nearly choked; he'd been so intent on his own thoughts he hadn't even seen the man slow on the sidewalk, study the window and finally come across. Moe shook his head as the door opened and the would-be customer took a couple of steps inside. "Sorry, I'm closed." He looked up into the man's face—and up. Big fellah, he thought uneasily. Big and overwhelming, the way he just pushed his way in. Used to getting his way.

"Now, listen," he said rapidly. "I need a costume." At first Moe couldn't understand him: the man had an accent, a bit of singsong to his words. Moe shook his head once more as the word "costume" registered. The big man took another step, closing the distance between them. "And if it's money you're wanting, I've got it." He pulled a wad of money out of his pocket. Moe forced his eyes from the man's face to look at the money, and his stomach made the nervous twist that said he'd not be able to eat dinner. Was that really a fifty bunched so casually in with the rest? What sort of maniac carried that kind of money around loose in a pocket, on these streets after dark?

A maniac he didn't want to argue with, Moe decided, and turned to walk back into the shop, very conscious of the foreigner behind him.

Foreign—Irish, that's what that accent was. He leaned

130

one elbow on his counter, turned back to face his customer, managed a smile. "Look, there's nothing," he
said persuasively. "Tomorrow you come back, you could
have your pick: Jesse James, Darth Vader. King Arthur!
Whatever you want. But—closing time on Halloween
night?" He shrugged vastly. The Irishman was frowning
slightly, as though he was having trouble of his own,
following Moe's thick Yiddish accent. When he finally
did understand, the frown grew threatening, and Moe's
smile turned nervous; he put his hands in his pockets
to keep the man from seeing how they shook. "Well,
all right. Maybe I can find something in back." He
walked around the man, went through the divided curtain that separated the tiny shop from the long, skinny
storage in back. "You don't mind a little frayed, maybe
a missing button?" he called back. His voice echoed in
the unusual openness.

"Doesn't matter!" the man yelled. "Just *hurry up!*"

He could hear the fellow out there shuffling his feet;
heard pages of newspaper crackling. Well. There was a
pink fairy princess costume for a little girl, maybe six,
with torn wings. There was a Headless Horseman suit,
complete with lit pumpkin, it didn't smell so good, but
this Irishman wouldn't fit half his body in the shirt and
as for the pants—! A few others, mostly for skinny
women or small men. One other thing, the only costume
left on the Revolutionary War rack. Might fit; might be
long, and some men didn't like wearing the tights and
knee pants. Moe yanked at the hanger and pulled down
the costume, grabbed the handled box of accessories—
musket, red coat, white pants, black vest: knee boots,
a tall hat and white powdered ponytail wig. It was a job,
getting himself and all that back through the curtain.
"Here," he mumbled, thrusting the jacket forward, "this
will maybe fit." He looked up to find the man glaring
at him in a towering fury.

"Are you having a bit of fun with me, is that it?" he
snarled. Moe felt himself caught in a pair of hard hands
and jerked back and forth. The voice went up to a roar,
the man released him with a shove that sent him flying,

off balance, into the counter. "Get that damnable rag out of my sight, and get me something decent!"

The Irishman looked absolutely murderous, and Moe had no doubt, suddenly, that he was sharing a locked storefront with a man who knew how it felt to kill other men. Something about the set of his shoulders, the way his eyes were. *One of those mad Irish, they shoot and bomb each other, bomb housewives and schoolchildren—haven't they enough without coming here to bother people?* he wondered indignantly.

But he couldn't imagine anything more foolish than to die over a lousy costume. He shook himself with what he hoped was dignity—and feared only made him look like a trembly rabbit—pushed himself away from the counter and started toward the back with every intention of simply letting himself out the back door and running for his life. A blare of red and green caught his eye just short of the curtain. He'd forgotten the Dizzy the Clown costume; it had been in the window so many years, unrented, that one arm was sun-bleached. It looked like an extra large; he thought he remembered it was. Clown suits were made oversized, anyway. He let the Redcoat costume fall, pulled the hanger from the window display and held it out. "Here," he said flatly and shoved it into the man's arms. "So, it's too big, well, there's nothing else." He tried to make his chin quit wobbling as he brought it up so he could look the man in the eye, so he could add with a semblance of dignity: "This doesn't suit, take your business elsewhere."

"It'll do." The man dropped some of his paper money on the counter.

Moe glanced at it, left it there. He nodded toward the other wall. "The changing room is over there." The man dumped his raincoat down next to the money and his newspaper, grasped the costume with one large, square paw and stepped into the little curtained booth, pulling the drape across with a rattle of rings against a steel bar. Moe, who was leaning against his counter to keep his quavering knees from giving out, watched the curtain shift back and forth. Maybe it wouldn't hurt, he'd get his nephew to put in one larger changing room for men that size. He turned away then, afraid the man would come out, catch him staring and take offense. It would be very wrong to offend this Irishman. He picked up the folded section of newspaper from the counter and turned so the room's best light was behind him.

It had been folded over to page four—society section, not what he ordinarily read, and creased open to the article headed MASKED BALL TO FETE IRISH PEACE ACTIVIST. Peace activist! Moe barely managed to repress a very indignant snort. The man in that changing booth had nothing to do with any peace activist!

Behind him, in the booth, Michael McPhee finally got his jacket off and hung on the hook; he could leave his pants on under this bit of foolishness, thank God. He twisted around to get a better angle on the whole mess, got one leg up to insert it in the one-piece clown suit and almost lost his balance. He caught himself with one hand before he could fall and swore, softly, using every word he could think of. There was a draft on his backside; he reached around and pulled the curtain into place, managed to twist his head around to cast a suspicious glance at the proprietor. Moe stood at the counter, apparently absorbed in reading the paper. Michael shrugged; the article didn't mean much. The man wasn't paying any attention to him—fortunately, after his gaffe over the Redcoat costume. *Watch that, Michael McPhee*, he told himself sternly. Sean O'Reilly wouldn't like mistakes like that. Sean would be quite frankly murderous with his henchman if Michael failed to get himself into that rich man's party and get his hands on Brigit O'Donnell.

Moe himself would have been horrified had he looked up when Michael McPhee lost his balance, because for one long moment, the man's whole back had been exposed—including the pistol tucked into the back of his trousers.

A full, harvest moon sailed free of the rooflines to the east, cast blue light down upon concrete sidewalks and the walls of tall buildings. As Vincent emerged from a drainage culvert deep in Central Park and looked up, it seemed caught momentarily in the bare twig-fingers of an elm. He heard traffic noises from Central Park West, from Fifth Avenue on the other side of trees and grass. Here in the park: a bird, high in the branches of a fir and well behind him. An answering, muted cry. Nothing else. Wind hissed along the grass, sending dry leaves spinning over the sidewalk. He stood very still for some moments, watching the moon free herself from the elm. It *was* a magical night. He adjusted the hood of his cloak, bringing it forward so that his face was partly hidden, only a gleam of pale hair showing.

He stepped out onto the sidewalk, then, moving rapidly along it, staying in shadow as much as possible out of habit.

He paused as he heard traffic along one of the streets that cut through the park, heard a girl's high voice over the sound of a clattering, old and poorly maintained car. Someone—two of them—laughed, and, coming out of shadow, were walking straight toward him: two pirates, a woman in a short black costume and tiny black-and-white cap, net stockings and very high heels she could barely walk in. She was complaining laughingly; they were laughing at the way she minced along. A fourth behind them, sex undeterminable but probably the date of the second pirate. Vincent hesitated, remembering his words to Father, then mentally shrugged. Call it a test, he thought, and walked past the four. "Hey, neat mask!" one of the women called out as he walked on. "Andy, did'ja see that guy?"

The apartment building was on Central Park West, not far from Catherine's building, but its penthouse was several floors higher. He looked up from park shade across the street, considering his next move thoughtfully.

In the end, he simply walked up to the second floor, waited until the elevator stopped at ground level for a load of passengers and dropped onto the top of the car. It carried them—and him—up, remained where it was long enough for him to climb onto the maintenance ladder and find the door at the top. He came out in blackness, a valley of roof between two heights, climbed the nearest to find himself looking down onto John Brennan's terrace.

By comparison, Catherine's little garden was a postage stamp—a very shabby postage stamp. This ran the entire roof of the building, an L-shaped garden along the south and east walls of the apartment. Colored lights illuminated a rectangular pool, various individual shrubs, a climbing vine. Vincent waited until his keen night vision could take in all of it, letting eyes and ears adjust to his surroundings. Now that the moment had come, he felt it keenly. In a minute, he would walk along the ledge, move out onto the brickwork that shielded the owner's view of unfinished tar-paper roofing, rusty metal and greened concrete on the north of his building; he would edge down until he reached the point where the vine's supports veered left, where the wall was only about seven feet. And he would leap down onto this wealthy man's terrace, walk through those glass doors below him and let it be assumed by those inside that he was one of them. He could hear music, the clink of glasses, a babble of talk from a hundred throats, laughter.

In a minute, he would cross from his world to Catherine's. If he could get his feet to move now, to take the first steps that would bring him there.

Brigit O'Donnell would be there. Perhaps she was already. Somehow, he would find her alone—for the least moment, surely; he couldn't let himself dare hope for more time than to tell her "thank you." That would be enough. Before he could think any more about what he was about to do, he simply straightened up and did it.

The terrace was dull-finished clay tiles that clicked faintly under his boot-toes when he landed. A rubbish of crunched-up, brown leaves whispered across the tiles and over his boots, crackled as he walked through them.

Wind—but a wind with no hint of fall in it—fluttered the hems of his cloak.

Charles had wanted to get a cab; Catherine talked him out of it. "It's warm, Dad, and it's not that far. Besides," she added teasingly, "aren't you always telling me you never get enough exercise?" He eyed her sidelong, irresolute on the sidewalk. "You look great," she added. "In case you were thinking about people laughing at us walking from here to there."

"Ha," he said. But he took her arm and started down the sidewalk. "Guess if you don't mind, I certainly don't. You're something to be proud of, anyway."

"You look great, Dad," she repeated softly, and tightened her grip on his elbow.

Even with two elevators leading up to the penthouse, they had to wait a few minutes, and the car they took was nearly full. It went straight up to the top, discharging twenty people onto a landing where perhaps forty costumed people already hovered. "Wow," Catherine said. John Brennan's costume parties were well-known—infamous, as John himself often said. People put a little extra effort into dressing for one of John's parties, and she found herself facing a Jawa right out of *Star Wars*, gleaming red lights for eyes and all; with the Jawa, a young woman in full belly-dancer regalia. Beyond them—a pirate, a pirate king, Blackbeard complete with candles—unlit—in his beard, a skeleton, two men dressed as Zorro, a parlor maid and Sherlock Holmes; a medieval hero, his pointy-hatted lady and a dragon—on skates. A second, startled look assured her the skates were enormous felt boots, not real roller skates.

Charles pulled his yellow domino into place and adjusted the string, settled his hat at a jaunty angle and fished the invitation out of his gray jacket before taking his daughter's arm again. "Quite a mob, isn't it?" he shouted somewhere near her ear.

Quite a racket, too. She nodded, adjusted her own mask so she could see better—the hackles dancing above her eyes were a little disquieting to her peripheral vision.

She had forgotten how madly impressive John Brennan's penthouse apartment was; they'd done a cover story for *Architectural Digest* a year or so before when he'd divorced his second wife and remodeled to remove every last trace of her. His living room would have held her own modest apartment three times over; the ceiling was twenty or more feet high. The walls no longer bore the second wife's single-tone design; the new designer had done the lower half in dark wood, the upper half in oyster-shell white, had re-hung formal chandeliers. It made the room seem less chilly—but that might also have had something to do with the size of the crowd of people presently filling it.

Charles handed his invitation to the butler who stood at the head of the stairs coming up from the elevator alcove. She had to look twice to recognize Andre, even in his impeccable suit: his entire head—hair, eyebrows and all—had been done in blue so bright it nearly glowed, and he wore a set of those silly sparkly balls on springs: deely bobbies, she thought they were. The face under the deely bobbies was Andre's terribly grave, absolutely correct face, however; Catherine was glad for the size of the crowd because she was able to duck out of sight before the laughter bubbled over; she was afraid Andre might be hurt if he knew she was laughing at him.

"Wow," she said again, as they came into the living room. There was a full-sized dance band, a long table of wonderful-looking and -smelling food and a crush of caterers to serve it. Half a dozen men wandered through the crowd with trays of drinks, as unnerving as Andre in full, formal servant's attire and masks or makeup. The middle of the floor had been cleared for dancing and there were probably twenty couples out there.

Her father threaded his way through the crowd, hand now in hers, bringing her with him. He stopped for champagne, turned to toast his daughter, then swung around again as a man in a bread-loaf helmet and ornately embroidered tabard, chain-mail arms began working his way toward them. Catherine blinked: John

Brennan's face had been painted the same color as his steel helmet; he looked like the tin man made into a knight. "Charles!" he exclaimed warmly, and held out both hands. Charles shifted his glass to his left so he could shake, then brought Cathy forward. "Didn't expect you so early, good to see you, man. And surely— this isn't Cathy!" He goggled in mock surprise.

She smiled and extended a hand to forestall his next remark: knowing John Brennan, it would be a variant on "My, how you've grown." To his credit, he shook her hand, professional adult to professional adult. But almost at once he turned back to Charles, and the conversation, as she might have expected, shifted to corporate law.

They'd be at it for hours, unless someone broke them up. She turned slowly in place, trying to see through the mob—to perhaps find a familiar face. It wasn't easy: no one's real face was visible. There were a few dominoes, like her father's, but most everyone wore much more elaborate face coverings—making her own simple white feathered owl mask look quite plain indeed—or was made up to a professional degree.

Like the pair of skeletons out there, waltzing across the dance floor like Fred and Ginger—their faces had been done in exquisite detail with skulls that glowed an eerie blue-green in the shadows. Or the little man with the gnome's face who was looking at her blankly—or so she thought, until she realized it was the back of the man's head under that face. And he turned around, revealing a duplicate mask, this one with real eyes under it. Unsettling.

Over at the bar, though: didn't she know those copper sequins? That skintight dress that might have been made for the Supremes, back in the early sixties? And while she couldn't see the face under its ornate mask, close as the bar was, there was no mistaking those earrings: silver and rhinestone monstrosities right out of the fifties, they looked like young cousins of John Brennan's chandeliers, and ran across the woman's collar bones, right onto her dress. Marie Hackenson had got them at a

Christmas party years before, part of the white elephant gift exchange, and she'd spoiled someone's joke by actually wearing the things. "Marie?" she asked. And, a little louder: "Marie?"

The woman looked up, tilted her head to one side and laughed in sudden delight. "Cathy? Is that you?" Cathy clapped her hands together, met Marie halfway and hugged her fiercely. Marie eyed her critically, and grinned. "You look terrific! Hey, everyone's here, come on!" She tugged at Catherine's hand: Cathy caught her father's eye, indicated her direction with a jerk of her head. The hackle feathers bounced and swayed, marking her passage through the growing crowd.

It wasn't exactly "everyone" of course: not with Jenine settling down in Santa Monica, Arnold working on his thesis at Oxford and his twin sister Alexa at the Sorbonne; with Martha and her new husband on a cruise of Greek islands. Most of the rest were here, though, and ready to talk about old times, current events—with lighthearted malice about the ones who weren't with them.

"We never see you anymore," Ellen said.

Cathy smiled. "Sorry," she said lightly. "Been awfully busy." She sensed rather than saw Jeff—Marie's current boyfriend—frowning and shaking his head in Ellen's direction. Catherine's decision to leave her father's firm and work for the DA was pretty much a taboo subject: none of them could understand why she would do something like that, and that being so, she couldn't find reasons that seemed adequate to any of them.

At least they were willing to leave it alone; she knew people who weren't. People she never saw at all, anymore.

Jeff came up behind her and slipped a casually possessive arm around her shoulders. Cathy gave Marie a grave wink. Marie was notoriously jealous of her men, but she'd always handled Jeff's outrageous flirting with Catherine. "So," he looked down at her. "So. Have you met Brigit yet?"

"Not yet."

"She's really remarkable."

Marie's mouth quirked under her mask. "Jeff's taken a tremendous interest in her *cause*," she said dryly. Jeff laughed and Catherine looked up at him, face grave and eyes alight with mischief.

"I can imagine."

Greg moved over behind Marie, rubbed her shoulders. "Did you hear she sold that book *Three Hundred Days* to Hollywood?"

Marie gave a little, genteel snort of laughter. "Right," she said. "*Romeo and Juliet* with Irish accents." Greg chuckled.

"Come on," Jeff protested. "It's a terrific story!"

Greg nodded; he'd stopped laughing. "She has guts. This peace thing's gotten her death threats from both sides. Her mother and her husband were both murdered."

"Her father's IRA," Jeff said. "Wanted for one of those bombings in London." Catherine nodded. She knew all that; she'd read everything Brigit O'Donnell had written, everything she could find about the woman. She was glad Jeff and Greg had silenced Marie; somehow Marie's usual little carping remarks seemed very out of place, under the circumstances.

She looked up as John Brennan came across the room at his usual high-speed trot and leaned over Greg's shoulder. "Cathy. I was going to introduce your father to Brigit. Care to come along?"

She nodded, detached herself from Jeff's arm. "I'd love to."

Behind her, on the other side of the glass that separated living room from terrace, a dark cloaked figure paced along a lit walkway that snaked from the reflecting pond to a small, white, wrought-iron bench. Back again. Vincent watched Catherine separate herself from the crowd of young people, follow the red-and-silver-clad man into the party. When he could no longer see her, not even the feathers that shivered in rhythm with her step, he turned and walked back the way he had come, stopped and gazed thoughtfully at the double terrace doors. Sooner or later, he must walk the five or six steps from this place to those doors, take hold of the handle, turn it, pull the door open and step into that room. Sooner or later . . . He took one step, a second. And stopped.

John Brennan slowed his pace so Catherine, with her awkward skirts, could keep up with him; he collected Charles from a group of older men all discussing some esoteric point of property, and led them both past the piano, past a glowing skeleton whose eye sockets pulsed with the music, past a couch barely visible for the number of guests seated on it, perched on its back, gathered around it. Just beyond that, there was a small clearing, then another tight mob of people packed around the base of a broad, curving flight of stairs. Brennan mumbled something over his shoulder, began working his way into the center of this group. People moved aside for him, making enough room for Charles and his daughter to follow. But as they reached the first of the marble stairs, a man in a leather short-sleeved jacket and a horned Viking cap laid a hand against Charles' chest, stopping him cold.

"Hold up, there," he said. It came out more like "Huld opp, theer." His other hand deftly drew the cavalry officer's sword. "Let's have a look here." The right hand stayed where it was, against Charles' chest; he ran his left thumb over the blade, testing it thoughtfully. John Brennan was back, both hands fluttering. Emily Post didn't cover social embarrassments like this, Catherine thought with amusement.

"I'm dreadfully sorry, Charles. Mr. Cavanaugh here is one of Brigit's bodyguards."

"No offense sir," the Irishman said as he let the sword slide back into its scabbard. "There's been threats. Or-angemen, Croppies."

Charles made a two-handed gesture that waved aside the apology and the need for it; his forehead wrinkled as he took in the man's words. "Croppies, did you say? I'm afraid I don't understand that."

"No reason you should." It was a woman's voice, soft and low but the sweet, musical lilt cut through the babble of voices and laughter around them. "It's from an old war." Brigit O'Donnell came around Cavanaugh's side. "An Irish Catholic uprising against the British and their Protestant allies. The rebels," she smiled faintly, "had short-cropped hair, you see."

Catherine had to think a moment. "That was—what, two hundred years ago?" Brigit nodded. "That's a—that's a long time to remember a haircut."

Brigit was physically smaller than Catherine would have expected, somehow: about her own size. She wore an Empire gown such as Napoleon's Josephine might have worn: high waist, low throat, short puffed sleeves and long gloves. The effect would have been voluptuous on a Josephine. On Brigit—one was first aware of her as small, fragile. The mask she wore, though—Catherine blinked in surprise. It was her own, save that Brigit it's was brown. The delicate rosebud of a mouth under the brown owl's beak smiled and it was a sweet, gentle smile. The eyes were approving, though: as though she hadn't expected an American girl to know such a bit of Irish history.

She might not have, if Brigit O'Donnell's books hadn't led her to get several books on Ireland from the library, and read them cover to cover.

"We Irish have long memories," Brigit said, and there was an underlying distress to her words that belied the gentle, softly accented sound of them. "My father taught me all the songs about the brave Croppy boys when I was still in the cradle."

Charles sketched a bow. "I stand instructed. I'm afraid," he added ruefully, "that history was never my subject. And most of what I did learn, I've managed to forget."

Brigit nodded and gave him another of those lovely smiles. "Forgetting is a trick that Ulster could stand to learn," she said. Before Charles could reply, John was back at his side, touching his arm and making a face.

"There's Samantha," he said. "She'll never forgive me if I don't bring you over to say hello, Charles."

It was Charles' turn to make a face now; a wary one. Samantha was John's first wife and she'd tried hard to attach herself to Charles on the rebound from her divorce. She still flirted with him in an embarrassingly heavy fashion. He sighed, took Brigit's fingers and squeezed them gently. "It's been a delight," he said. "Please excuse me. Duty," he added wryly, "beckons." And he followed his friend back across the room. Catherine turned back to see Brigit's eyes—preternaturally solemn and alert behind those brown feathers—on her. But when she smiled, Cathy felt as though she'd known the woman for years.

"I like your mask," Brigit said lightly. "You know, I wrote a story about an owl-woman once. Just a little fable," she added rather shyly. "For children."

Cathy shook her head. "Children of all ages. I read it just last year, and I just loved it."

"Did you now? It's not easy to find, that one."

"It was given to me by a friend. A very special friend," she added softly, more to herself than her companion. "You have a real gift. I wish you wrote more children's stories."

The dark blue eyes behind the brown owl-woman's mask had a remarkable depth to them: Catherine felt as though she could see the tragedy of Ireland going back hundreds of years in those eyes. Dierdre must have had such eyes. "I wish I could," Brigit said softly. "But there are darker things than ghosts in Ireland now. And you can't hear the fairy music for the gunfire."

Vincent looked down, thoughtfully; the breeze picked up the hood of his cloak, momentarily ruffled the surface of the little pond. When it stilled, he could see himself: the thick, golden mane of hair that spilled from the hood and across his shoulders; the white shirt with its fall of ruffles; the black leather gauntlets that covered hands which no one would mistake for costumery. And above the blue-white ruffles of shirt—broad forehead, brows that were scarcely visible against skin of the same color; the broad, flat cat's nose with the soft, curling fur that covered it, cat's upper lip. Brilliantly white, pointed teeth behind those lips. Deep-set, light blue eyes—the most human-looking thing about his face—gazed back at him above high cheekbones.

Abruptly, he turned away from the reflection and strode toward the door, caught hold of the handle and turned it. Concentrated party struck him like a blow, holding him in place for a long moment: the sound of a hundred and more people trying to hear and be heard over a hundred others; the sound of trumpets, piano, a saxophone and a full set of drums, of feet scraping across hardwood floors, the clink of glasses, of plates on glass tabletops, loud hoots of laughter and applause here and there in the crowd. His sense of smell reeled under the mix of two hundred perfumes, the scent of stage makeup and expensive cosmetics, hair spray, the glue used to fasten masks and costumes together; the smell of hot hors d'oeuvres, wine, whiskey and rum; the familiar and—in this setting extremely odd—scent of candle wax and raw pumpkin. There was a jack-o'-lantern on the floor near the door, the candle flame bending in the breeze he was letting in. Vincent pulled the door closed behind him, and became part of Brigit O'Donnell's party.

Halfway across the living room, brown and white owl-women stood at the base of the stairs, chatting like old friends. Brigit approved of Catherine's chosen profession, and listened intently while Cathy talked about it. "I love the work. For the first time, I—feel—" She half-turned as chill air blew across her bare shoulders, froze in place as she saw a familiar black-cloaked figure standing against the doors of the veranda. *Vincent?* Vincent here? It stunned her into silence. The orchestra had started playing again, dancers filled the floor between her and the veranda and when she shifted a step to the side and could see the doors again, there was no one there. Brigit's touch on her arm brought her back to herself.

"Catherine? What's wrong?"

"Nothing." But her eyes went back to the doors and stayed there. She felt rather than saw Brigit shake her head at her bodyguard; felt Cavanaugh shake his own head in mild despair and step back from them once more. "I thought I saw someone I know. Would you excuse me?"

She didn't think anyone could possibly have left the party yet, and she was willing to bet another couple hundred people had come since she and her father arrived. John Brennan's living room must be rapidly reaching critical mass. And why she had to choose this silly costume, with the awkward framework that held the skirts out sideways, so they were a full five feet side to side!

At least they were ordinarily wide front to back, not much wider than she herself was: she managed to thread her way through the talkers, watchers, then through the dancers. She started as a waiter loomed up in front of her, horrid red devil's mask peering at her over the silver tray of canapés and drinks he shoved in her direction; slid around a pair of truly awful demons and past a mermaid and her partner—some cowboy from an old television series, she thought vaguely. A sheik and his belly-dancer girlfriend tried to play keep-away with her, and she thought she'd never get by them.

It was too warm here; she suddenly couldn't tell where the walls were and all the people around her were strangers: they were too close to her, she couldn't get through them, the windows were as far away as they had been. . . . She shook her head, drew a deep breath and then a second. The mild claustrophobia faded, left her for good when she looked around and saw her father's familiar back almost within reach. When she turned back the way she'd been headed, she could see just the least hint, just a tantalizing corner of a black cape and then, as she edged around a woman clad mostly in red feathers, the definite shape of a cloaked and hooded man, standing at the buffet. She squared her shoulders and increased her pace.

A clearing—she had found a space where there weren't fifty other people. Just beyond it, another pack but on the far side of them, the table with hot chafing dishes and several bowls of oddly colored, smoking punch. And there— She edged around the Frankenstein monster to grab a handful of black wool. "Vincent?" she whispered. He turned: the face above an ambassador's formal suit and sash was a pasty-white vampire's—a man she'd never seen before. The man glared down at her, icily in character, exposed long, white fangs. She made him an apologetic smile, ducked under his arm, turned away.

Vincent—here? She didn't know what to think! But she had come this far; she might as well check the veranda first, before working back into that mob. At least on the veranda she might be able to *see* him, if he was there. She gathered her skirts as close as the boned underskirt would permit, edged through the people standing between her and the outside and pushed the door open, shoved it closed behind her, before she walked swiftly across the brightly lit area before the doors and into shadow.

There was no one—no one readily visible, she corrected her thought. He'd have seen her leave the party; he'd know she was here. "Vincent," she whispered cautiously. She took another step, deeper into shadow, and pitched the whisper as loud as she dared. "Vincent!"

There was no reply.

Eleven

I⫟ was more of a different world than he could ever have imagined: the sheer size of the room, the number of people in it. The very cut of the costumes they wore spoke of wealth, of costly fabrics sewn with care; the hairstyles of the women done with a precision that spoke also of the expensive skills of others. Vincent stayed near the veranda doors at first, walking back and forth near the glass wall, watching from a slightly aloof distance— studying those he had just joined. Watching for the one woman he knew—he could tell where she was, deep in a pack of people near the stairs—watching for another woman, one he felt certain he would know when he saw her.

Oddly, he no longer was afraid; once he'd taken the first step into this party, he had left fear on the other side of the doors, out there keeping company with the warm, skirling wind. He was wary at first, but even that faded a little as he walked around and then among John Brennan's invited guests and no one challenged him, or even spoke to him. They were too busy, he thought, with their own pleasure—their own concerns.

People in servants' clothing and masks or outrageous makeup had passed him with trays of glasses or other trays containing exquisite-looking little bite-sized pieces of food; several had been offered to him but he had taken none: the drinks contained alcohol, he was certain; he'd no taste or head for alcohol. And sheer amazement had completely taken any appetite he might otherwise have had. He had paused once, enchanted and speechless with delight when a waiter leaned toward him, proffering a beautifully chased silver tray with a crystal bowl embedded in ice. Caviar, the man had said. Beluga caviar. Something the czars had eaten—a delicacy the Princess Anastasia might have spread over thin wafers of toast at a ball similar to this.

He was near the dance area now; the blue glowing skeleton drew his eye as he passed it, the music touched his ear but it was too jazzy and too fragmented to make much impression on him. It shifted to a waltz. He moved to a place where he could stand and block no one's gaze, stood watching.

There. A small woman in a narrow gown and long gloves, a mask of brown feathers, dancing with a man in a horned helmet and a domino. She moved lightly—smoothly for several steps, then shifting to a nimble little jig of some kind. This was nothing like the dancing of others he saw around them, and it puzzled him until he realized she was trying with only partial success to dodge her partner's heavy feet. What little Vincent could see of the man's face showed his despair, his grim determination to finish this obligation and have done with dancing forever. Anyone watching could almost hear the short bits of conversation between the two: "Ah, damn, Brigit; I'm sorry!" "It's all right, Thomas, don't fret it." "But I—ah, damn!"

Brigit O'Donnell—for it was she, dancing with her large bodyguard—was watching the people around them; as her partner turned her, her eyes caught and held Vincent's. When her partner swung her partway around, she pressed to bring him back so she could look again. The music stopped; people applauded, the level of voice-sound went up to fill the gap left by music. The musicians laid down horns, the drummer stood and stretched; the pianist let the cover down over the keys and reached for the drink sitting on the small table next to him. Brigit O'Donnell stretched as tall as she could, peering through and between couples standing on the dance floor.

Vincent stayed where he was, somehow certain she had seen him, that she was Brigit O'Donnell, that she would come to him. He saw the man with her touch her arm, saw his suspicious eyes, saw rather than heard Brigit's rather exasperated laugh. He lost her for a moment, but when the crowd shifted once more, she was coming straight to him.

Fate, surely, he thought, and gave it no further thought. Tonight was meant, he had known that all along. "Brigit O'Donnell?" he asked softly as she stopped before him.

She smiled. "Herself," she replied, and held out a hand. His hesitation was so slight, she could not have noticed it. Then he reached out to take her small, white-gloved fingers in his leather-gauntleted ones.

He was vaguely aware of the people around them, of a familiar presence a distance away that was Catherine. And then of nothing but this woman, who held his hand in a friend's grasp, and who looked at him as a friend would.

"I did not mean to interrupt your dancing," he said finally. It broke a long silence.

She smiled up at him. "An act of mercy. Thomas is a good friend and a brave man, but a dancer he is not." She leaned near to study his face, and to his own surprise, he did not pull back from her regard. What an amazing job of costumery, Brigit thought. But his clothing was quite plain—black woolen cloak, patched and reinforced with black leather, a cavalier's shirt and close breeches—gauntlets and slouched boots. It was the mask that gave the costume its push into wonder. And yet—and yet, such a mask. Perhaps a stage makeup. His voice went well with his look—deep, resonant and bearing a hint of gentleness under its strength. "How extraordinary," she said softly. "You look as though you might have ridden with Cuchulainn, or sailed with Theseus—" Her voice faded away to nothing.

Another time, she would have made him self-conscious and shy. Not tonight. "Only in my dreams. And sometimes in books like yours." He'd had words carefully thought out, just what he would say; they no longer mattered. "Your writing has helped me through dark times. You've touched me, made me think." He suddenly felt foolish; she must have heard such things from all those here tonight. "I just—wanted—to tell you that. And to thank you."

The smile faded from her lips as he spoke but it remained, warm, in the dark eyes behind the owl's feathers. "Come," she said softly. "Take me outside."

Cathy saw them standing together as she came back into the party, shivering the last of the cool night air from her bare throat. She had almost begun to believe she'd been mistaken, but there, indeed, was Vincent: there in the very midst of John Brennan's party. Vincent—and Brigit O'Donnell. Cathy stared for a long, astonished moment, then began working her way around the room toward the piano.

People knew Brigit by now and moved aside for her as she led the way straight across the dance floor, thereby avoiding Cavanaugh and his cohorts. They, of course, were grouped near the entry and about the stairs, where they expected her to return. A few of those who let the two pass turned to stare after Brigit's companion and to comment in whispers at his back: "Who's that with Brigit?" "Don't know. What a mask." "Yeah. But the walk—must be one of Josie's friends from the Strasberg Institute, doing full character, don't you think?" "Well, yeah. But what kind of a character is that?"

It was stuffy and hot in that party; Brigit hadn't realized just how stuffy until she and her unknown companion came out into the garden. She headed unerringly for the outer wall, propped her forearms on it and turned back to look at him.

Catherine stood irresolute a short distance from the veranda doors, a little line between her brows. What to do? Vincent had chosen to come—but she found herself wishing he'd told her what he was planning. And what, she wondered, would Brigit do if she discovered that her companion's mask was no mask at all? She shifted once or twice, actually took a step toward the veranda, stopped once more. If he was getting his opportunity to speak to Brigit, she couldn't interrupt him. But then again—

She took another step and a man's hand came out of the mob behind her to touch her bare shoulder. She jumped and swung around, her skirts banging into an upholstered chair and rebounding into one of Brennan's waiters. The man backed and moved around her with the obvious ease of an evening's practice.

A tall, lean and dark young man stood just behind her, hand still extended to touch her again. He reminded her of Errol Flynn in *Captain Blood*—all dark good looks and flashing teeth, a close-fitting, practical pirate's garb his costume. Of course, Flynn had never worn an eye-patch like this one had. One very blue eye widened at her from a little too close, and he sketched her a rogue's bow. "Masks make life so interesting," he said cheerfully and rather archly. Ordinarily it might have amused her, this kind of come-on; right now she didn't have time for it. "Under those feathers, you might be anyone: a childhood friend, an old lover." She gave him a dismissive, socially correct smile and would have turned away, but he caught her forearm and short of rudely yanking it free she couldn't get away from him. "Come on, now, help me out," he pleaded. "Am I getting warm?"

"Afraid not," she said dismissively but softened that with the little smile once more. Unfortunately, he seemed to take the smile as encouragement.

"A famous writer then?"

"You're getting colder." She could just see around him, now that she'd shifted her stance once more; the veranda windows were right there where she could almost touch them—but she couldn't see anyone outside.

Her companion laughed and looked at her ruefully. Even *that* was a come-on, as was the way he stood just a little too close to her. And even with just the one eye visible, he was making constant eye contact. She was reminded of Jenine's going-away party, Jenine and someone else talking about the guys at one of the downtown watering holes on Friday night, someone who just *knew* he was irresistible and how long it took them to convince him they were fully capable of resisting. I don't *need* this tonight, she thought irritably. But he was talking again; maybe she could find something to use as an exit line. "Uh oh. Have I just tripped over my sword again?" He laughed. "The butler's the real pirate. I slipped him a ten-spot to tell me what the guest of honor was wearing."

Right, Cathy thought tiredly, but he was amusing despite her dislike of the type. "I don't think you'll get a refund," she said dryly. "Brigit is also wearing an owl mask."

"I'll consider it money well spent," he replied with heavy gallantry. "I'm Donald Pratt."

Her eyes strayed to the veranda once again. Two people out there—the redhead in the skeleton costume and her matching companion. Damn. She turned back to Donald Pratt, held out a hand. Be nice to him for a few minutes, then find someone to dump him on. Someone who liked the Mr. Wonderful type. "Cathy Chandler," she said.

He took her hand and held it instead of shaking it. "Well, Cathy Chandler! Shall I run up the Jolly Roger and steal you away for this dance?"

Dance. The orchestra was beginning to play again; the glass wall showed no one on the veranda except a faint glow that was shiny paint on a skeleton's black leotard.

She brought up a smile and rather guiltily hoped it didn't look as forced as it felt. "Why not?"

He must have sensed he wasn't really wanted; but men like this Donald Pratt made a habit of not noticing such things, apparently in hopes they'd go away. He certainly made the most of taking her in his arms and sweeping her out onto the dance floor. Catherine bit back a sigh, and braced herself for a rather long half hour or so.

By design, Vincent had moved them along the parapet until they were shrouded in darkness, and he could no longer clearly see Brigit's face, keen as his own night vision was. He knew she could make out nothing within his hood save shadow, perhaps the line of his cheekbones or his hair in the reflected city lights to the south of them. She had propped both arms on the rough stone, and was now gazing out toward those lights: toward buildings soaring upward, sparkling like concrete and granite Christmas trees or a queen's jewel box. They could hear traffic—engines running up through the gears as traffic lights changed from red to green; the unmistakable roar of busses, a constant blare of horns all up and down Central Park West. A helicopter high overhead.

A breeze stirred dry leaves around Brigit's feet and lifted her hair; she inhaled deeply and let her head fall back, turned to look at her companion. "The night has a special magic to it, don't you think? This night especially." She let her eyes move away from him to take in the bend of young trees against a gust of wind, to the shadowed, still park below and east of them, back to that clutter of lighted buildings. "In the old religion, they called it Saowen," she said softly, almost as though she spoke to herself—as though she'd forgotten him. "The night when the wall between the worlds grew thin and the spirits of the underworld walked the earth." He caught his breath as her words sank into him, catching him with a barbed truth she hadn't intended. She looked back at him and smiled. "A night of masks and bale-

153

fires," she said, her cadence almost a troubadour's chant now, and he felt a passing sorrow that Father could not hear her speak. "When anything is possible, and nothing is quite as it seems." And that, certainly, was true. She turned back to look at the city lights, shoulders tightening as a siren blared below them—a police car racing north. "Your city has its own magic as well. The lights, the towers—listen to it." The siren died away, fading in distance; another replaced it, was drowned by a racing engine and half a dozen horns. "In Derry," she said softly, "the night has a darker music." She sighed. "Bombs, gunfire. The screams of dying men." She brooded on the lights now.

"Yet—you always return," he said, and his question was there for her to hear.

She shrugged, brought up a smile. "Oh, I've thought of leaving—but Derry's my home, and whatever else I might be, I'm a Bogside girl." The smile became rueful, then faded once more. "My father's daughter. My— husband Ian's widow."

The words came more easily this time; how could he have thought her difficult to talk to? "When you wrote of Ian in *Three Hundred Days*, I felt as though I knew him. You made him live again with your words."

Light touched a gem on her cheek, sparkled as it slid down her face and another followed it. She seemed oblivious to them. "It's been two years since he got into that car," she said quietly, "and an hour hasn't passed that I haven't spoken of him, or written of him, or thought of him."

"I don't want to waken painful memories," he began, but she shook her head so hard the hair flew, mingling with the brown hackle feathers, silencing him.

"Oh, it hurts, it hurts." She smiled up at him, her eyes brilliant with more tears. "But it's such a sweet pain." She swallowed, gazed beyond him. They stood side by side in silence for some moments. "Ian and I were born six streets apart," she said finally, softly. "And yet, in different worlds." She laughed painfully; her eyes had gone distant and tender with memory. "A stiff-necked Orangeman and a Croppy girl from Bogside, we were—were daft enough to fall in love, but not so big a pair of fools to think that he could live in my world, or me in his." She sighed. "So we tried to create a new world that we could share together." She became conscious of his eyes on her, of the stillness in him—of something that was a compassion beyond mere sympathy. This man knew, she realized suddenly, knew bone deep the truth of her words. "Well, you know how that ended!" She fell silent, and he waited until she chose to speak again. "It could have been me, you know," she said into that silence. "And there are times I wish it had been." She let her eyes close, opened them to find his gaze on her.

The music stopped; Catherine would have made an excuse and gone back into the crowd but Donald Pratt somehow—rather skillfully—managed to wring the next dance from her. They'd come to a halt near the main entry, where there was a little fresh air moving up the stairs with the guests who were still coming. Catherine moved against Pratt's hand on her elbow, turned so her back was to the steps, so she could face the veranda she couldn't quite see from here—thanks to the sheer number of costumed backs, shoulders and masks between her and the glass. She bit back a sigh and managed to pay at least polite attention as Pratt launched into another what she was certain must be a highly successful line. She couldn't recall the last time she had been so thoroughly bored in a good-looking man's company.

A few paces away, the blue-faced Andre moved to block a single costumed man coming late to the party—a large, bulky man made even bulkier by the clown's costume and the rainbow wig that stuck out all around a white-face mask. The clown's eyes shifted, passed over the blue makeup, caught momentarily on the bouncing, glittered Ping-Pong balls. He would have slipped around the man then; Andre moved to block him. "Your invitation, sir," he said.

Michael bit back a sigh. Of course they'd have men to check; drat and blast his poor timing that brought him face-to-face with a man like this. He offered an embarrassed smile and began to slap at the vicinity of his waist. "Invitation? I have it here somewhere." The Irish lilted in his voice; he hoped Sean was right in saying there'd be plenty of Irish here tonight, because he'd never been good like some at losing the brogue. The butler stood immovable in front of him, looking down at him with that supercilious lack of expression that Michael McPhee hated nearly as much as he hated the snobby hint of English accent such men overlaid their own American patois with. "Damn," he said softly. "I lost it somewhere. I had one, I swear I did." The butler wasn't going for that, either.

"I'm afraid I can't admit you without an invitation," he said flatly.

Michael glared at him through the eye holes; the bloody mask stank of plastic and so did this made-up rich man's servant. "I'm telling you I was invited!" he snarled in a sudden outburst of rage. "Are you calling me a liar, now?" But that wasn't the way to go about it. He fought himself back from the brink of a good Irish fury before it cost him his only chance to get next to Brigit O'Donnell. The butler was looking definitely skeptical; O'Donnell had bodyguards enough to fill a bus and they'd be on him any moment, if he kept shouting like that.

The butler was speaking, still in that smarmy, hoity-toity accent. "Mr. Brennan's instructions were quite firm. Perhaps I should summon him."

"No, no," Michael said soothingly—and he hoped without any of the alarm he felt. "You needn't bother yourself. I remember where I left it, the very place." He smiled into the blue skeptical face. The man didn't believe a word of it, and they both knew it. "I'll just get it and come back."

"Very good, sir," the butler said woodenly. Michael

turned away before his smile could turn into a snarl, before he could fling himself on the bastard, and he started for the elevators.

It was fate, surely: the doors opened and a bulky man dressed as Henry VIII waddled out of the metal box, followed by a bevy of young women clad—barely—as Vegas showgirls. Michael was scandalized—but not so scandalized as to miss this chance. He averted his head as he moved up next to the man in the velvet knee breeches and the broad-brimmed feathered hat. And while the blue-faced butler was checking invitations, he slipped right by them all, and into the party.

He was luckier than he knew: as he edged his way between two separate mobs of people, a man in brown leather and a Viking's horned helmet passed him on the way to join the butler. Cavanaugh had heard McPhee's angry voice, and was on his way to making certain no situation was developing out there. The music had started again, and he was having a hard time making headway through the dancers.

Not far away, Donald Pratt laid a possessive hand against Catherine's back and took hold of her right hand. She let him lead her into the dance, but without paying much attention to him, the music; her feet followed his automatically. She looked across his shoulder as they came near the windows, and when they turned she became aware of his rather thoughtful eye on her. "Hey!" he protested lightly. "I can't be that bad a dancer!"

"You're not," she said, and gave him an answering smile that couldn't have been a very good one by the look on his face. "I'm sorry, I'm not very good company at the moment."

"I'll be the judge of that," he retorted and actually winked at her. At least, she *thought* it was a wink—hard to tell with that eye patch. "He's a lucky rogue,"

"Who is?"

"Whoever the hell you're looking for."

Oops, she thought and felt a sudden chill across her neck. That would never do. She smiled again and this time must have done a better job of it; her brain was churning dizzily, trying to seriously figure out how she could get *rid* of this guy. Short of absolute rudeness, however, not much seemed to touch him. She managed to keep up a mild banter with him, kept an eye out for another female to push him at; somehow, no one she knew was around except Marie—and Jeff wouldn't talk to either woman for a month if she left Marie in Pratt's clutches. She let him snag them champagne, hoping to drink him a toast, empty the glass and use it as a farewell; that didn't work, either. Maybe a trip to the women's room—sure, and he'd escort her there and wait outside for her return.

She saw her father's gray Civil War hat working across the room with relief at first, but the look on his face broke that bubble. Charles would be the last man in this entire room to take her away from a handsome and suitable-looking young man. He came on through the crowd, stopped to sketch her a bow. "Don't I know you from somewhere?" he demanded archly. She smiled and bit back half a dozen scorching replies. "Having a good time, sweetheart?" He turned to eye her companion appraisingly. "And who might this be?"

She presented him. "Donald Pratt, this is my father, Charles Chandler."

"Donald Pratt?" Charles shook his hand firmly. Catherine recognized his "Father checking references" tone of voice with a sinking heart. "Not the Donald Pratt of Bender, Sachs and Pratt, surely!"

For one moment, she thought he'd hesitated, and the look in his one eye was a little odd. He shrugged deprecatingly and smiled then. "Ah—well, actually, yes."

"Never dreamed you'd be so young!" Charles said with the enthusiasm of a man who has placed a social equal. "Al Prasker, one of my partners, is still nursing his wounds from that licking you gave him in the Scott case." He touched his daughter's shoulder playfully. "Oh, Catherine, be careful! This one isn't as harmless as he seems." You don't know the half of it, she thought in despair, but managed another smile as she nodded.

"How do you two happen to know each other?"

"Well, actually, we don't." Donald laid a hand across the small of her back with a possessiveness she was beginning to actively dislike; it took her an effort not to pull away from his touch. "But I'm trying to rectify that," he added, smiling down at her. She swallowed another rude reply, somehow didn't grab for Charles' arm as he turned and went in search of John Brennan. A big man in an aged and slightly mildewed clown costume brushed against her arm, knocking her slightly off balance and into Pratt; she glared after him, scowling at the multicolored frizzy wig as it worked its way slowly into the crowd.

Michael McPhee was keeping a wary eye out for the blue-faced butler—though he'd likely be guarding the broached front door for the rest of the night—and more importantly, for Thomas Cavanaugh in that ridiculous horned helmet. But Cavanaugh couldn't possibly know him in this striped thing and this mask. All the same, a little belated caution never hurt. Unfortunately, he wasn't getting much of anywhere with finding Sean O'Reilly's daughter. He brushed aside the servant walking around with the silver tray of caviar— Caviar, for God's sake! he thought angrily, and was suddenly grateful for the all-covering plastic mask that hid not only his face but his true feelings for all these gentry. He ran a hand into the pocket slit in the side of his baggy clown overall, made sure of the pistol tucked into his waistband, slid it cautiously around to just under his buckle. No sense having one of these bloody rich bastards knocking into it, was there now?

Vincent had lost the last of his shyness, and knew it to be her doing. Brigit O'Donnell had a way of sharing herself even beyond what he knew of her through her books, of accepting him at face value, that made him feel as though he'd known her for years. They had moved away from the parapet as other couples came out to look down on the park and the city, and now they walked along one of the narrow paths Brennan's landscape architect had created to give the sense of acreage on this once-bare patch of roof, passing between a pair of young trees decked in white lights, down into a flagged open area that held a glass-topped table, several chairs, an enormous bronze globe.

She was talking now about her childhood, sharing a totally different world with him. "My father used to tell me of New York, when I was just a little girl. He came here a dozen times—never *quite* legally, of course," she added dryly. "Raising money for the Cause, collecting for the widows and the orphans." She gave a little sigh. "And for the weapons to make more of them. He always promised he'd take me with him, one day, across the ocean." The thought visibly saddened her. "One day," she repeated softly.

This was her first visit to New York, he knew that; but he could feel her need to talk. "He never did?"

"My father—cast me out," she said, and now the lightness was forced. "It was three years ago, on my wedding day. He came to the church, called me a traitor and an Orangeman's whore, and I've not seen him since." They walked on a few paces, stopped near the reflecting pond. "By rights, I ought to hate him."

She looked up as he shook his head. "There's no hate in you," he told her. "Only grief."

Such a glorious look the man had to him, and such knowledge of the ways of the heart. She was more than half aware, somewhere deep down, that the face was no mask. The Irish of her accepted that, as she accepted Saowen and the breaking down of the walls. "Aye," she said softly. "How can you hate the man who taught you what love meant?" She shivered, turned her eyes from his to look at the water.

"Are you cold?" he asked.

But it hadn't been the air that affected her. She stirred, fought down the chill some said was Sight and buried deep the vision it tried to show her. "Cold? No. It's naught but a brisk fall evening!" She looked at him, sidelong, considering, and finally smiled. It was an urchin's grin, and promised mischief. "But—I'd borrow your cloak, if you're willing to lend it."

He didn't understand. "My cloak?"

She nodded. "Thomas and the others, they'd give their lives for me. And I love them for it." She cast her arms wide in a gesture of frustration. "But sometimes, I want nothing so much as to get away from them for a few hours."

"They're only trying to keep you safe," he protested mildly. But he told her nothing she didn't already know—he could see that. She looked properly, smolderingly Irish all at once. Rebellious.

"I'm sick unto death of safety!" she burst out passionately. "I look at that city out there, and I want to touch it, to walk its streets and meet its people, listen to its music!" She flung out a hand, taking it all in. "I want to see all the things my father told me of, and I can't!" She met his eyes squarely. "Can you imagine how that feels?"

She'd struck something deep; she couldn't tell what. He was still and silent for a long moment. Finally, simply, he said. "Yes."

She laughed, showing fine, strong teeth. "To hell with the risks!" and then became somberly intense. "Sometimes, we must leave our safe places, and walk empty-handed among our enemies."

There was nothing at all he could find to say to that. Nothing, he knew with a certainty that went to his very core, that he would want to say. He reached up slowly, before he could let himself think what he did, and pushed the hood back, unfastened the throat, then held the black fabric out so he could settle it around her shoulders.

He watched her go, a slight figure smothered in black, the hood pulled low over her face, the hems dragging the ground all around her until she caught them up before her and held them close to her chest. She slipped through the veranda doors and a roar of party billowed out across the roof garden. Vincent stood in shadow, waiting until she vanished unchallenged into the party, before he

turned toward the north and pulled himself back onto
the ledge. Another roof—there. So. He dropped several
feet, with only the least thump marking his passage,
moved along the darkened flatness and found the little
emergency hatch that would get him back into the elevator shaft.

He let himself down the ladder a step at a time, hung
there in the blackness, waiting for a car to come up. He
wondered a little at himself, then set it aside. This was
not the time for introspection; he was living a truly curious adventure, and it would surely be wrong to do
anything but follow where it led.

The elevator stopped just below him and he landed silently on its roof, bracing himself for the descent. Catherine was still there; he knew she was worried about him—
say, rather, concerned. He wished there was some way
he could assure her that everything was all right.

Cavanaugh stood near the veranda doors, scowling all
around him. Brigit had simply vanished; the last anyone
could remember seeing her was a good half hour before.
She could be anywhere in here—as much as he'd lectured her on the foolishness of it, she could even be outside, a clear mark for any sniper who knew where she
was, where this man Brennan lived. And thanks to that
bloody article in the newspapers, that included only a
mere eight million!

But that would just be Brigit, wouldn't it? Taking no
thought for herself and what she meant to people. He
squared his shoulders and started for the outside, brushing past a little man in a black monk's cloak coming in.

The cloak wove through the crowd, seeking the path of
least resistance, moving from clear space to clear space—
and there were a few of those now, as some of the early
people began to leave. And so Catherine looked up and
caught sight of that familiar wool and leather hood, hurrying past her. She frowned; there was something not
quite right about the person, but there was absolutely no
mistaking the cloak this time. She stuffed her champagne
glass, mostly full, in Donald's hands, cutting short what-

ever silly thing he was babbling about now and slipped around him, in pursuit of that still-visible hood. She heard Donald's protest behind her, then forgot about him as she forced her way through a clutch of people gathered around the stairs, stretching out the usual good-byes. Her nose wrinkled; that clown again. The fabric really smelled awful, as though it hadn't been washed or cleaned in years. Imagine wearing *that* to a party like this! She had pushed him with her skirt, murmured an apology as she turned sideways to pass him. He mumbled something back, but she felt his eye on her. Well, if he was upset, that was certainly too bad. She gathered up her skirts two-handed and made her way down the steps. The elevator doors were closing, its sole occupant Vincent—

Not Vincent. She stopped, staring, as the head came up and Brigit O'Donnell's face was framed by the hood. Brigit tipped her a wink and laid a finger to her lips warningly. And the door closed, the elevator began sliding down the shaft. She was still gazing uncertainly at the polished steel doors when she became aware of Donald just behind her. Donald. Of course she couldn't get rid of *him!* "Hey," he said. "That was Brigit O'Donnell, right?"

"Something very strange is going on here," Cathy said flatly, and her hand sought the elevator button, pressed it hard. "And I'm going to find out what!" With a faint groan and squeak, the second elevator slowed, positioned itself before the doors. They opened, and the clown pushed past her and into the empty car. She glanced at him. "Would you hold the car a moment, please?" and turned back to Donald, who was smiling like a man who'd caught the gold ring. "Donald, I don't mean to be rude, but—" She spun away from him as the doors clapped together and the elevator started down. She slapped the button with her palm; too late, kicked the doors and swore furiously. Donald spread his hands and grinned.

"Hey, no problem!" he said. "We—uh, we pirates can—we can find stairs!" he finished in triumph, and caught her by the waist. "C'mon!"

She'd have liked nothing better, suddenly, than to trip him up at the head of those stairs and leave him sitting at the top on his backside. She let that picture entertain her all the way down a very long flight of fire stairs.

Below her, Brigit walked out of John Brennan's building and onto the sidewalk, then stood waiting. Before she had a chance to wonder if she'd done something entirely foolish, she saw him: Vincent came up behind her, magnificent and tall in his cavalier's shirt, pants and boots. His face—she no longer thought of it as a mask—was a lion's or a man's, both mixed: a man's deep, strong blue eyes looking at her over the flat, furry muzzle of a large cat. It was the face that fitted him, it was all a part of the magic of this night—it matched the strength of him, the deepness of his feeling and the overall sadness of him.

That it was not a human man's face—how could that matter to a woman who all her life had seen handsome men's faces hiding beastly, black souls?

She smiled up at him, saw the answering smile that moved his lips a little and warmed his eyes. He sketched her a bow that wouldn't have shamed a king, and held out an arm for her, to lead her across the street and into Central Park.

Bare moments later, Catherine came through the door, breathing hard from the burst of speed she'd managed coming down the last stairs and across the lobby. Donald was right behind her, unfortunately. She looked around as she came onto the broad sidewalk and swore under her breath. There was no one in sight who might have been Vincent or Brigit. The doorman— She ran up to him. "Have you seen a woman with red hair? Wearing a black cloak?"

He nodded with such enthusiasm his hat slipped and nearly fell off. "Yeah, sure! Looker like that, I'd have to be dead not to notice." He gestured at the sidewalk before them. "She met a guy in a cat mask."

"Where did they go?" Catherine demanded.

"They went off into the park—north, I think."

She nodded her thanks, started across the sidewalk. Donald was right on her heels, though; she sighed and stopped short. "Look," she said earnestly. "I have to go after them. It's a personal thing, I can't explain. I appreciate your help, but there's no need for you to leave the party."

She might have saved her breath. He was already shaking his head. "I can't let you go off in the park alone! Hasn't anybody ever warned you about all the things that go bump in the night?"

"Donald, I'll be fine. Really—!"

"While we're talking," he overrode her sweetly, "they're getting away."

She couldn't argue with that; without a further word she turned, gathered up her skirts and sprinted across the street. He stayed right behind her. At the first possible moment, she promised herself firmly, *somehow* she was going to get rid of this jerk. And be damned to hurting his feelings!

Twelve

T HE sky was clear; the wind had died away to nothing. The full moon appeared twice its normal size, a second moon shone from the depths of the Reservoir. People walked along the paths—some costumed, many not. Somewhat apart from those others, a woman in long, slender skirts walked with a man: a tall man, with moonlight turning his ruffled shirt radiantly, eerily blue, picking out blue-white highlights in his thick tangle of long hair. Brigit, cloak slung over her forearm, walked beside him in silence, drinking in her surroundings. He turned away from the water, led her under trees, where he felt less vulnerable. She slowed, stopped in shadow almost as though she understood his need for the darkness, removed her mask and smiled up at him. "I'm beholden to you, Vincent. You cannot know what this means to me." He felt her eyes studying him, gravely; his own eyes were searching the way they had just come. Something out there made him uneasy, and yet there was no indication anyone had paid them the slightest heed. Certainly no one had followed them out into the open park.

"Or perhaps you can at that," she said finally. He turned back to look at her. How very odd: he realized that she saw him for what he was, and felt no fear or repugnance in that. And he, even more oddly, felt no fear of her knowledge.

But it was after all Saowen; the wall between the worlds was paper-thin and thinning more still.

Brigit turned to walk slowly down the sidewalk; he came up beside her and for some moments they ambled along in companionable silence. "Will you be telling me of her, then?" Brigit asked gently.

"Who?"

She gestured, a movement of one hand that stopped just short of his arm. "Your lady. The one who's breaking your heart." She looked up at him sideways. "You didn't come just to say you liked my books," she added lightly. "Something about Ian and me struck close to home."

He opened his mouth, closed it again. Finally nodded. "She brings me such joy," he whispered. "Such pain as I have never known." He considered this unhappily. "I have no place in her world, and she has none in mine. Our bond endangers everything: people I love, secrets I am sworn to keep." He looked at her to see sympathetic eyes watching him. "The beliefs I have lived by. Everything."

She nodded and this time let her hand rest on his arm. "Aye. That sounds like Ian and myself, sure enough. They don't understand, do they? Father raged—" She sighed, shook her head and fell silent.

"Yet you went on," he prompted. "Despite everything."

Brigit laughed, a dry, bitter little sound with no humor to it. "Oh, yes, we went on! Till he died for it." She stopped, and her hand on his arm brought him to a stop, brought him around to face her. "Are you asking me for counsel then? Forget you even knew her," she urged him flatly. "And both of you will be happier."

Vincent gazed down at her in silence, disengaged his arm gently and turned away from her to look out through the trees; a stray beam of moonlight came through bare branches to lay across his shoulders. "You wrote that the price of your love had been high, but you would pay it willingly until the end of your days." He looked back at her. "That you would change nothing, regret nothing—"

She closed the distance between them and caught his arm in both hands, shook it as hard as she could. "That's damned unfair of you, you know, quoting my own words back at me! After I gave you all that good advice!" But then she smiled, and finally went on softly: "Your brain tells you all the sensible things to do, but the heart knows nothing about sense. And the heart is as stubborn as the Irish." She shrugged helplessly, held out his cloak; Vincent settled it over his shoulders. His fingers froze on the fastening, his other hand tightened on hers and she looked up at him in sudden alarm. "What— what is it?"

Someone *was* there! He'd thought it before, and now he was certain of it: someone coming for them, for the two of them in particular, with evil intent in his heart. He could feel his anger rising, threatening to consume him: was this woman never to be left alone, to do the good she was capable of? He laid a gloved finger to her lips, pressed her back against a tree and stole into shadow.

Michael McPhee was utterly frustrated: it had been a fool's errand to begin with; of his own choosing he'd never have gone after the wretched girl at that party. And now what? Here he was, in New York's Central Park—surrounded by murderous gang lads, doubtless!—stalking her through the dark! His night vision had never been good and since the explosion in that pub four years back it had gone worse, he was half-blind out here. He got a better grip on the pistol, and walked on. This way—he was nearly certain that it was Brigit he'd seen crossing from the water and into shadow, and that long brute with her. . . . Well, he'd be certain of them both, soon enough.

A low growl brought him up, heart pounding painfully. Had they lost one of the zoo animals? Before he could move, a blur of white shirt flung itself at him, and he gasped. Was it the man he'd seen with young Brigit? But the face! Ah, God, what kind of mask moved like a murderous beast's face?

Michael McPhee set his jaw and brought up the gun; Vincent roared in fury, drowning the man's terrified yell. The gun went flying and Michael found himself hurtling forward, caught by costume and the shirt under it. He saw nothing but a blare of white light then as he was slammed back into a tree trunk, and collapsed unconscious to the pavement.

Catherine heard the roar and knew it at once; fear lent wings to her feet and she pelted down the sidewalk, temporarily leaving Donald Pratt behind. He caught up with her a short distance into the trees, looked down where she did. The clown from John Brennan's party lay at full length in the middle of the sidewalk, out cold. Pratt knelt, pulled the mask away, checked his pulse, unaware that Catherine's attention was not on him. She was gazing all around them, searching the shadows. "Is he dead?" she asked.

Donald stood, began brushing dirt from the knees of his costume. "He's out cold, but he'll live. Just maybe a concussion." He bent again to smooth his breeches; Catherine had turned away from him and stood quite still. A distance ahead of them, she saw him: Vincent. Moonlight touched the narrow line of shirtfront revealed by his cloak, but he otherwise stood in shade. And then Brigit's pale face and white throat, the front of her dress and her long gloves, as she stepped onto the pavement to stand beside him. Vincent retreated a step, a second; he touched Brigit's arm but his eyes stayed on Catherine's as he moved fully into shadow, turned away and became one with the night.

"Vincent!" So little sound came that even Donald Pratt did not hear her agonized call. But Brigit saw the look in her eyes as she came running toward them.

Donald became aware of her and stopped fussing with

his costume. "Well. Brigit O'Donnell, I presume," he said, and somehow contrived to sound as though there was nothing unusual about the circumstances of their meeting. "What happened to the other guy?"

Brigit offered him a wry smile. "He had promises to keep." Her eyes caught Catherine's meaningfully. "But I'm thinking he'd rather have stayed."

Just those few words. Catherine nodded faintly at her behind Donald's back. Suddenly everything was—if not exactly all right—no longer so muddled and upsetting. And a thought pricked her with uneasy amusement. *Was I jealous?* Was it something that ridiculous that had motivated her this past hour? But she could worry about that later. Right now, there was an ugly situation brewing and someone would have to get it under control. For starters, get Brigit O'Donnell out of this park and back into the care of her bodyguards. "Brigit," she asked crisply, "what happened here? Are you all right?" She saw Donald glance at her, surprised at the sudden strength in her voice.

Brigit nodded. "I'm fine." She gestured, taking in the unconscious man at her feet. "But it's not for want of this man trying." She glared down at him.

Cathy bent over with her, to study the exposed face. She'd never seen him before, but the other woman certainly had. "Why? Do you know him?"

She gave a very unladylike snort of anger that scarcely sounded like the Brigit O'Donnell Catherine had talked to earlier. "Oh, him and his sort!" she burst out. "I've known them all my life. His name is Michael McPhee." She made it sound like curse words. "He's a fine IRA man."

"As long as you're all right," Catherine said calmly. "We'll call the police."

Donald touched her arm and shook his head. She frowned; something about *him* wasn't quite the same, and his own voice, when he spoke, flattened out, losing the "tomcat on the prowl" cadence that had nearly driven her mad. "No need. Actually, I can handle it from here, thank you."

"You?" she asked skeptically.

He cast her a rueful glance and reached into his shirt. "I'm afraid I wasn't quite honest with you, Cathy." Brigit looked at one, then the other, shook her head in bafflement. Donald pulled out a black folder the size of a wallet, flipped it open to expose a badge and a photo ID card.

"Interpol!" Cathy read the card aloud; she still sounded skeptical, and Donald shrugged, visibly embarrassed. He flipped the ID closed and restored it to its inner pocket. "I thought your father was about to blow my cover for a moment back at the party. All that lawyer talk." He tossed her one of those irking, toothy smiles but when he turned to Brigit, who was watching them both uncertainly, he was suddenly gravely correct. "My apologies, Mrs. O'Donnell. We received a tip that an attempt would be made on your life, and I was supposed to keep close to you. Unfortunately I met the wrong owl."

Brigit shook her head and a very faint smile touched her lips as she visibly relaxed. "It's perfectly all right. All owls look alike by night." She spoke to his back; Donald was bent over, searching the ground while he fumbled with the scarf around his throat. When he straightened, he had McPhee's pistol in its folds; moonlight glinted on the barrel, then vanished as he wrapped the scarf around it. "Evidence," he said in explanation. "Have to be thorough. We'll drop you back at the party, Cathy. No reason everyone's Halloween should be ruined."

"No, I'll see it through." He wanted to protest; she overrode him. "As long as the masks are coming off, I'm with the district attorney's office."

The stunned look on his face almost made up for an evening of his silliness. All the same, she had a sneaking feeling he found what she'd said alarming, and wondered why. "Are you? This *is* a night for surprises." He indicated the fallen man with a nod. "Well, if you'll keep an eye on Sleeping Beauty here, I'll bring my car around." She nodded; as Donald vanished into the trees, back toward Central Park West, Brigit O'Donnell stepped closer to her. They waited in silence for some time; finally, headlights came down the roadway a short distance off and they heard the late-model automobile stop.

It took the efforts of all three of them to get Michael McPhee on his feet; he was only about half-conscious, scarcely capable of walking, but between them they couldn't have carried him. Donald Pratt flashed his ID, then a snub-nosed pistol. McPhee seemed unaware of either or of the man himself. But he walked to the car, mechanically, leaning heavily on both women, while Donald followed with his gun at the ready.

They got him in the backseat, and Donald ushered Brigit into the passenger seat before he got behind the wheel, leaving Catherine to walk around and get in the back next to McPhee. She edged into the corner, as much to keep an eye on him from what distance she could as to stay as far as possible from the unpleasant odor of mildew. He ignored all of them; his eyes had been mere slits while he walked and now were closed, his mouth sagged open, head rolling from side to side as Donald pulled out into traffic, turned right on Fifth and drove toward downtown.

For several minutes—three traffic lights, a crowded pedestrian crosswalk, a tieup behind a horse-drawn carriage—Michael lay in the seat like a sack of grain: face pasty white, air wheezing into his open mouth. As Donald turned left, he rolled his head side to side uncomfortably and began to moan. Catherine saw Brigit's pale, worried face as she slewed around in the passenger seat. "I think he's coming to," she told the Irishwoman. She saw Donald's head flick partway around, saw his eyes in the rearview mirror—they touched on his prisoner slightly, fixed thoughtfully on her before traffic forced him to bring full attention back to the street.

"Oh, God," the man in the corner groaned. "My head hurts something fierce!" He brought up a shaking hand to touch it, took it away and moaned again.

If he was after sympathy, he wasn't getting it. Brigit

fixed him with a black look. "You ought to be grateful it's still attached to your shoulders, Michael McPhee," she said severely.

He sighed. "Ah, don't take that tone with me, woman! You know I wouldn't harm you." Silence. "Damn it!" he shouted, and caught his breath on a pained little gasp. "It was Sean sent me," he went on in a considerably softer tone.

"Am I supposed to care?" Brigit stormed at him. He winced at the sound of her voice. "He made it quite clear he does not have a daughter!"

"He's dying, girl!" McPhee overrode her, shocking her into silence. "There's not much time left to him. He wants to see you again," he urged quietly. "He sent me to you."

"Oh, aye, he did! With a gun in your hand!" she snapped, and the moment of shock was gone, buried in anger. She swung back to face forward, went on in a pained whisper: "My own flesh and blood! What did I ever do to make him hurt me so?"

Where were they? Catherine was uneasily aware they were doing a lot of traveling and were well away from any of the police stations in the area—particularly far from the federal marshal's offices, where they should be going on an illegal entry matter. She leaned forward; Donald's shoulders were tight, his neck stiff, and what she could see of his eyes in the rearview mirror was daunting. McPhee distracted her before she could say anything.

"You got it all wrong," he said flatly. "It wasn't you I was after, girl, it was that fellow with you, with the black cloak and the lion mask!"

Cathy swung around to stare at him. "Vincent?" The name came out in a tight, frightened whisper; the breath froze in her chest. Brigit was shaking her head violently.

"He's a friend!" she protested sharply.

"A murdering Orangeman was what he was!" Michael McPhee shouted her down. "We had the word, girl! It's Sean they're after, but they have no love for you, either!" He was clutching his aching head and panting; he had

174

to stop and catch his breath. "I was to keep you safe, and to bring you safely to your father, don't you *see*?"

Brigit might not, but Catherine did; the unease that had been growing the past hour or more suddenly had a shape: murder. And a name and a face to go with it. She caught hold of Donald's shoulder and leaned across the seat to look out the front window.

"Where are we?" she demanded. "We're supposed to be headed Downtown, this isn't—"

His answer was to slam on the brakes and turn the wheel violently; her hand tore free of his shirt and she was thrown back into the seat and against the door, Michael McPhee falling on top of her. She heard Brigit's shout of surprise as she caught the door handle to keep herself from toppling onto the driver. A horn blared; there was a long, deserted and utterly black block and then lights all around them, suddenly; the car's tires screamed on the smooth concrete of a parking garage. An empty parking garage, Cathy saw uneasily. Facing onto a very empty street. She braced her elbows against the seat and the door, slipping the seat belt off so she could throw herself forward once the car came to a halt.

Too late. Donald had already cut the engine, stopping the car right in the middle of the ramp, and was already turned around. The snub-nosed gun he held easily covered all three of them.

The good-looking, rather vapid Errol Flynn face was set, the eyes black and hard. She wondered she could ever have thought him a brainless womanizer. And when he spoke, his voice had a lilt that had not been there before: an Irish accent that was the least musical she'd ever heard. He met her eyes briefly, raised one dark eyebrow and indicated first Brigit, then McPhee with the pistol. "The best thing about Croppies," he said crisply, as if instructing her, "is they're as stupid as they are ugly."

He turned the gun in Brigit's direction. "You, out," he said flatly. She moved, slowly, eyes fixed on the weapon as she worked the door handle and scrambled out. At once, he threw his own door open and was

175

somehow standing several paces from the car. Fast on his toes, Catherine thought measuringly. Fast, determined and armed. All the same, she didn't doubt her chances of overpowering him, if she could get close to him. He was too dependent on the gun, and he'd never take a woman seriously as a physical threat.

He got Brigit over next to him, then bent down to meet Cathy's eyes, gesturing sharply with the pistol. "Come on, my darling." She did, carefully. Michael McPhee, at another gesture, slid across the backseat and came out after her. Donald retreated one cautious step at a time, until he was between them and the car, until he had the three of them bunched together.

Catherine pushed her fear aside; fear wouldn't help any of them. She'd do better to try and defuse the situation; if that didn't work, to stop him. She edged herself between him and Brigit. "Don't do this, Donald," she urged quietly. "Put down the gun. Don't let this get out of hand."

He might have been made of stone and deaf both; his attention was all for the man in the faded clown costume. He had lost the angry edge he'd shown briefly in the car, to become all cold purpose. It chilled her, but when he shifted a step, she stepped between him and the others once more. He gave her a terrible look, then let his gaze pass her, to fix on Michael McPhee. The man was pathetic for all his size, his own hair and face incongruous above the clown suit. "Do you remember William Harland?" Donald whispered.

Cathy sensed McPhee's nod; she didn't dare turn to look at him. His loud, truculent voice made her jump. "A lying, murdering Orange bastard, he was."

"You and your lads didn't even have the courage to face him when you gunned him down," Donald said, his hard, low voice cutting through the echo McPhee had raised. "You waited until he was good and drunk, and caught him leaving the pub."

"It was no more than he'd done for better men than him," McPhee snarled. Catherine took a step forward, stopped as the little gun swung around to fix on her.

"Stop it, both of you!" she shouted. "Donald, you don't need to do this!" Silence. She could hear her heart thudding wildly against her ribs, could hear McPhee's breath coming in short little gasps. "Turn him over to the police," she urged and could hear how desperate she sounded. "He'll pay for his crime."

"Oh, he'll pay for it, sure enough," he replied meaningfully.

Brigit's hand touched hers, startling her; she jumped painfully. "It's no use, Catherine," she said and there was as much anger as sorrow in her words. "You cannot talk sense to them. Not to any of them!" She turned to glare at Michael McPhee. "It's like a sickness with them now, and there's not a drop of human decency left in the lot of them."

The pistol shook momentarily; Donald's knuckles were white as he took two steps toward the Irishwoman. "Shut up!" he shouted at her. "I've heard enough of your damned pious speeches." Brigit opened her mouth, shut it again in silence as Catherine gripped her fingers. Donald moved swiftly, backing McPhee and Brigit away from Catherine—just far enough so that Catherine could no longer even pretend to shield them. "Empty your pockets," he snapped. The big man set his jaw and glared at him defiantly. The snap of the hammer going back echoed from concrete ceiling to floor and back again. Brigit made an involuntary move, caught hold of McPhee's hand and gripped his fingers, hard.

"Michael," she whispered painfully. "Do as he says."

It was pitiful to watch the fight go out of the man, as much from her touch as the sight of that pistol. To watch his face sag and go grayish in the uneven light; to see his shoulders droop. He fetched a short breath and delved into the side slit of his costume, holding it back with one hand while he pulled out the contents of his pants on that side, and then the other. American money in crumpled wads, a matchbook; cigarettes cascaded from a red-and-white box, rolling across the floor; coins bounced and rolled away from him. A wrapped peppermint, a second. A key on a thick brass ring, attached to a red placard bearing a hotel name. Donald watched the pile grow, smiled as the key rang against the smooth, oily floor and the plastic made its own faint clatter, almost lost in the shuffling of the older man's unpolished shoes.

There was a deep rumble, somewhere near, almost like thunder. A train, Cathy thought, and saw the intent in Donald's eye. She shifted her weight as unobtrusively as she could, cast Brigit a warning glance she hoped the woman would take as an order to stay still and keep quiet.

"My name is Jamie Harland," the armed man said softly. "William was my brother."

Catherine swallowed. It was hard to make any words come in the face of so much hatred; somehow, she forced them out. "Your brother is dead," she said softly but with finality. "You won't bring him back with murder."

She had to raise her voice at the end, to be heard above the roar of engine and clatter of metal wheels on metal rails. Donald was shouting above it. "I'm no murderer! This is an execution! For Ulster," he roared out, "and for Billy!" The structure shook with the passing train; the sound filled it, echoing from post to post, growing from loud to unbearable. The single pistol shot cracked above it, but Catherine heard neither her cry of protest nor Brigit's. Michael McPhee had thrown himself forward, hands crooked into claws, grabbing for the Orangeman's throat; the bullet stopped him in mid-flight. He fell forward without a sound, measuring his length; his face was mercifully not visible.

The rattle and clangor of train was fading into the night. The two women stood very still, watching Jamie Harland, who let the arm that held the gun fall to his side, limply. Would he kill them, too? Cathy wondered, and wondered why she felt so unafraid. Jamie Harland stared down at the body of his fallen enemy, but she knew he had enough of his attention on them. He knelt, caught up the hotel key and stood looking at it.

"Damn you to hell," Brigit said evenly. Her face crumpled then, she turned and Cathy caught her close to hold her while she wept.

He never even looked at her. His eyes caught Cathy's; he gestured with the pistol, indicating the car. "We're going for a ride. You drive." Silence. "Get going," he snapped.

Catherine held her ground. "Where are you taking us?"

For one moment, she thought he might simply shoot them; it was in his eyes and in his mind. "There were three of them that killed William," he said finally. "I got the first a year ago, and Michael McPhee here—he was the second." He flicked a chill smile at her. "You might say he was—sort of a bonus. It was the other one I was hoping she'd lead me to." He glanced at Brigit, brought his eyes back to hold Cathy's and held up the key like a hunter's trophy. "To a gentleman name of Sean O'Reilly," he added lightly, playing his accent like a harp. "Who, I'm thinking, might just be found in a certain hotel, and ill, too. But maybe a visit from his loving daughter will cheer him up." She could feel Brigit begin to tremble in her arms, but to her credit, she said nothing, merely pushed herself upright and walked back to the car. Cathy stood irresolute, weighing her odds, but Donald took a step toward her and she suddenly knew she could not bear for him to touch her. She whirled away, caught hold of the driver's door, fought the long satin skirts into place and pulled the door shut with hands that were beginning to tremble.

It still wasn't fear for herself: it was reaction to Michael McPhee's sudden death, to the unbearable shift from one personality to another as the man next to her shed one mask after another. He twisted his mouth into lover's smile under killer's eyes, and let her see the gun he held ready to use on her, just against the edge of her skirt.

It seemed to take her a very long time to get a steady enough grip on the key to turn on the engine.

* * *

In the time Vincent had been gone Above, the wind had died down, and the dust and smoke were rapidly settling; in his room there were faint halos around the two candles he had lit on his return, the lamp on his table that stayed burning except when he slept. It was still cold enough to warrant gloves and an extra layer of jacketing; Vincent had left his cloak tied at the throat, and his arms were tucked inside the heavy fabric. Father came into the chamber and blinked, peering doubtfully through the gloom. It took several moments for his eyes to adjust and see Vincent seated in his favorite high-backed chair, slumped down, legs stretched long before him. His eyes were fixed on the toes of his boots, but he looked up as the older man came near.

"Lana said you'd returned, Vincent. Am I—disturbing you?" Vincent shook his head, gestured. Father limped over to take the empty chair close to him. They sat in silence for several minutes; Vincent apparently brooding on his feet, Father waiting for him to speak, then trying and discarding several openings to conversation. "Did you find Brigit?" he finally asked.

"Yes." Vincent brought his eyes up briefly. "And so did a man with a gun." Father let his own eyes close briefly, shook his head. Such a thing could not surprise him; little of the violence Above could. Vincent's voice showed his astonishment, his pain; the other could almost envy him that unworldly innocence. Almost. "She's given so much," he whispered to his boots. "And gotten only violence and grief and pain." He brought his gaze up, looked at his older companion searchingly. "How can they hate so?"

Father shifted in his chair, touched Vincent's hand and shook his head. To explain without pouring all his anger and hatred into the boy—it was a narrow line he walked at times like this. "Sometimes," he said finally, "during my first few years in the tunnels, I would lie awake at night. Wondering if I'd done the right thing. I was full of such anger, I wanted to avenge all the wrongs I'd suffered." He looked up to find Vincent's eyes still on him.

"Yet you never went back up." It was not quite a question even though he clearly did not understand.

"No. If I had, I think my anger would have consumed me." He looked up in alarm as Vincent drew himself upright and then leaped to his feet. "What's wrong?"

"Catherine—!" It wasn't an answer, it was a whispered cry of fear and pain—response to her silent cry for help. Before Father could say anything else, Vincent was gone.

Thirteen

In terms of physical distance, the hotel wasn't far at all: a dozen crosstown blocks from a parking garage in a slightly seedy neighborhood to a definitely seedy four-story brick building with a sign that ran from the second floor to the roof and spelled out OTEL—the H burned out, possibly years before; the hotel's name—if any—not lit. It was possibly the longest trip Catherine had ever taken in a moving vehicle. Jamie Harland sat sideways on the seat, so he could keep a close eye on both women, and while he kept the gun low, she could still see the tip of the barrel across his leg when she glanced that way.

It was a very quiet journey: once in the car, Jamie kept a tight-lipped silence. Catherine concentrated on driving, afraid that the least off maneuver on her part would convince the man she was trying to wreck the car or to draw attention. He'd shoot them both, she had no doubt of that. In the backseat, Brigit was by and large a shadow; she moved only once, as though she might lean forward to speak. Jamie rounded on her and she returned to her former position. After that, she watched New York going by her window and kept her head turned away from him.

By a stroke of good fortune, there was a parking place just across from the hotel's entrance: Catherine had been half-afraid she'd be unable to find anywhere to leave the car nearby; and that the man would decide to incapacitate or kill one of them, rather than trying to walk any distance with a pair of hostages. *Carefully*, she thought as he shifted his grip on the pistol and motioned her onto the pavement. He had already been unstable when he shot Michael McPhee; he was practically trembling just now with the nearness of his last victim.

For one terrible moment, Catherine thought Brigit might refuse to move; Brigit apparently thought so, too; then Jamie came around the car and stood in the street, yanked on Catherine's arm so she was bent over and the gun pointed right at her face. Brigit got out and shut the door behind her. Jamie smiled, kept his hold on Catherine's arm so it would look as though he was her escort and motioned Brigit to his other side, just ahead of him. "Walking me darlings," he said with forced cheer. Neither woman smiled, and after a moment, neither did he. They crossed the street and went up the two cracked steps; Brigit held the door for them.

The lobby had been painted a dingy brown a long time before, and the years hadn't been kind. The linoleum was one of those aged patterns of roses and ferns designed to look like carpet and the original colors could only be guessed at, particularly in the dim light. There were two seat-sprung leather chairs, a lamp between them with a forty-watt bulb. An old man sat in one of the chairs, squinting at a newspaper; he didn't even bother to look up when they passed him. The desk clerk was asleep in an equally aged chair behind the counter. Jamie Harland gave the elevator one dubious look and waved the women toward the stairs.

Second floor—third. The flooring here was a linoleum at least as ancient and cracked as that below, the walls were a water- and grease-streaked cream or yellow.

Doors ran down both sides of two short corridors. Jamie fished the key out of his pocket and consulted it, looked in both directions, gestured with the now openly carried pistol: right-hand corridor. Catherine and Brigit exchanged glances; Brigit's eyes were growing desperate, Catherine wasn't certain her own face didn't look fully as frightened. But she shook her head minutely, hoping Brigit would understand she must not do anything now, not while the man was ready for it. The Irishwoman touched the back of her hand lightly as they walked on.

The hall smelled faintly of old cooking grease and ancient coffee, of mildew and spilled, stale beer. They heard the racking cough long before they reached Sean O'Reilly's door, last one on the corridor and backing, unless Catherine had lost her sense of direction, on the rear of the building. As they came up to the door, they could hear that thick, painful cough again, the heavy clink of a thick bottle against a heavy-duty drinking glass. Silence followed by another bout of tubercular coughing. Brigit put a hand against the wall for balance and let her eyes close. Jamie snatched at her other arm and turned the key in the lock silently; with infinite care, he turned the knob and began to ease the door open. It protested, and he swore furiously under his breath.

The coughing stopped; bedsprings squeaked as if in answer. A high-pitched and querulous man's voice called out: "Michael?"

Jamie swore again and hit Brigit in the middle of the back with his open hand, propelling her into the room; before Catherine could react, he had her by the elbow and had slung her in next, following closely upon her heels.

The man in the bed was unflatteringly lit by lamps on the two end tables: thinning gray hair was damply plastered flat to his head, beads of sweat dotted a seamed, gaunt face that should have belonged to a much heavier man. He sat up in the bed, blankets twisted around his feet and legs, a sleeveless undershirt plastered to his breastbone and hanging loose everywhere else. A bottle of Irish whiskey and a tumbler half-full stood on the far nightstand. The smell of whiskey and sweat mingled unpleasantly in the room, even with the window partway open and the wind blowing the curtains, sending cool, fresh air across them.

Brigit moved almost before the man in the bed could register who stood there; with a pained little cry, she flew across the floor to drop onto the edge of the bed and throw her arms around her father's neck. He caught her close, murmured something against her hair and patted her shoulder. It was a long moment before he recalled the others standing at the foot of his bed. Catherine rated a brief, puzzled glance, but Jamie—there was no mistaking what Jamie Harland was, if not precisely who. He stiffened and put Brigit away from him.

"Very touching," Jamie said with broad sarcasm. "Brings a tear to my eye, it does."

"And who the hell might you be?" Sean demanded. "And where's Michael?"

Jamie sneered. "Burning in hell, old man, where you'll be joining him soon." Catherine touched his arm and he shook her off violently. She caught herself on the end table, the whiskey bottle tilted and she barely kept it from falling onto the bed.

"Jamie, he's an old, sick man!" she protested softly. She might not have spoken for all that the man with the gun responded; Sean cast her an angry, reproachful glance, turned back to face his enemy with squared shoulders.

"I'm still strong enough to spit on the likes of him," he said flatly. "Go on, do your worst, I'm dying anyway." Brigit made a faint cry of protest; laid a hand on his arm as he began to cough. Her agonized gaze caught Catherine's; Catherine, with one wary glance in Jamie's direction, filled the hotel water glass to the top with Sean's whiskey and handed it to him. He managed to swallow a little—enough to ease that horrible, racking and visibly painful cough.

Jamie laughed unpleasantly. "Oh, you'll die soon enough. But not until you've seen your daughter die before you."

Sean would have dropped the glass if Catherine hadn't been there to catch it. She backed away from the bed, aware of Brigit getting to her feet to step back and square her shoulders in a gesture that was clearly taken from her father. Chin high, she looked at Jamie Harland, but his gaze was still fixed on Sean, so he could enjoy the spectacle of his enemy's face crumpling.

"No, please," the old man whispered, and fought off the coughing fit that wanted to overwhelm him. "Not Brigit, please! She's never—she—it's not her you want, it's me!" He choked. "Dear God, have mercy!"

Jamie Harland's smile was a triumphant flash of teeth; his eyes were black and hard, pebbles in a set face. He brought the gun up and held it at arm's length. "I'll give her the same mercy you gave Billy," he said evenly.

Brigit set her jaw and took one step toward him; there was no sign of fear on her. Jamie's finger was tightening on the trigger when Catherine spun around and threw the whiskey in his eyes. He screamed and began clawing at them; she threw herself at him, ripped the pistol out of his hand and threw it onto the bed behind her, spun on one heel to slam her back against him, ramming her elbow into his belly with her full weight behind it. He sagged; she followed through, slamming him back into the dresser, where he hung by one elbow while he continued to try and paw alcohol from his eyes.

Cathy turned back to see the gun: up, level and pointed. Sean O'Reilly had pounced on it, and now held it two-handed. The barrel trembled a little, but at such a short range, he couldn't possibly miss. And Jamie was for all purposes blind, paying no attention to anything but his pain. Sean caught her eye and gestured her away with the pistol. "Back off, now," he said. "I may be dying but at least I'll be able to take one more murdering Orangeman with me before I go." Brigit, who had taken one hesitant step toward him, looked at him as if he were some fantastic monster.

"Father," she whispered. "No!"

He cast her one hard glance, turned his attention back to his enemy, who had now staggered away from the dresser and watched him with wary, reddened eyes. "I don't like it any better than you, girl, but it's got to be done. He's no better than his brother, murdering scum." Silence. Brigit took a step back, away from him; her father glared at her. "It was his sort murdered your mum!"

"Yes," Brigit said flatly. "And it was your sort who killed Ian." And with two more steps, she put herself deliberately between the two men.

"Get out of the way!" Sean yelled.

"No." She set her mouth in a hard line and folded her arms. "It has to stop."

"Do as I tell you, girl, I'm your father!"

"Oh, are you now?" She laughed, but there was no humor to it. "That's news to me! Go on, if you're so bound and determined to kill him. What's one more body? Think what a fine hero I'll be, once I'm dead!" He might have been turned to stone by her words; he still glared at her, but could find no words to answer her. The gun remained fixed on her and on Jamie Harland behind her. "Well? Go on!" Her voice went up a notch as she taunted him. "What are you waiting for? I'm nothing to you, just a traitor, an Orangeman's whore!" And as he still sat frozen in the bed, she screamed, "Shoot!"

For one horrible moment, Catherine thought he might; his finger tightened on the trigger, the hammer went back, shivered. And then his hand trembled, his arm—his whole body. He looked down at the gun in horror, as though he realized for the first time what he held, and he let it fall to the bedding. "Brigit." Her name was the least of pleading whispers. He let his head fall forward then, and wept.

Brigit's face softened in pity, she let her arms fall slack and would have gone to him but Jamie had been waiting for such a chance; he threw an arm around her throat, dragging her off balance and back against him. And from his belt he drew the scimitar-shaped pirate's sword that went with his costume—a blade of fine, well-honed steel. The light gleamed along the edge as he laid it against Brigit's throat and began pulling her back, a careful step at a time. "Come along, Brigit darlin'," he cooed, the tension in his voice ill-matched to the sweet words. "We'll be leaving this party."

Catherine took a step to the side, watching for the least chance to help the other woman and knowing there wouldn't be such a chance because Jamie had her across the room, hard against the window. He shouldered the curtain aside, threw one leg over the sill; his boot clanged on the metal fire escape. Brigit cast her father one frightened look; the older man scrabbled at the covers as though he'd leap to her defense no matter the cost to himself. Jamie gave him a warning eye and slid the blade along white skin. Sean froze. Jamie shifted his glance threateningly; he had Catherine's measure now and he wasn't going to let her within arm's reach of him, either. She stopped at once, watching helplessly as the man shifted his weight on the windowsill. He gave Sean O'Reilly a look that was a black covenant between them. "I'll find you again, old man."

Sean gasped as a long, white-clad arm with an extremely hairy hand shot through the open window, caught Jamie and dragged him outside. Brigit, released, almost fell; Sean began coughing painfully, but before he was doubled over by pain, he saw the shadows of two men silhouetted against the curtain: Donald and a man much larger than he, an extraordinary head of hair, a—a cloak? Sean bent over then, and did not hear the infuriated roar, an answering high-pitched male shriek. Brigit caught her balance on the side of the bed and sat, wrapped her arms around her father and held him in a fierce grip. Catherine came around the bed just as a limp Orangeman was hurled back into the room. She knelt to feel his pulse—he was only unconscious, not even badly hurt—and then dragged the awkward skirt from under her knees so she could stand and look out. The air was clean and crisp after Sean's hotel room; there was no one on the fire escape landing—no one visible up or down the ladders. She sighed and pulled back into the room.

Jamie lay like a straw dummy on the faded linoleum. Brigit and Sean held each other closely, desperately; her tear-wet face lay against his shoulder, and he stroked her hair, smoothed it back to kiss her forehead, whispered soothingly against her ear. She caught hold of his hand and brought it up, held it against her face.

The desk clerk had heard the shot and called the police; he hadn't come to investigate on his own. Catherine admitted two blue-jacketed patrolmen just as Jamie Harland began to blink and mumble to himself, and try to sit up.

To his credit, Sean O'Reilly didn't try to make her an accessory to any lies; he put Brigit away from him and said, "Well, it was a good game, but it's over, isn't it?" But he was barely able to sit, visibly incapable of leaving the room under his own power. One of the policemen went down to call an ambulance for him. Two more patrolmen came with a detective in a rumpled and seat-sprung brown suit; one of them put Jamie Harland in handcuffs and took him out, while Brigit, Sean and Catherine answered questions. Catherine directed them to Michael McPhee's body.

No one mentioned Vincent; Jamie wasn't coherent about what had attacked him and Catherine took responsibility for the man's other bruises. The police seemed to think Jamie's protests had more to do with an unwillingness to admit that this delicate-looking woman had knocked him cold than anything else, and dismissed his wild assertion that he'd been attacked by a two-legged seven-foot-tall lion.

The rest of it wrapped up rather quickly: a pair of Irishmen illegally in the country, a third dead and the gun that had killed him right to hand. Both men's prints on it but only one of them capable of having done the deed, and only one of them an Orangeman to the Catholic of the other two. The shabby-looking detective read Sean his rights almost as an afterthought as the stretcher bearers came into the room, a goggle-eyed desk clerk right behind them. Brigit held her father's hand all the way down the elevator, across the lobby and to the door of the ambulance. She shivered as the siren came on and the vehicle pulled away, heading uptown. Catherine wrapped an arm around her shoulder, watched as Jamie was put in one of the police cars and driven off.

The second police car waited in the street, next to the row of parked cars, lights now turned off. A handful of onlookers stared at it, at the building; at the desk clerk who stood just inside the lobby doors, the two women on the curb. Catherine glanced up along the "otel'" sign toward the roof and smiled; a tawny head came into sight over the wall, and Vincent looked down at her.

"I can arrange for you to stay with your father, if you like," she said. Brigit nodded, managed a brief, teary smile. Catherine hesitated. "You know that—"

"That there are warrants out on the man?" Brigit demanded bluntly as Catherine sought to find a tactful way to say what she must. "And he must be arrested, too? Yes. I've lived with that," she added simply, "since I was six." She sighed and stood gazing thoughtfully in the direction the ambulance had gone. "We won't have long together, not even three hundred days. But we have to take what we're given." She turned to meet the other woman's eyes, managed a true smile. "Three hundred days, a few months—" She paused, glanced up toward the roof. She knows, Catherine realized in sudden wonder. Knows all of it, and wishes us well.

"Or a single night," she whispered. Brigit nodded emphatically, and as one of the patrolmen touched her arm, let herself be escorted to the second car. Catherine watched it go, looked around to discover with a start that their audience had vanished. Even the desk clerk had gone back to his desk and was probably already asleep again. She glanced toward the roof. And felt a little pang of unhappiness as she saw no one there. He could not have gone, not without speaking to her—not again this night!

But he hadn't. Of course he hadn't. Vincent came across the sidewalk. His eyes warmed her. "Brigit will be all right," she said. He nodded; his eyes remained fixed on her, and she thought he would have touched her if he had let himself come nearer. And then he turned away, began to walk away. To leave her. She drew a steadying breath and went after him, catching hold of his near hand. He turned back in surprise. "Don't leave." She could see it in his eyes: he had been Above tonight, done so many things beyond his usual activities. Perhaps he saw it as enough for good and all, maybe even intended to return to the tunnels and stay there, as he'd tried to do during those first hectic months she had known him.

It took her a moment to realize she had the key, the right words, to find the voice to speak them. Her voice trembled. "She told me that this is a special night. Saowen. When—"

"When the walls between the worlds grown thin," he said softly, and his fingers tightened on hers. "And the spirits of the underworld walk the earth."

She nodded emphatically. "Vincent, we can't waste this." He gazed at her for a very long moment, but she knew he would give in. She could see it in his eyes. And when he nodded, she gave him a relieved, wonderful smile—a radiant smile answered by his smile—and took his arm so he could escort her down the street.

There was a taxi from the corner back to Broadway, and then up Broadway past a brilliantly lit City Hall, on up the glittering thoroughfare to Times Square. They walked through Times Square, surrounded by people in masks, people in costumes—people in ordinary clothing who found nothing unusual about costumes, masks or the tall man in his cavalier's shirt and lion's mane and face—the slender, beautiful Marie Antoinette in an owl's mask who looked up into his face with such open love, who laughed with him, pointing out various sights along the street.

A little farther, they found an older couple leaving a hansom cab and Catherine drew an unprotesting Vincent into the open, horse-drawn carriage, sat back in the curve of his arm as they continued north.

He had never imagined being a part of so many lights and happy people, and said so. He admired the Empire State Building but liked the Chrysler much better, particularly now he could see it from so many angles previously denied him. He looked at everything, engraving it all in his mind to keep forever, taking pleasure in the sound of the obvious pleasure in Catherine's voice as she pointed out museums and parks. He was enchanted by the statue of Atlas in front of Rockefeller Center; impressed by the bulk of the Guggenheim, sorry with her that he could not see inside the museums they passed.

The crowds remained heavy, the automobile traffic thick for some hours; it was not until he heard a clock chime three that there was a visible lessening in the number of people on the sidewalks, and the traffic was shifting its pattern, until there were fewer private cars, more yellow taxis. They were walking now themselves, looking in expensive shop windows at an astonishing variety of items, at curious fashions in clothing, strange sculpture or paintings in the windows of galleries. There was a boat at some point during the evening—he could not later remember if it was early or late, only the whip of boat-generated wind and droplets of water touching both their faces as they stood in the very front of the ferry and watched Liberty Island and the Lady glide past them. Docking at Staten Island and standing in the stern so they could look at the brilliance of the night city across the river.

And then they were back in the midst of the brilliance: lights and more lights; a clock rang four, then five. They walked for hours, down broad streets and narrow cul-de-sacs, past neat rows of houses and apartments. Through small parks. Six chimes; they sat on a bench with the smell of river in their noses, the sound and lights of passing boats, and talked: less now about themselves, more about what he thought of New York and its people, what she thought. When he looked up, he could just see the lights of the Statue of Liberty, down the river from them—strings of lights following the lines of a bridge upriver.

It *was* a magic night; and the walls had crumbled forever between them—walls he had not even known still existed until the last of them fell. He wrapped his cloak and an arm around Catherine, who sighed happily and leaned against his chest. They sat like that for some time, in companionable silence, and watched the sky fade from the never entirely black of a city night to the deep blue that precedes dawn. Catherine sought and held his fingers, brought them to her lips.

He could see more clearly now: the bench was at the edge of a long walk that paralleled the river, it sat in a long, narrow strip of grass and small trees. He roused himself with a little sigh and a shake. "I've lived here all my life, Catherine. And yet, somehow, it's as though I'd never seen the city until tonight."

She smiled at the surprise in his voice. "You've seen so much of the violence and hatred of my world," she replied gently. "I wanted you to know that there's beauty as well."

He looked down at her for a long moment. "I have known that," he said finally, "since the night I found you, Catherine." She looked up at him and his heart stopped; so much love in one face, and—all for him. It filled him with warmth, and with wonder. He brought up one hand to lay against her cheek, felt her lean into him. Early light made her face pale, but her cheeks were flushed.

They both jumped, and she caught her breath in a startled little gasp, as the flat slap of sneakered feet came pounding down the concrete toward them and someone yelped in surprise; the feet stopped. A middle-aged man in red nylon shorts and a wrinkled T-shirt stood staring at them, mouth open. As they moved apart, he started to laugh. "*Jeez*, you gave me a start!" he said hoarsely, and before either of them could reply, he flapped his arms back and forth and took off again. "Halloween was *yesterday*, guys!" he shouted back at them, and even through his labored breathing they could both sense his annoyance.

Catherine turned to look behind them, toward the east; there was a definite lightness where the sun would follow shortly. She swung back hastily as Vincent stood and pulled the hood over his head for the first time in many long hours. "I must go," he said. She looked at him, wordlessly; finally nodded, and held out a hand to touch his fingers. He stood looking down at her, knowing his heart was in his gaze, knowing she could see it there, and then he turned away and walked rapidly back into the city. He knew where he was, more or less: there was a condemned building not far away, an opening in its basement behind a rotting wooden coal bin. He'd be back in his own world, he thought, within the hour—and there was relief in the thought, but more wistfulness than he would once have expected.

Catherine sat where he had left her; she did not watch him go. There was no point to that, she thought with a deep, happy sigh, since he was with her. Always.

Fourteen

It was an odd Christmas: Catherine's father was in Florida, most of her friends were in Colorado or Europe, skiing. She celebrated quietly with her closest friend Jenny and Jenny's latest boyfriend, and the next morning drove Brigit O'Donnell to the airport to catch a plane for Ireland. Sean O'Reilly had died two days before Christmas, a bare week after Jamie Harland was bound over for trial for the murder of Michael McPhee, for kidnaping and armed menacing. Much later that night, when Vincent came onto her balcony, she gave him the one small gift she knew he would accept from her: an old and thick leather-bound volume of Irish verse, tales and songs—and another, smaller package, which was a copy of *Three Hundred Days* which Brigit had signed for him.

The winter was a cold and harsh one; they could seldom meet on her terrace and he would not enter her apartment. Knowing his strong feelings about attempting to cross the barrier between their worlds, she never pressed the issue, but saw him as often as she dared in her basement, or visited him in the higher reaches of the tunnels—walking with him sometimes for hours through winding, pipe-lined passageways or narrow tunnels roughly hacked from living rock, to concrete paths poured for water. They talked, and even now continued to learn more about each other.

She did not often presume upon her welcome among the true residents of the Underground, knowing and sharing Father's legitimate worries for their safety—and knowing how great the reaction would be among her own kind if such a society were uncovered.

But when Charles Chandler suffered his stroke and died later that spring, she abandoned her world and took sanctuary with Vincent, until she could deal with her pain and guilt enough to go back Above. That stay altered many of her perceptions of life Underground; it seemed also to change Father's perceptions of her, and she thought she sensed in him more acceptance of her, a trust in her that had not been there before: as though he had finally accepted the depth of her love for Vincent, the fact that she could be trusted with all his secrets. But she realized the older man still worried about Vincent, and this love that he saw as an impossible and surely ultimately tragic one.

Vincent still had not entered her world, save those occasions when he walked the streets in secret. The one Halloween night when he had dared appear with his own face had truly been a night touched with special magic, for all its terror, and Catherine doubted it would ever be repeated.

They had now known each other—almost two years, she realized with sudden wonder. Two years since he had found the chilled body of a young woman flung under a tree in Central Park and left there to die; two years since he had taken pity on the horror brutal men had made of her, brought her Underground and saved her life. Given her life, and the strength to go on living— at least, she admitted to herself, had touched strength in her she hadn't realized was hers, until he showed it to her.

Two years. They had done nothing the year before to mark the date. This year, Catherine decided, would be special. This year, they would celebrate. And, perhaps, another barrier would come down.

April twelfth. A few very bright stars competed with the lights of office buildings, high-rise apartments, lights on the streets and across the park, still visible through small, early spring leaves. Late as the hour was, there were still people about, taking advantage of this suddenly relatively warm evening after a particularly harsh and late winter storm. Across the street and farther along the park, more lights, strings of white lights lying across young trees, turning them into something out of fairyland. She was not surprised to see runners still jogging past on the street below: there were always runners, no matter what the hour or the temperature.

She turned away from the ledge and went back inside, leaving the terrace doors ajar. The long brass fireplace match gave her the usual difficulty lighting, until she took it in both hands. The long flame wavered in the light breeze that ruffled her hair and fluttered the silk flowers on her mantel. She wrapped a hand around it protectively, held it down to the first of many white candles grouped at one end of the mantel. When they blossomed in their individual crystal holders, casting rainbow lights along her walls, she moved across to the table set just inside the terrace doors, and took the engraved glass chimney from the hurricane lantern centered on the thick lace tablecloth that had been one of her mother's favorites. The tall white candle caught, the chimney enhanced the light, shining on polished silver, plain white china plates, crystal goblets and a silver ice bucket. Glass-topped end tables cast reflected light against the ceiling, lighting the room further.

Candlelight warmed her slightly flushed face; she straightened, extinguished the brass match and returned it to its usual place on the mantel before she could lose it as she so often did. She smoothed the long, black dress, resisted an urge to touch her upswept hair. It was fine, everything was fine. She turned back from the fireplace as a stronger current of warm air bent the candle flames, and looked up to find Vincent standing in the opening of the French doors, watching her.

She so seldom heard his approach; only rarely did she sense him as he always sensed her. But first sight of him—always, she felt as though her blood had turned to champagne; as though happiness and love were like color described to a blind woman—until she found this one man of all the men in the world. *That is what love is*, she thought happily, and came across the room, onto the terrace. The candlelight from the table, the mantel, those few candles and the two hurricane lamps she had lit on the terrace all touched his face from beneath, enhancing the strength of his cheekbones, the deep-set eyes. She held out her hands; he took them and her fingers tightened momentarily, hard on his, as though she would never let them go. "Two years tonight," she whispered. His eyes fixed on hers, his hands wrapped gently around one of hers and she touched his cheek, let her hand rest on his shoulder. His touch gave her the strength to go on; suddenly, in his presence, she was uncertain what to say that would persuade him. If she could persuade him. "I thought maybe—we could go inside. By the fire." She smiled up at him, turned aside so he could see the table, just inside the terrace doors. "Where it's warm," she added, and then forced herself not to say anything more. The next step must be his choice.

He gazed down at her a moment longer, looked thoughtfully into her apartment, then away. She realized she was holding her breath, let it out quietly, and waited.

He turned his gaze down to look at the tiled floor at his feet. So long this had stood between them; this line between their worlds. He could never be a part of hers, his very looks prohibited that. But beyond appearance, his lack of understanding of her world—no, it was simply impossible. Of his own, he would never cross her threshhold; in two years, he never had. But that she asked it of him, that Catherine—who never asked him for anything—asked this: he hesitated, would have shaken his head, would have taken a step back from her, and somehow could not.

She felt the resistance leaving him; her smile returned, the warmth of it darkening her eyes. She stepped back, turned away from him and walked into the room, as she would for anyone else who came to visit.

And her movement released him, took away the last of his uncertainty. If such a thing—truly a small thing—gave her so much pleasure, then how could he deny her? He took a step, a second that came down on the door frame—and the telephone rang. He stopped at once, hovered in place. She turned back and shrugged, rather helplessly; deep inside she was swearing. Damn, damn, damn! Of all the times for someone to call! But—who, at this hour?

Probably a wrong number, she told herself, and let the answering machine pick it up. Her short message ran: just her phone number and an invitation to leave word, a beep to signal the caller to start talking. She didn't expect anyone to talk: wrong numbers and random obscene callers usually hung up at once, it was too late at night for anyone selling magazines. But the beep was still ringing in her ears when Jenny's voice—urgent even through the tinny little speaker—filled the room.

"Cathy? Cathy, are you there? Cathy, it's Jenny! Pick up!" She was talking so fast the words were scarcely intelligible. Cathy looked back at Vincent, shook her head in helpless apology and caught up the receiver.

"Jenny, I'm here. What's wrong?"

"Cathy?" There was an ambiguous little not-quite silence, as though Jenny was trying to get her voice under control. "Are you okay?"

Cathy frowned at the phone, glanced over at Vincent once more. To her surprise, he had not yet backed away from the doorway as he so often did. As though her phone caller might see or sense him through the instrument. "Yeah, I'm fine. Why?"

"I don't know," Jenny admitted, and now she

sounded hesitant. "I just had one of those weird dreams, and you were in it."

Somehow, Cathy kept the irritation out of her voice. After all, she knew what it was like to wake alone from a particularly ugly nightmare. That was bad enough; Jenny's dreams— And besides, it really was almost funny: all the things a midnight call could have been, winding up only as one of Jenny's monster dreams. She brought up a grin, hoping she could put across to her friend a sense she was interrupting something—without having to come out and say so. "Well," she said, "I'm fine." She cast Vincent another glance; he was still there, and that took away the last of her anger.

"You're sure?"

"Positive," Cathy said, and put as much undercurrent into the word as she dared. *Jenny, you dolt, I'm not alone, can't you figure that out?* Apparently, she couldn't.

"Why are you still awake?"

Cathy giggled. "Go back to sleep, Jen," she said, and hung up the phone. Jenny's bad dreams could wait; tonight she had something much more important on her mind. Vincent stood waiting as she came across the room to him, hands outstretched, and there was no reserve in his eyes now.

The traffic over on Fifth Avenue was not as heavy as it had been, but the busses rattled the windows of the apartments in this older building. The windows facing the avenue were dark at this hour; even the ones on the top floor, those occupied by a seated man. He sat just outside a sliding glass door, a phone at his one elbow, telescope at the other.

He was so average-looking as to nearly be unnoteworthy where he sat; on the city streets, for all intents and purposes he *was* invisible: not quite six feet tall, medium brown hair worn short but not too short; slender but not thin. He wore a long-sleeved dark plaid shirt and tan chinos, high-top tennis shoes; his skin was pallid rather than simply untanned. Only his eyes—if anyone went to the trouble of looking into them—would give away that he was not, particularly, as average as he seemed. As normal. They were a pale brown, almost tan; there was a degree of intensity to the way they fixed on the telescope, on the subject he was watching across the intervening expanse of park.

He ignored the clink of ornaments on his brother's coffee table—his sister-in-law's stupid Mayan pottery, all over the place—and kept his gaze fastened on the telescope. That big man—all he could see was the fellow's back now; he was blocking *her* once again. What was he doing there anyway? He'd come before; just somehow, he'd be there. As though he'd used teleportation or magic or something. And the look on her face when she went to him—! The man with the telescope swore viciously under his breath until the big man moved and he could see into the apartment once again. Could see her, talking into the phone and looking exasperated.

He was lucky, wasn't he? Lucky to have the connections he did. Like his brother John having this place; it was the best view he'd ever had for his favorite pastime. And to have it all to himself, not to have to answer anybody's prying questions about what he was doing, why—what he thought . . . They were down in Mexico somewhere, John grubbing in a ditch for old pots, Debbie with her camera and sketchbooks. Nice of John to say he could stay here. Of course, that was as much guilt on John's part as brotherly love. Guilt because John's baby brother had had—call them problems—fitting in. That was what the family had always said.

He didn't care. He had a place, a good place—the right kind of place, high up enough so he could look down on the city, as he had every right to do. A place in a good neighborhood; there wasn't any point to looking for what *he* wanted in some place like Queens or the Bronx, for God's sake! Here, he had clean rooms, good food, a little money besides the Navy's medical discharge pension he got every month. More importantly, he had use of John's excellent telescope and his binoculars. And on his second night out on John's terrace, he'd found *her*.

Getting her name and her phone number—well, that had been easy. A guy knew enough of the right people, he knew things; with connections, he'd had the name, the phone number within hours. He had other things now—he'd think about those later, though; about what he'd do with them. He adjusted the focus, glanced at his watch as it double-beeped the hour; moments later the countdown alarm went off. And he smiled as Catherine Chandler cradled the telephone and started to walk toward her terrace—toward that man. The phone had been pulled out as far as the cord would reach, onto the terrace and on Debbie's umbrella'd table. He reached for it, hooked the receiver between his ear and his shoulder and began to press the buttons. An almost infinitesimal silence, followed by the connecting click, a ring. Another. He took the receiver lightly between the fingertips and thumb of his left hand, brought his eye back to the telescope.

Her shoulders sagged as the phone rang; she stepped away from the big man, obviously apologizing to him for having to pick up the phone again. He was grinding his teeth as he looked at the man's back. That *hair!* He looked like a goddamn hippy with that hair! And a cloak, for God's sake, who the hell did he think he was? His attention shifted away from the man then; Cathy had picked the phone up on the second ring, the man had moved aside so he could see her, her living room—and now her face. A pleased smile spread across his face. Anticipation. Tonight, he would bring down another of the barriers that separated him from her.

Damn Jenny anyway, Catherine thought crossly, and snatched up the phone before the machine could take the call. "Hello?"

"Cathy?"

She frowned. Odd, whispery voice—unpleasant voice, but familiar, too. Whose? "Yes?" she said warily.

Only silence and the faint echoing noises of an open

phone line answered her at first; *Count of three and I hang up*, she thought and folded in a finger. *One* ... "I can see you," the voice said.

"See—?" Her lips moved, no sound came. And she turned to look out the French doors, even as a corner of her mind assured her there was no one there but Vincent. Nothing out there save a dark expanse of Central Park, and well across the way, other apartments, condominiums, buildings. . . . There were lights everywhere, out there, but nothing near.

And a voice, chillingly, against her ear, as though their eyes had just met: "Hi!" it said brightly.

She froze, not even daring to breathe, listened to the sounds of the phone line again, to a distant breathing, and felt the hair on the back of her neck standing up. Someone spying on her—fear redoubled then, as her eyes shifted and her gaze caught Vincent's; he turned to look the direction her eyes had gone.

"Yeah," the voice said softly, meaningfully. "I can see him, too."

She slammed the phone back into place and ran across the room, caught hold of Vincent's cloak with hands that wanted to shake: "You've got to get off the balcony! Someone's watching us!" She forced her fingers to let go of the cloth and pushed him, hard. He leaped back into deep shadow, taking her momentarily with him; his eyes darted across the city spread out on three sides of them, hanging over them. Catherine gave him another shove. "I'll meet you down below—Vincent, please go!"

She was afraid for him, more than for herself—for his secret. And he knew he must be, too. He turned and moved away from her at once, heard her hurrying back into her apartment, slamming the doors shut and locking them behind her.

She dragged the curtains across, blew out the nearest and brightest candles and caught up the house key she kept near the door, dragged the short camel-hair coat out of the closet and threw it around her. The phone rang again, startlingly loud, and because she had half-expected it, she jumped and cried out, banging her shoulder against the door jamb. She stopped, frozen into immobility by the voice: "Open the drapes, Cathy." It filled the room—*her* room, her apartment. She turned and fled, yanked the door shut and triple-locked it behind her. She could hear that voice, following her down the hall: harsh, whispery, menacing. "Open the drapes."

Across the park, he stared for another moment at the darkened terrace, at the opaque curtains covering the French doors and blocking his line of vision. "Open the drapes, Cathy," he demanded. There was no answer. He finally hung up the telephone, sat back from the telescope with care so as not to jostle it and thought.

She would come around. She would understand, sooner or later. She'd be flattered by his attentions. He understood women. But that man who had been with her tonight—what was wrong with his face? And what was wrong with her, that she encouraged such a horrible creature to come to her?

She must not think of herself as worthy of a better man—one such as himself. From now on, he would help her to realize just how worthy she was.

It was even cooler in the basement than it had been on the terrace; or maybe that was the chill constricting her heart, the terror-induced sweat drying in the air coming in from the subway tunnels beside and below them, through the entrance Vincent had broken for her nearly two years before.

She forced herself to stop pacing, to look into the darkness behind the massive oil burner and the long-abandoned, antique coal-burning furnace. But thought of the opening back there upset her further, leaving her even more depressed and helpless-feeling than she had been. The one who spied on her balcony, if he somehow found *this* place . . .

Vincent stood unmoving where she had found him moments before, leaning against the aged brick wall.

"Do you have any idea who it might be?" he asked finally.

She shook her head; hairpins struck the concrete floor in a series of high metallic pings, and a section of her hair fell across her shoulders. She ran her hand through it, dislodging the rest of the pins and letting it all loose. "There was a call," she managed finally. "On my machine yesterday. But I didn't think anything of it. I thought it was just a prank call." That was why that voice had sounded so oddly familiar, when he spoke her name.

She didn't think it was a prank now, Vincent knew; he needed no special sense to see the fear in her eyes. But if she feared as much for him as for herself, his terror at the moment was all for her. Men who stalked women—men like that weren't safe, they killed. "What do we do now?" she asked. He knew nothing, he realized; nothing that could be of help, and his heart sank. In this, he could be of little or no use to her, except for moral support. And his responsibilities—.

She remembered them, too. She shook her head again, and her voice was steadier this time when she spoke. "We can't go to the police, we don't know what he has. Maybe he's taken pictures." She swallowed and looked at him unhappily, drove both hands through her hair, dislodging a last pin. "Vincent, the balcony's not safe anymore. It was the one part of my world that belonged to us!" She was suddenly furious. "I will not let him destroy it."

He could only touch her arm; there seemed to be nothing he could say. Moments later, he left her, to return to his own dark world. Catherine shivered, shifted her grip on the ring of keys and began the return journey to an apartment which was no longer the haven it had been.

Fifteen

S<small>HE</small> hadn't thought she would sleep; somehow, she did, deeply for at least a couple of hours. Mercifully, the phone didn't ring at all—she wasn't certain she could have handled that, even if it had turned out to be an ordinary call. She put a blank tape in the answering machine before she left for work and put the one that had been in it inside her little portable tape machine, checked the batteries and the lightweight runner's headphones before stuffing it all in her purse.

She couldn't bring herself to listen to it on the bus—she hated covering both ears in the best of times, hated the thought of someone coming up behind her unnoticed because she was "plugged in." She could *not* listen to that voice under such circumstances, not without a wall at her back. She hadn't realized how vulnerable something like this could make a person feel. She'd wait until she got into the office, until she hit a free moment between projects.

She dropped her things at her desk, went in search of coffee and detoured through the computer room on her way back. Dave Osmond was already at work, pulling a list of people out of the data file. He was a graduate student who worked days, went to school nights, studied evenings—God knew when he slept. He still looked like a skinny fifteen-year-old who'd got his full height and was waiting for the rest of the growth to catch up; he was shy like a kid, too. But he was damned good on the department's data processing program, and with Edie taking a couple days off, Dave was her best bet for a favor. He kidded around with her rather diffidently for a few minutes, found out what she wanted and said he'd be able to get her a complete printout of her cases since she'd come into the DA's office—at least, if she only wanted names, dates and current disposition. She thought that would be enough to jog her memory, and since it seemed to be all she could get in one day, she'd take it.

If there was an answer to be found somewhere in the work she'd done here so far, she didn't intend to put off finding it. Already, she was beginning to dread the thought of going home to that apartment, all by herself. To someone who was watching her, watching her terrace—

But she couldn't let herself think that way. "Think of it as a puzzle," she told herself firmly as she started back to her desk. "Think of it as a riddle, or someone else's problem, and solve it." She was rather pleased to notice the coffee she was carrying wasn't sloshing. Sign of a steady hand, good nerves.

The stuff on her desk was the usual mess: important, but none of it immediately vital. Moreno had five ugly binders that needed to be sorted through and put in date order, the high points red-inked and set out for him on a separate, single sheet of paper—but that was for next Monday. Joe—she frowned as she made room for her coffee and briefcase and dropped into her chair. That kicked off a warning bell, but she couldn't think why. He hadn't left her his usual stack of notes, though: none of his "immediate and more immediater" messages that made her laugh or swear, depending on her workload and what he was adding to it. Something to do with Joe—she'd remember, eventually. At least there weren't six things due last week.

She took a swallow of coffee, made a face at the cup— it was too strong to be drunk as cool as it was now, but she wasn't going all the way back down the hall to reheat it, either. She dragged her shoulder bag out of the drawer, hesitated with her hand on the zipper, finally shrugged and pulled the tape player out of it and dropped it on the pile of file folders in front of her. There was a possibility the phone call last night and the one earlier—the ones on this tape—were related to a matter she had worked on. Someone getting even on his own behalf, or because of a friend or relative. If so, she had every right—and an obligation—to work on it here and now. She couldn't be certain her watcher had nothing to do with her job, but suddenly it didn't matter. She had to *know*.

In any event, she'd give the tape an hour before she went on to other things.

Fifteen minutes; half an hour. She'd copied down the earlier message in large block letters on a legal pad, stared at them as she ran the tape back again and again. Her thumb was getting sore. Victoria's message once more, fuzzy with a bad long-distance connection, her high, cheerful voice announcing fresh powder at Aspen. Right after that, a click, the beep that separated messages, and that voice. Male—she had written *that* right after the content of the message, and had not been able to get any further in her analysis.

"I like that red sweater you wore today. But I didn't like your hair. Don't wear it that way again."

Bossy—bossy like someone's father. But that didn't necessarily give her an age. *No noticeable accent*, she printed finally, and sighed. So he wasn't from the Bronx or from Atlanta. And what did that leave? She ran it back once again, adjusted the right headphone; it was digging into her ear and bending the cartilage painfully. Her fingers froze on the foam rubber as the movement brought up a previously unnoticed background noise. She rewound the tape, slammed the play button down and cranked up the volume.

There. Right in the middle of the message, a high-pitched beeping. Familiar—? She frowned deeply, rewound again and shifted the earpieces back and forth, increased the volume again. There was a definite noise under his voice. Microwave bell? Doorbell? But it seemed very close, near the receiver; it sounded like it echoed off something, maybe. Damn, she thought in rising irritation, I should *know* what that is! She ran it back again, shifted in her chair and jumped in alarm as a large hand came down into her line of vision to rap against the desk.

She caught her breath raggedly, pulled the earphones off and dropped them—she hoped casually—onto her penciled notes, rendering them unreadable. Joe, still in his coat, was scowling down at her. She looked up at him, then rather uneasily at the thick computer printout dangling from his free hand. Bless her rotten luck, it *had* to be the one Dave promised her.

Joe waggled his briefcase under her nose. "Forget something this morning, Radcliffe?" She stared at him blankly and he sighed ostentatiously. "Brian Crater? His deposition?"

Oh, God. I forgot! "I'm so sorry," she said. He looked at her stricken face and smiled briefly.

"It's okay, I got it." He lifted the printout; pages slapped together as he set it on the corner of her desk. "Dave caught me on the way by. This is for you."

Yeah, she thought sourly. *Great timing, Dave.* "Thanks," she said, gave him a bright smile and wondered how she could divert his attention. He glanced down at the stack of fanfold, back up at her and dark eyebrows drew together heavily over his nose.

"Look," he said abruptly. "Is something going on here I should know about?"

She raised her own brows. "No. Why?"

He still wasn't buying it; he had that "coddle Cathy" look on his face that she ordinarily found as exasperating

as she did touching. Just now, she wasn't touched at
all; she absolutely *had* to keep him out of this. "Because
you missed a deposition, and you requested a status list
on all your prior cases," he said dryly.

She desperately needed a diversion. Joe would never
understand why she had to stay away from the police,
he'd be frantically worried about her. And as for telling
him the truth . . . An unexpected answer to her need
came rather diffidently into view just behind Joe, smiled
shyly and wriggled fingers in a "Hi, but don't let me
interrupt" wave. Good old Jenny, Cathy thought with
relief, and smiled back. "Jenny!" she said delightedly,
more to alert Joe to the other woman's presence—to shift
his attention—than anything else. It worked; he
dropped the fanfold, and turned to look.

"What are you doing here?" Cathy asked. Jenny
hardly ever came to Cathy's office; she didn't want to
be a pest, she said. Didn't want Cathy's bosses thinking
she was hanging around all the time.

"Surprising you and taking you to lunch, I hope."
Her voice rose on the last words, making a question of
it.

Catherine looked at her in surprise, then down at the
dainty little gold watch that had been her father's last
Christmas present to her. She couldn't have spent an
entire morning glued to that tape player! "It can't be
lunchtime—it's only eleven o'clock," she said accusingly.

Jenny shrugged. "I'm hungry," she said simply.

Cathy laughed. "You're always hungry!" She turned
back to Joe, who leaned against the corner of her desk,
arms folded, portrait of a man exhibiting great patience.
"You want to go over that deposition right now?" she
asked. He relented, grinning, shook his head.

"No, it can wait. But I do want to know about this,"
he added as he stepped back. He flipped a thumb over
the corner of the computer printout, and there was no
give at all in his eyes or the set of his mouth.

Cathy dropped the tape player, pencil and legal pad
in her purse—it barely zipped around the long tablet,

but she was not going to simply rip off the top page with Joe standing there, watching her like a hawk. She pulled her jacket on, slipped the strap of her bag over her shoulder and nodded once at Jenny. "We're on," she said, and grinned at Joe as she passed him. "I order those to keep my files up to date," she lied glibly, let the grin widen and leaned closer to coo at him. "But you're cute when you're worried." Just as she figured, that last comment got him at about belt level; he made a terrible face, and she scuttled past him to grab Jenny's arm and get her out of the office before her friend could say anything.

She almost managed it. Jenny half-turned to look back at him wide-eyed and demand, "Why are you worried?"

Cathy tightened her grip on Jenny's elbow and hissed, "I missed an appointment. Can we drop it?" Jenny, to her relief, let it drop. She wasn't sure if Joe would; she didn't dare look back but she could feel his eyes on her, all the way down the corridor.

The coffee shop was ordinarily packed from noon until late afternoon; just now, it was early enough the two women had no problem getting one of the large booths to themselves, and the coffee was hot and fresh, the waitress prompt with it and with menus. Cathy glanced at the menu, at Jenny, and ordered salads for both of them. Jenny was in one of those states where she wouldn't notice what she ate—or that she was eating at all. Just now she was sipping hot coffee without tasting it—obviously, since she usually dumped a full packet of sugar in it.

Cathy drew a deep breath, but instead of asking the obvious questions, let it out and drank coffee instead. Why call me so late at night? What was the dream? What—? She suddenly wasn't entirely certain she wanted to know, even though ordinarily she could never quite believe in Jenny's dreams. People dreamed true in certain kinds of books and movies—not real life. Not— not people you actually *knew*, she thought uneasily.

Jenny looked at her glassily over the heavy rim of the

blue restaurant coffee cup; her gaze focused suddenly, and she made a face at the almost empty mug, set it down with a clatter. She ran a hand over dark springy curls and sighed. "I'm sorry, Cathy. Truly. I just—" She stopped, cleared her throat.

"Tell me about it. It must have been—unpleasant," Catherine chose her word carefully, "if you called me that late at night."

"Yeah, right." Jenny smiled shakily. "I really do have better manners than that. Normally. It was just that—" She paused, gazed down at her coffee cup. Cathy waited. "It just—"

"Tell me about it," Cathy repeated. Jenny nodded faintly. The waitress came by with a coffee pot in each hand, refilled their cups from the caffeinated one and moved on.

"That's why you came in today, wasn't it? To tell me about it?"

"I just—"

"Well, I—" Jenny shrugged, picked up the packet of sugar Cathy dropped on the table in front of her and turned it over between her fingers until Cathy took it away from her, ripped the end off and poured the contents in her cup. Jenny took up her spoon, slid it into the cup and let it dangle forgotten from her fingers. "I just—"

"Stir the coffee, Jen. Before you melt the spoon." Cathy gestured; Jenny smiled vaguely and did what she was told; Cathy took the spoon out of her fingers and laid it in the saucer. "And tell me what it was all about. You know it helps when you do that with a dream. Talk about it; get it out of your system."

Her friend looked down, touched the edge of the spoon as though she had never seen one before, shrugged. "I—I know, you always say that. And it does help sometimes. But—this time, I feel like I'm putting a curse on you." She gazed across the table with wide, unhappy eyes.

Cathy sighed in exasperation but managed to keep most of the irritation she felt out of her voice. Jenny wasn't being deliberately obtuse. "I'm going to throw something on you if you don't tell me about this dream," she threatened, and reached for the salt shaker. "Come on, Jenny, not all of your bad dreams come true."

"I—all right." She drew a deep breath, fixed her eyes on Cathy's and poured it all out in a rush. "You were— I don't know where you were. But there were flowers all over the place. And all of a sudden, the lights went out, and you were in the dark." Her words were coming breathlessly now, her breathing almost a pant. "You wanted to move, but you couldn't, and there was this— this hand. But it wasn't connected to anything, and it was trying to touch you."

She felt a little bored or maybe embarrassed—the way one did when other people described their dreams in detail; all the same, it was odd to hear Jenny describing *her* as part of a dream. As though she had no reality outside Jenny's dream, or as though Cathy were a different person. Jenny was watching her helplessly, waiting. She nodded, said, "Uh huh," as encouragingly as she could. Jenny gulped and went on.

"You tried to scream, but you couldn't!"

Defuse this, she thought suddenly. The waitress was going to wonder what was going on if she came over with salads and one of her customers was having some kind of fit. Besides, it was starting to give *her* the creeps. "A severed hand is coming at me," she said solemnly, "and I'm going to scream. Guaranteed, I will scream."

It helped a little; at least, she was able to distance herself from the spookiness of Jenny's disembodied hand. And Jenny managed a little smile—almost as though she was biting back laughter. "Well, then you were running," she went on and the smile vanished.

"Is the hand still after me?" Cathy asked.

This time Jenny didn't smile. "I don't know, Cath," she replied somberly, "but you were running. I don't know if you were running away from someone, or maybe to someone. But you couldn't catch your breath. You—couldn't breathe," she finished unhappily. There was a silence. The waitress set salads in front of them.

Cathy managed a brief glance at her watch; she couldn't afford to take a long lunch hour today. Not after this morning.

"And then what?" she prompted.

Jenny swallowed, shook her head. Her eyes were wary, and when she spoke, Cathy thought what Jenny said wasn't exactly the truth. "And then I woke up. And I guess I needed to hear the sound of your voice," she finished lightly. "So I called you."

Called. The tape in her bag . . . She fixed her eyes on her salad and picked up a forkful of greens, cheese and ham, but her appetite was suddenly gone. She felt Jenny stiffen across the table.

"What? Cathy?"

"Mmm? Oh. It's just so strange that you have these dreams."

"Why?"

She looked up, set her fork down. "About a minute after you called, I got another call from some guy."

Jenny's eyes went wider. "Who?"

"I don't know. I don't know him. But he said—" She shrugged, tried to make light of it. "Something that scared me."

"What did he say?" Jenny demanded.

"It's not important." Cathy took up her fork and picked through her salad. She looked up and managed a smile. "But if I ever find out who he is, I'm going to strangle him, and then your dream will have a happy ending."

Jenny's fork dropped onto her plate with a loud *clack* and rattled onto the table. "Oh, God," she whispered. "I don't believe you said that."

Cathy shook her head. "Why?"

The other woman shook her head in turn, dark curls bouncing around her face, momentarily shielding frightened eyes. "I wasn't going to tell you," she whispered finally. "But that's what I saw. You couldn't breathe. Something was around your neck. You were trying to pull it off but you couldn't. You were being strangled." There was a chill little silence. "You died, Cathy."

* * *

It was one of the better conversation stoppers Catherine had ever run up against; she opened her mouth, couldn't find anything to say, ate her salad in silence and watched Jenny toy with her food. Finally she set the plate aside, reached across the table and touched her friend's hand. Jenny jumped convulsively and this time her fork hit the floor. "It's all right, Jen," she said quietly. "It's not—" She had to turn away briefly to deal with the waitress, to assure the woman they didn't need another fork, just the check; to assure her the food was fine but they had run through their hour and had to get back to work. She left a larger tip than she might have otherwise done; the waitress was making coffee when they left, her high-strung party of two probably already forgotten.

She left Jenny on the next corner, at her friend's insistence. "You're sure you're all right, Jen?" she asked, and the woman nodded firmly, dark curls bouncing around her solemn face.

"I—look, Cath, I'm sorry if I upset you; I just—" She spread her hands wide in a helpless shrug.

"It's okay. You just remember your dreams don't always come true, or even happen the way you think. Maybe it just means," she added with a smile, "that I'll be stuck in Moreno's office this afternoon with his cigar." Jenny gave her a smile in return, but her eyes were still dark with remembered fright.

"I have classes this afternoon and one from seven to nine. Call me later, will you?"

"Promise," Cathy said, and left her. She ran most of the way back to the office; Joe would probably be out to lunch or eating at his desk at this hour. Maybe she could get that damned fanfold out of sight—and with some real luck and a busy afternoon, out of *his* mind.

It was sunny, breezy and a little brisk downtown; below the city, it was dark between the lanterns and lamps that illuminated tunnels and high-vaulted chambers. Wind scoured tunnels that gave onto the outside world or that connected in just the right way to other tunnels and corridors; dust lay thickly on everything and filled the air, as it so often did this time of year. Father's desk was clear of all save a single volume, and he was standing, gazing down at the closed cover, when Vincent came to speak with him. The Tiffany lamp had been turned off hours before, since it illuminated nothing but dirt. Father's eyes hurt from trying to read and he'd finally given it up.

Vincent's eyes were heavy; he'd spent the rest of the night and most of the morning walking, moving through the tunnels as he did when he was trying to think. His face was seldom very expressive but Father knew his looks and his moods. He was terribly worried; concerned enough that Father could see it across the poorly lit room with his own eyelids scratchy and swollen.

"I was with her last night," Vincent began abruptly. "On her terrace, above the city. A man called. He—he is watching her. He saw us both, together."

The older man sat, hard; his fingers closed on the edge of the desk and dug into the wood. The very thing he'd feared; the one thing he'd managed to convince himself was impossible—unlikely at the very least, knowing how high above the city she lived, how much of the city around her terrace was Central Park. *Watching. Oh, God.* He looked up to see Vincent leaning heavily across his second-best chair; his eyes were black with worry, his forehead creased with it. "You're certain he saw you?" he asked finally.

Vincent nodded once, sharply. "I—when she looked up from the telephone and across the park, I could see her fear, I could feel it. I looked where she did, to see what had terrified her so." He fell silent, took a fold of cloak in his fingers and pleated it, concentrating his gaze on what his fingers did.

God. Worse and worse! Father touched the back of his hand; Vincent's fingers went still, cloak bunched between them. "Vincent, if someone has seen you—" He shook his head. "If you go to her, he'll see you again."

It wasn't what he wanted to say; he didn't know what

he wanted to say, or how to say it. Other than to flatly forbid Vincent to leave the tunnels, and how could he do such a thing? He had no right to do that. Vincent brought his head up to meet the older man's eyes and his were suddenly angry. "How can I leave her alone?" he demanded harshly. "She must be protected."

"If she is in danger, we'll find a way to protect her. There are other ways—" Ways which do not endanger *you*, he thought unhappily, and knew it was a lost cause even as he spoke. Vincent was already shaking his head, and that look was in his deep-set eyes: part stubbornness, part love, part despair.

"This is Catherine. *I* must protect her."

"Of course," Father muttered and turned away to cast up his eyes. There was no real answer he could make to that, nothing Vincent would accept. He had always known that what existed between the two of them was no fluke, no passing fancy. And so, he must be the practical one. "What is she doing to find this man?"

"All she can. But she's alone in this. She refuses to ask for help." He met the older man's eyes. "She is afraid for me and for our secret."

"He probably knows that," Father said softly.

"And he will use it," Vincent whispered, "to torment her." His eyes showed his misery. Father laid a hand on his shoulder, but he knew there was no reassurance he could give, nothing he could say to take that fear and worry away.

Sixteen

CATHY had the elevator to herself, an odd circumstance owing to the unusual hour. Almost all the lower echelons and clerical staff were at lunch; Moreno was out for the day, people like Joe with real offices used the quieter hours to lock themselves in with matters that needed extra concentration.

She came out of the elevator just as Rita Escobar—one of the newer assistant DAs—came out of the file room with an armful of expando envelopes. Her black hair was even more tousled than usual, as though she'd been driving her hands through it, there was a smudge on her ordinarily flawless face, and her jaw was set, her black eyes grim.

Cathy scarcely noticed; in fact, Escobar had to call her name twice before she realized the woman was there and trying to get her attention. Her eyes had been caught by a gruesomely bright Hawaiian print shirt, then by the rather nice-looking man inside the shirt. She'd seen him before—she realized he must be part of the building's maintenance personnel; he had a leather pouch of tools depending from his belt and there were parts of the hall water fountain scattered around his feet.

The shirt was white with blue, purple and pink hibiscus all over it. Bright blue, purple and pink hibiscus. Jenny and her damned flowers all over the place . . . Cathy shook herself and somehow managed not to jump a mile as Rita Escobar's elbow caught her on the upper arm and Rita's spicy perfume assaulted her nostrils. The woman was talking rapidly and angrily, had been for some minutes; Cathy hadn't taken in a word of it, her mind and eyes were fixed on the maintenance man. The guy knew where she lived, knew her name, her unlisted phone number—*could* it be someone here in the building . . . ? "Huh?"

Escobar cast her a black look, drew in a deep breath and ran it out again. "Are you ready for this? The judge just threw out the Santos case! There was a defect in the search warrant!"

She could hear that voice, almost blanking out Escobar's once again: not the words on the tape she carried but when she'd looked out across the terrace last night. "I can see you." This man with the garish shirt—he looked up, met her eyes, turned his attention back to the pipes he was working on—what kind of voice did *he* have? "What are we going to do?" Escobar's voice carried an edge, cutting through her fuzzed thoughts.

"File an appeal, I guess," she said vaguely.

"You don't think we can get a conviction without the notebook?" Escobar demanded dubiously. She cast a curious glance in the direction Cathy was looking, saw only a youngish man—too white, his hair brown, straight and much too short for *her* taste—and dismissed him from her thoughts. "Or maybe we can try to track down that accountant again?" she asked even more dubiously. "Get him to testify?" It must be almost twelve, Rita thought sourly; her watch was out of reach, under this awkward pile of cardboard and paper. She had to get cracking on this if it was going to get done before the end of the day; she had to get a go-ahead from Chandler first; what, was the woman half-asleep? As if

222

in answer to her thought, someone's digital watch beeped shrilly.

Cathy jumped convulsively; the breath stopped in her throat. That sound—*that* was what she'd heard on the tape! The guy had one of those high-tech electronic watches that sounded the hour, alarms. . . . Alarm bells were going off in her head, the man had just slid the front panel back onto the fountain and tested the water pressure; he glanced at his oversized black-faced watch, pressed a button, shoved tools back into the belt bag and was walking straight toward her. No way, she realized in sudden terror, he couldn't have seen her watching him just now. He knew, he must know that she knew. . . .

He smiled warmly and gave her a very grave wink as he passed, slowed enough to murmur, "Thanks, but I'm *very* happily married." He vanished into the stairwell, leaving her openmouthed and feeling more than a little silly. She blinked and turned to see Rita Escobar watching her curiously.

"Excuse me?"

Cathy grinned. "*Don't* ask," she laughed, and in a nice, briskly normal voice added over her shoulder as she started for her desk, "File an appeal."

"You got it," Rita shouted behind her.

It was reasonably quiet in the office. She was within a few feet of her desk when she saw the flash of brilliant red, and stopped cold. Color and unexpected shapes sorted themselves out and she went cold and still as she stared at a green glass vase holding at least two dozen long-stemmed red roses. Flowers everywhere . . . She forced herself to approach the desk, to touch them. The fragrance was thickly old-rose, unexpectedly strong for hothouse roses. The card—there had to be a card. She turned sharply as she saw movement out of the corner of her eye, but it was merely Joe going by, brown bag in one hand and coffee cup in the other, heading for his office. He rolled his eyes expressively and grinned. "Reel 'em in, Radcliffe!"

She managed a weak smile; her fingers found the small envelope that had been tied to one stem; eased the pasteboard card from it. It was from one of the nearby florists—the name and address were stamped on a corner of the card. Under that, printed: *You're starting to feel me with you, aren't you? Could you feel me in your room last night? I was there.*

She dropped the card as if it had burned her fingers; dropped into her chair, and stared at blood-red roses.

Terror froze her only for a few moments, but it seemed as though she hadn't breathed for hours. Her chest hurt and her hands wanted to tremble. *It's a lie,* she told herself firmly, flatly. *No one was there, I would have known!*

Logically, it had to be a lie: he was angry with her for closing her veranda doors, for pulling the curtains, for refusing to talk to him. He'd merely tried to come up with something to terrify her, as—as punishment? Was that how he'd think of it? By the tone of his voice on the tape, she thought it might be so. Fortunately, he must not realize there was something that could frighten her even more—he had hit her with fear for herself, for her physical safety, this time at least. He hadn't mentioned Vincent.

That gave her the strength to get back to her feet; but she had to hold onto the edge of the desk for another moment, until the room quit swimming. She would not look at the roses; she would not let herself see the picture that tried to form in her mind, herself asleep, a shadow of a man creeping into her bedroom, hand hovering over her face. *No!* she ordered herself; the picture shattered and she walked across the hall, down to Joe's office and tapped on the glass before she could change her mind.

He was eating a sandwich, going over one of the files piled on his desk. "Got a minute?" she asked.

He swallowed, nodded. "Sure. What's up?"

She leaned against the door, closing it, took one of the chairs. She had no idea where to start, suddenly wished she'd thought more carefully before coming after him. "If—let's say someone calls you in the middle of the night." She considered this, paused to choose her next words with even greater care. "And they hang up. How would you go about finding that person?"

He looked at her curiously, frowned as he took a sip of coffee. "Well. What did this person say?"

"Nothing really." She tried to smile; the look on his face told her it wasn't her best effort. "I just want to find him."

"You know what departmental procedure is regarding crank calls."

"I don't want the police involved," she said flatly. He stared at her. The silence stretched and she fought hard to keep from fidgeting.

"All right," he said finally. "You call the phone company?"

She nodded. "Yeah. They said—actually, they said this summer there're going to be some new things on the market. But right now, I'm on my own. Unless I want to change my number."

He took a bite of his sandwich, tucked it into one cheek and spoke around it. "That's a possibility."

"No." She shook her head. "I want to find him."

He considered this as he chewed. The frown deepened. "What about a wiretap?"

That meant police and they both knew it. "No."

"Tracing unit?"

"I've ordered one. It's going to be installed tomorrow, but I don't know if he'll stay on the line long enough." She spread her hands helplessly, aware his eyes were narrowing, fixed on her.

"Does this have anything to do with that list of your prior cases?"

He was too damned smart, that was his problem; why the hell had she come in here? "I—I don't think it's a prior case."

"Is he threatening you?" He didn't really need to ask; the look on her face was enough. He'd never seen her scared, not even with all the cases she'd taken the past year and a half. All the ugly places in the city they'd sent her. "Come on, Cathy, what's this guy saying?" he demanded.

"Nothing," she said. He gave her a look and she sighed. "Benign things."

The look didn't change. "Like what?"

"Like—benign things!"

"Like give me an example," he said with exaggerated patience.

"Like, he likes my sweater, hates my hair, I don't know!" She was shouting at him, words spilling out of her. She shut her mouth with an effort and glared at him.

He picked up the phone and held it out to her. "Call the cops," he said flatly.

"Why?"

"Why?" He wanted to shout at her. "Because he's *watching* you!" He started to dial; she came across the room, threw herself onto the desk and slammed the bar down, breaking the connection. He glared up at her; her jaw was set and she shook her head angrily. "Cathy, call Greg Hughs, right now!"

"No! I don't want to overreact. People like this fantasize, but—but they don't do anything."

He wanted to shake her until her teeth rattled. "You want me to pull some files with some not so pretty pictures? You don't fool around with creeps like this!" But she wasn't giving an inch, no more than he was; he finally had to give it up and put the phone down. Something about the way she looked, the way she was reacting . . . "What does this guy have on you?" he demanded suddenly.

Her eyes widened and he knew he was on the right track; but she gave him a smile that was nothing but a turn of lips and replied dryly, "My phone number, and my address."

He could feel the anger drain out of him, leaving him helpless and frustrated. There was so damned much enigma to this woman, so much he didn't know about her. Somehow, he'd never felt before this that he had any right to ask. "Where are you keeping your gun?"

"In my nightstand."

"Carry it in your purse," he said, and to his relief she nodded. And he hoped that somehow, in all that, she'd found an answer. When she left his office, most of the tension was gone from the set of her shoulders. Fortunately for him, he couldn't see her eyes as she walked back to her desk; they were haggard with fear.

He sat in his brother's darkened living room and stared at closed terrace doors; he thought about the telescope, the binoculars, the telephone. About flowers: had he been careful enough in purchasing them? Had he put enough distance between himself and the bouquet, so that no one could attach one to the other?

What would she think? But women liked flowers, didn't they? Women liked getting flowers, and long-stemmed red roses were best.

Bee-beep. He glanced down at the black bezel of his watch as it beeped the hour. Only three more hours; he could call her then, and ask her how she liked the roses. Maybe this time, she would really talk to him.

She checked the apartment carefully when she got home: each room, each cupboard and closet. Reluctantly, then, the terrace. There were messages blinking on her answer machine; she let it alone, unable to face it just yet. It was a weight on her mind as she fixed a sandwich and sat in the dimly lit kitchen to eat it. The living room was dark with oncoming night; she couldn't bear to go in there, to turn on lights. If he watched, he would see them.

She finished the sandwich and realized she hadn't tasted it at all. She stood up, then, took her loose house key off the rack and let herself out of the apartment, heading for the stairwell and the roof. Whoever this watcher was, he surely couldn't see anything up there; he wouldn't expect her up there. And somehow, she had a feeling, just this once, that she was expected.

She was; Vincent stood behind the little square turret that housed the stairs and the elevator machinery. He

227

might have been there for hours, waiting for full darkness; there was a tired droop to the corners of his mouth as she came to take his hands. "Did he contact you?" he asked.

She nodded, swallowed. "He sent me flowers."

He had felt her terror earlier in the day; it had knifed through him and left him weak and ill, knowing there was nothing he could do to reach her at work. It had taken everything in him to wait until dusk before coming Above and onto her roof. "It was more than just flowers."

She couldn't bring herself to tell him what the card had said; the one thing she was certain of was that if he knew he would insist upon staying close enough to protect her, or that she go where he could keep her safe. Maybe that was what the enemy wanted: for Vincent to be within his reach, or for her to lead him to the tunnels. The message on that card was all a lie, it had to be, she wouldn't let herself think otherwise. She must say something; she could feel his eyes on her, his growing worry. "He knows about you," she said finally. "About us. And—until we find out what he wants—" She couldn't go on; her throat hurt, ached with unshed tears that were fear for them both, for his world, fear for herself, anger . . .

Vincent was shaking his head. "He wants you," he said with certainty.

"Vincent, no! You have to stay away!"

His fingers tightened on hers, every fiber of his being shouted no! He could not abandon her, how could she ask it, whatever the danger? "I feel your fear, Catherine," he whispered finally. "How can I leave you alone with that?"

She gripped his hands tightly. "Because I can handle fear," she said. "But if anything ever happened to you—" She could almost see it, as clearly as Jenny's dreams must be, and it was terrifying, unbearable. Her knees trembled and the tears that had threatened for hours broke free. She felt his arms around her, caught at his padded shirt and clung to him, weeping helplessly. The warmth of him, the masculine scent of him, the slightly scratchy cloak with its faint odor of wool, leather and smoke, was reassuringly all around her; his arms were. It gave her back the strength she had suddenly lost. He was there for her; he would always be there for her—he would be, if she could weather this crisis and keep him safe from discovery, until she herself could find this watcher and deal with him.

He held her close. "Come Below tonight," Vincent urged her softly. She brought her face up so she could look at him, kept her grip on his shirt. He could see the twin lines of tears coursing down her cheeks; after a moment, she shook her head as he had feared she would. As he had known she must.

"I can't let him do that to me," she whispered. "I can't." She leaned against him again, his shirt blotting her tears. "Vincent, we're alone in this."

There must be something, a way, must be—! But he sorted rapidly through the few options he knew, and realized she was right. He took her in his arms once more, realizing bleakly it was all he could do: hold her, share himself with her, his strength and hers. Whatever was out there, who or whatever it was, it could never be equal to that strength, that bond.

It was all they had.

He cradled the telephone with deceptive gentleness, a faint click the only sound in the room. It was the fourth time he'd tried her in the past few minutes: there was a single light in her apartment, but with the curtains closed, he couldn't tell where she was. If she was there, if she had listened to his voice on her machine when he finally left his message . . . Somehow, he knew she was not. She was with that—that—that disgusting, ugly creature again.

She was gone, out with him. He fought air into his chest, expelled it in a gust. It was better to think they were abroad in the city, rather than to think she sat in her living room with him, listening to the machine. Maybe laughing at the pain in his voice . . .

She was his, his alone, she must be his! Tonight, he'd—tonight? He let his head fall to one side, sat in the dark of his brother's living room, and considered this. Tonight. She was like the other women, not knowing what she really wanted. What she needed. He would have to show her, before it was too late. He smiled. Tonight, then. Soon.

It was full dark when she came back down the stairs, peered nervously up and down the carpeted hall before letting herself out of the stairwell. She had her keys ready, the three locks undone and herself inside in record time. She didn't let out the held breath she'd taken in the stairwell until she switched on the living room light and glanced around at apparent normalcy.

The answer machine was still blinking. She swallowed, squared her shoulders and walked over to press the replay button.

She shouldn't have been surprised to hear that voice; she still jumped when it filled the room, and she fumbled with the switch that would lower the volume. He wasn't whispering now; he was almost shouting; snarling at her. "Why aren't you there?" he demanded. Silence, and then: "You're with him, aren't you? Of course you're with him. Why do I even ask? Whore!" She wasn't particularly prudish after so long in the DA's office, but she wasn't used to such words directed at her; it would make her ill if she let it. The silence stretched for several long moments; she could hear his breath, and then a flat, chill "No more. Okay, Cathy? No more." More silence, then disconnect, the machine beeped and shut off. She was trembling as she reset it to record incoming calls.

She looked around the warm, friendly little room that had become so alien. As though she had walked into a stranger's living room. The fabric of the curtains over the French windows felt harsh against her skin and the nerves of her fingers and hands prickled the way it did when she'd come down with flu the previous winter.

No, she thought fiercely, and gripped the curtains

hard, setting wrinkles. *No! He cannot run my life like this!*
She flipped off the overhead lights at the wall switch,
plunging the room once again into darkness, yanked the
drapes apart and unlocked the doors, walked into the
night air.

It was not nearly as dark here as inside: lights from
the street and the park, from other buildings nearby, let
her see the darker shadow of the retaining wall, the
potted geraniums she had put out the week before. Light
touched the glass tabletop and gleamed on the metal
railing around it. She ignored the tingling between her
shoulder blades as she took another step into the open
and then another; impatiently forced aside the urge to
turn on the outside lights, to light candles, to explore
every shadowy corner and niche where a man might be
crouched, waiting for her to pass by so he could come
up behind her, grab her ... "Not in my own home," she
told herself in a fierce undertone.

The feeling eased, just a little, as she stopped at the
brick wall; the metal rail that ran around the top of it
was cold, slightly damp under her fingers and she withdrew them. Out there ... the man could be anywhere.
Any of those myriad lights: the building to her right,
the building three down that soared above hers. Any of
those on Central Park South, or the ones on Fifty-eighth
she could see beyond it. The office buildings and apartments downtown that a friend of hers from New Mexico
had compared to foothills and mountains: rising tier on
tier, a boggling number of them jumbled together. The
highest floors there loomed above everything else in the
city; a man in one of those high-rise buildings could
see—whatever he chose, she thought bleakly. Even
across the park, though she had never before been properly conscious of windows and people over there; there
were buildings, apartments, condos, galleries. That
someone might stand on a terrace like hers, or just inside
a window, and look for people to spy upon ... Someone
with a good telescope or good bird-watching binoculars.
He's sick, she thought. *Disgustingly sick, to prey on someone
like this.*

But if he was the dirty one, why did *she* feel so unclean?

And was he watching her now—looking through his telescope, gloating over her uncertainty, her anger and helplessness? That decided her; she made herself turn her back deliberately on the world out there and walked from the terrace, pulled the doors closed and locked them behind her, let the drapes back down over the glass and started for the bedroom. Let him look at a darkened terrace and black windows. Let him wonder if she was with Vincent, and let him choke on the anger she'd heard in his voice and die of it. She was going to take a shower.

She turned on the bedside light and undressed quickly, hung the mustard-colored silk blouse on the closet doorknob and dumped everything else on the chair near the bed; she could hang it all up later. She caught up her terry robe and pulled the bathroom door closed behind her; after a moment's thought, she pushed it open again. In case the phone rang, or the doorbell did. It might be someone else—someone important, she thought sourly. Someone real. But if anyone called or came, she wanted to know.

The bathroom lights filled the little white-tiled room; it was almost as if the bedroom light weren't on at all. She tossed the robe over the pebbly opaque glass door and leaned into the shower stall to turn on the water and adjust the temperature.

Water roared out of the pipes, a white noise that would drown out most others. Well, that was fine; she didn't need to listen to an old building settle right now, and jump at every creak and pop, did she? She grabbed her new bottle of shampoo off the counter and stepped into the shower, leaned back out and frowned slightly, listening. Right, she would be able to hear the phone or the doorbell if either rang. *Get in there, lady*, she ordered herself with a rueful grin, and pulled the opaque glass door firmly closed behind her.

* * *

The silk shirt on her closet door swayed as the handle shifted, fell in a dark yellow puddle to the carpet. The door moved out across it, over it again. A man's sneakered feet stepped carefully over it; he knelt to pick it up, turn it over in his hands. He kept his ear carefully tuned to the sounds in the next room, his eye shifted now and again to the line of light and the steam drifting out. She would be in there for several minutes; he must not allow himself to think of her in there, showering. He must move, quickly. Women spent hours in the bathroom, but not always; they did not seem to spend as long under the shower as men did.

He held the blouse to his nose and inhaled gently, then let it slip through his fingers to lay on the floor once again. It smelled of her warmth, the fragrance she had worn, but it was not what he wanted. He cast a glance at the bathroom door, skirted the bed swiftly and stood beside the antique wardrobe she used as a closet. The shallow drawer underneath, she kept them there, he thought . . .

But he knew what was there, he might as well check the other drawers, in the other dresser, while he had a moment. He crossed the room in utter silence and bent over to slide out one drawer, then another. If he had looked up, he could have seen his reflection in her mirror. He didn't bother; mirrors were nothing to do with him; mirrors were women's things. Just as the contents of these drawers were: bottles and boxes, a cut-glass bowl of little pastel-colored cotton things. Perfumes. A lipstick. He opened it, sniffed, shook his head and set it aside. The left-hand top drawer was full of brocaded cloth rolled around jewelry—most of it not even real, if he was any judge. Intelligent women didn't leave gold and diamonds in dresser drawers, of course. The drawer next to it held stockings—neatly bagged or folded, clean or new in their plastic bags, nothing for him there.

No, he wanted the long drawer under the antique wardrobe. He went back to it, knelt and drew the drawer open. A strapless slip, neatly folded, and under that—His fingers closed on a lacy camisole, what his mother had called a bodice. She had worn this. Unlike most of the things neatly folded here, this one wasn't fresh-ironed and there was a subtle hint of scent to it, the fragrance she kept in the drawer and her. Her skin. He took it, pushed the drawer shut silently. Glanced nervously over his shoulder.

She was still in there, water running, and he thought he could hear her singing softly. How nice, he thought. She there, and me here—how domestic. She would be there a little longer. He moved across the carpet on silent feet and stopped at the dressing table—a sheet of thick glass held up by black columns, very Art Deco. Here was a bewildering array of cosmetics, hair clips and combs, a box of pins, more cologne in a pastel-colored bottle with one of those fancy squeeze bulbs, like his mother'd had. An enameled pin of a large cat that angered him; it reminded him too much of that distressingly ugly man—man?—she preferred to *him*. Little porcelain and glass gewgaws, a clear glass box containing a variety of ski resort pins, a postcard from someone in Jamaica wedged under the base of the lamp that lit the table.

A little round box, topped with porcelain roses. It looked old, it reminded him of one his mother had kept bath powder in that had once belonged to her mother. He picked it up, held it experimentally, shrugged. It fit neatly into the oversized pocket of his tan jacket; he was meant to have it, then, wasn't he? He folded the delicate little camisole with fond care and put it in the other pocket. Turned and hesitated, his eye on the bathroom. No, he must not. She would be frightened if he went to her now; he did not want her to fear him.

Cathy rinsed the last of the shampoo from her hair and ran her hands over it to sleek the water out. "God, why didn't I think of this before?" she mumbled into the shower head, and let water run down her throat.

The sound shattered her temporary peace, freezing her in place. Sound—she'd turned over the lightweight Lucite lipstick holder too many times not to know the clatter it made when it fell. She stared toward the bedroom she could not see from the shower stall, even with the door open, scarcely daring to breathe. The bedroom lights went out.

The bathroom stayed lit; in some ways, that made it worse. She was spotlit, marked—she couldn't move, wasn't certain she could remember how to breathe. "Oh, God," she whispered. Terror wanted to buckle her knees. Terror—no; she must not be afraid, Vincent would feel that and come, this man would see him. . . . She couldn't think straight! She could only see Vincent and her tormentor facing each other; that was enough to release her from that momentary thrall and set her mind working once more.

A weapon, any weapon. She pressed against the shower door, holding it carefully so the magnetic latch wouldn't click, turned off the water so she could hear better and threw the robe on. Covered, she felt less vulnerable, more able to think. But thinking would slow her; she must not think about him standing there in the darkness, just outside the bathroom door, watching her. *He is not there, move, dammit!*

Weapon: she knotted the ties of the bathrobe, slicked wet hair back from her face. There were things scattered along both sides of the bathroom sink, as usual. She ran through them quickly. Blow-dryer, bars of soap, a bottle of cologne and another of after-bath rub. A nail file—she rejected that; not enough of it to grip, not enough edge. Hair spray? Perhaps. But under the hair spray, in the drawer . . . She crossed the room in one silent bound, pulled the drawer open and felt for the long, thin bladed scissors she used to trim her bangs, eyes warily fixed on the darkened bedroom.

She moved then, before she could let herself think again, convince herself he stood there waiting.

How had he got in? She set that aside to think about later—if there *was* a later—came across the bathroom and leaned into the bedroom.

She half-expected to come face to face with him right then; there was no one in sight. No one in the open, at least: the light spilling from the open bathroom door illuminated most of the bedroom. She stepped into the bedroom, set her back against the wall, eyes darting from dresser to closet to bed, back again. She shivered; the bedroom window was open, curtains blowing in, cold air flowing across the floor and chilling wet, bare legs and feet. The living room—worry about it next. Her clothes were no longer on the bed, the closet door was open and the shirt she'd hung on it on the floor.

He could be anywhere except within easy reach of her. She moved one careful sidestep at a time to the bedside table. Her night vision was coming back after the brilliance of the bathroom lights—there was something on her pillow that hadn't been there: a cellophane-wrapped bouquet of long-stemmed roses.

Not my imagination, then. Her knees wanted to buckle; she couldn't let them now. She looked away from the roses with a shudder and fumbled for the ring on the drawer under the lamp, tugged it open.

The handgun that should have been there was gone.

Vincent had remained on the roof after she left; it was not sensible, Father would have lectured him for it and even Catherine would have protested. And he had promised both of them. But he couldn't leave; he'd tried. Even with his own life depending on it, he couldn't desert her. He sensed her tension and anger, her despair as she stood on her terrace. He could have seen her if he'd looked over the wall; he stayed hidden and assured himself that he was holding to at least a part of the promises he had made. He waited, knowing she was inside her apartment, locked in. Safe.

Or so he thought and hoped, until he became aware of the presence there—a sneaking, furtive and nervous presence. Surely not with her—but her sudden breathless horror told him otherwise. He had stood irresolute for one long moment, until the burst of terror decided him; he went down the fire escape ladder that led from the roof down to her terrace. Two rungs from the tiled deck, he stopped, let his head rest against the metal ladder, and concentrated, hard. This man who stalked her—he could not tell where the man was now, only that he had fled. Catherine was alone in her apartment, left with her fear and the shadow of the fear of the man who had been in there with her.

Vincent dropped down the two steps onto the terrace, stopped again, irresolute. If he went to her now, she'd worry about him rather than herself. She had so much to think about just now, he dared not distract her or add to her fears. If he simply watched, and waited—so long as he remained on her terrace, in her world and not between hers and his, surely this man could not trace him, could not discover the remainder of Vincent's secret.

He let his head down into his hands and leaned back against the wall. To feel so helpless, unable to do anything to protect her!

Cathy pulled the drawer all the way out, knowing it was no use. The gun was gone. *He* had it. But was he still here, ready to threaten her with it, to use it on her? She let the hand with the scissors down to her side, hiding the makeshift weapon in a fold of terry cloth, and froze. Someone in the living room, something moved in there!

Before she could let herself be afraid again, she moved with purpose, striding barefoot across the carpet, down the two steps. The French door drapes were pulled aside, letting moonlight and city lights stream in, partly lighting the room; a window was open, it was the curtains she had seen moving. The living room was empty, unless someone crouched behind the chair—and when she made herself move to look, there was no one there.

And something else: movement at the outside door caught her attention. It was the brass chain swinging gently back and forth.

The high-pitched double beep went off just behind her and she nearly screamed, spun around in a low crouch, scissors out and ready to maim. No one. In the uncertain blue-white light, it took her a moment to see the cheap multifunction digital watch lying on her mantel.

Seventeen

FOR one terrible moment, she thought she'd be sick; one fist pressed against her stomach, just under the ribs. The other she stuffed hard against her teeth and bit, concentrating on the pressure of teeth against skin until the moment passed. The scissors, she realized rather dazedly, were still clutched in white-knuckled fingers.

A faint sound—oh, *God*, did she hear it or imagine it?—outside the French doors; she was partway around, scissors out and ready. Another, much more definite at the front door, forced a little airless shriek out of her as she spun back. But that was a knock. That—*he* wouldn't knock, would he? "Who is it?" she demanded, and the high, thin voice scarcely bore any resemblance to hers— it filled the living room and made her skin crawl.

"It's me—Joe!" She'd already realized by the time he named himself who it was; no mistaking that voice. It took her a moment to get her feet to move, though, and by the time she got the light switch on, the door open, he had his arm up to hit the door panels again.

He was looking at her with concern. She pressed past

him to look up and down the hall. "Did you see him?" She could see nothing save a length of white-walled, neatly carpeted apartment hallway, heard nothing but the muted grumble of the elevator—probably on the return journey from bringing Joe to her floor. But he had to be out there, where could he have gone? "He was just here—!"

She had never been so grateful for intelligence and quickness in a friend: Joe's eyes narrowed as he cast one glance into her apartment before turning back to scan the hall as she was doing, "Who?"

"Him!" she panted. "He was just in here!"

No trivial comments about her robe, no pointless inquiries about her health, nerves, state of mind: with no one in sight in the hallway, he turned and caught at the stairwell door. Cathy grabbed him before he could get through it. "No!" It took all her strength to hang onto his arm long enough to get him to listen. "No—don't! He has my gun!"

He turned back, looked at her blankly, let the door close behind him as he hurried her back into the apartment. "Did he hurt you?" She shook her head. "Did you see him?" She shook it again, caught hold of the back of her couch and watched him close and lock the door. Movement at the French doors brought her head up and she nearly shrieked again; but the shadow she saw out there was familiar, welcome. Vincent edged forward enough to make certain she was all right, to be sure she could see him out there before he retreated into deep shadow.

Cathy looked back in Joe's direction, but he had been so intent on the locks he hadn't seen anything. Relief weakened her momentarily. Joe turned from the door, looked around until he located the phone and headed for it, jaw set as though he expected argument from her.

She squared her shoulders. "What are you doing?"

He scowled at her and turned back to the phone. "You know what I'm doing."

"No—!" She didn't have enough strength to cross the room at the moment, let alone fight him for the receiver, and the look on his face told her he'd win anyway.

"Yes," he overrode her flatly. "I'm not waking up to a call that says this guy got to you."

Got to me, she thought weakly, and suddenly she wanted to laugh. *As if he hasn't already got to me!* She became aware of the scissors still in her right hand, of the fact that she was standing in her living room in a terry robe and nothing else, that her wet hair was streaming cold runlets down her back. *Class, Chandler,* she told herself. *Real class. Get some clothes on before the cops come, why don't you? Greg Hughs has a big enough mouth without something to feed it.*

Thought of Hughs coming on her like this—her and Joe like this, however innocently—was enough to put muscle back into her legs. Joe looked up from his call as she moved, nodded when she gestured with her head toward the bedroom and tugged at the robe's collar. He turned his back on her as he began speaking into the receiver and she ran for the bathroom.

Vincent moved once more where he could see into the room, just in time to see Cathy go to change. The man there—the one she worked with. Joe. He would see she was safe, just now. Vincent stepped back, melting into shadow, heading once more for the roof. It was all he could do for her, save to be out of the way for a while. There would be police, they'd search the patio, the roof, the surrounding area. The stairs. Perhaps they'd catch the man. At the moment, he still feared much less for himself than for her.

He climbed steadily, thoughtfully, and came out onto the roof. North. He'd go north. There were pipes there, another roof—a jump and a climb both, unlikely the police would believe anyone could manage the distance and the nearly sheer wall. He'd be near, still, if she needed him.

Once out of harm's way, he sat where he could watch the roof of her building. What had happened to frighten her so? Perhaps later, he would dare go to her. He would wait, in any case.

* * *

It was cool in the park; the grass was damp with late dew, the air under the trees chill with oxygen. He touched the little porcelain box and made certain it was still deep in his pocket; reaching inside the jacket, then, unsnapping one of the breastbone-height snaps to touch his shirt and then the object that now lay inside his plaid shirt, next to his bare chest. Soft cotton and lace, tiny buttons . . . He smiled, and increased his pace. Let her think she had won this round, women needed to think they won, now and again. It would soften her toward him; and he would win, in the end.

She would come to him . . . perhaps even tonight, she would come to him. If he did not go to her. Either way, he must be ready.

She'd thrown on her heavy gray sweatpants and a mauve knit shirt, pulled on heavy white gym socks and sneakers. Her hair had mostly dried by the time Greg Hughs pounded on the door and now it was entirely dry. She'd have to get it wet again and condition it; the ends were flying everywhere. She'd run a comb and her hand through it once the shirt was buttoned and tucked in, barely glanced in the mirror at her white, drawn and unmade face, gone to sit on the couch. She still sat there, watching the fingerprint man dusting the Lucite lipstick holder and a couple of the brass tubes.

Joe had gone through the apartment an item of furniture at a time as soon as he got off the phone—touching little or nothing, looking intently at everything. He'd gone onto the terrace, and she'd held her breath until he came back, clearly having found nothing. No one.

But he wouldn't have stayed there, she assured herself. *Vincent—he must have heard Joe arguing with me, must have heard him calling the police. But he'd have seen them arrive; he's long gone by now.*

She considered that, remembered the intensity of her terror when she heard the lipstick holder go over, leaving her naked and scared half to death in her shower. Maybe he wouldn't be gone.

Joe had done more than call police and search her violated home; he'd also got hold of a twenty-four-hour locksmith he knew to come and change the locks on the outer door, install a third bolt, add another lock to the terrace. The locksmith had shaken his head over the terrace doors, his face showing that a determined attacker could simply kick them in with no effort at all. The regular door wasn't that much better; strong locks, lousy door frames—what good was that? But in deference to the stricken-faced young woman huddled on the couch, he said nothing, merely added a push bolt to the French doors and went to work on the front one.

I should get my purse, Cathy thought dully. *I can't let Joe take care of this*. But she watched without much interest as he pulled out his wallet and stuffed several twenties in the man's hand. The locksmith ran a hand through thick black hair, shoved the cap back over it and handed Joe three new brass keys on a wire. "It's a good lock. I don't think she'll have any problems." She continued to watch as he stood aside and let Joe try all three keys in the extra deadbolt, watched as the locksmith caught up his toolbag and left.

Movement to her left: she turned her head as Hughs came down from her bedroom, slapped his notebook shut. He grinned; Cathy thought he intended to be reassuring but, being Greg, he just exuded "don't upset the little woman, you know how they are." She thought of some of the more picturesque things Edie called him, and almost smiled. "Okay," he said, and expelled his breath in a loud rush. "I think we've got everything we're going to get tonight."

No fingerprints, then, she thought. Figured. This guy was too damned clever to be caught that way. Too good—God, what a word for it!—at what he did. Joe got heavily to his feet and walked the two policemen over to the door. "Did you find anything?" He didn't sound like he expected it; didn't look disappointed when Hughs shook his head.

"No. It looks pretty clean." He cast her a furtive glance, saw she was watching him and gave her a smile

243

that was almost sympathetic. "If we do get lucky on any of the prints, it won't be until late tomorrow," he said.

Joe caught his arm, stopping him on his way out. "If you do come up with something, I want the information to go directly to Cathy. If you can't find her, then to me. No one else."

Can't find—dammit, was he talking in euphemisms? She could feel irritation pushing aside the depression and lassitude that had gripped her for what seemed hours. Hughs looked at Joe, glanced at her, frowned, finally nodded. "Sure."

"Thanks, Greg," she managed.

"You want a cop outside?" He was asking Joe, not her; she forestalled both men with a firm shake of her head. Joe pulled the door open, let the fingerprint cop out and followed the detective into the hall. She wasn't certain she heard Hughs correctly, muttering against Joe's ear as he was—she wouldn't put it past him to use the old line about "Can't live with 'em, can't live without 'em." It didn't seem worth her while to call him on it. Besides, he was doing her a favor, keeping this quiet— but that reminded her.

"Greg?" she said, raising her voice over Joe's thanks, Greg's last remarks as she came over to the front door. He stuck his head back inside, looked at her inquiringly. "I owe you a favor. Don't file a report, okay?"

She could see "what the hell" all over his face and thought he'd tell her flatly no. She shook her head, smiled, and he shrugged.

"Okay," he said, and left.

Joe didn't follow them; she hadn't thought he would. *God, I can't handle any more tonight*, she thought wearily. *And I really can't handle a mother hen*. And Joe had on his best mother-hen face when he turned back to face her. "Thanks," she said, and hoped it sounded like "Thanks and good night."

If it did, he wasn't listening; he started for the couch she'd just deserted with the look of a man in search of comfort. "So, what's on TV tonight?"

She caught him halfway there and turned him back

toward the door, actually managed to push him two steps in that direction before he dug his heels in. He ignored the jacket she'd grabbed up to hand him. "Nothing is on," she said flatly.

"Radcliffe—"

"Thanks for checking up on me."

He folded his arms and glared down at her. "I'm not leaving. I'm sleeping right there, on that—" He turned to look at her sofa in sudden dismay, turned back to grin at her ruefully. "—on that little—short—dinky couch."

She shook her head so hard the hair whipped around her face. "Oh, no, you're not!"

"Yes, I am," he said angrily.

"No, you're not!"

There was an ugly little silence. "Why not?" he demanded.

She looked up at him stubbornly. "I have my reasons."

"Look." He sighed. "Whatever it is, Cathy, we can get you out of it!"

Away from the weirdo, he meant. But all that was between her and turning the weirdo in—all, she thought despairingly—was Vincent. Vincent, his secret, their secret—his world. "No, we can't," she said even more firmly. He looked at her for a very long time, and she could see the purpose and the anger dying out of him, leaving him uncertain and frustrated. He knew he was fighting something and he couldn't figure out what, or how to deal with it.

Finally he shook his head. "Okay. Lock your door." He held out the keys and put them in her hand with a flourish. "Put a chair in front of it. Hell—" He grinned weakly, and something warmer than mere concern for a colleague was briefly in his face. "—put one of your couches in front of it!"

She took the keys, waited patiently for him to get the door open, himself outside. "Good-bye. Good night."

He stopped and pointed a finger at her. "Lock it!" he said. She knew he was still there, waiting to hear her turn the deadbolt and the old lock, slide the brass chain across. She in turn stayed right where she was until she could hear his retreating footsteps—pressure and the faintest creak of floorboards under thick carpet; the distant noise of elevator doors closing behind him. Gone. She let the door serve as a backguard while she looked around her living room.

She'd bought that couch—that "little dinky couch" over a year before; the table next to it had been her mother's, from the summer place. The entire apartment was furnished that way: the bed set hers from the Long Island place and warmly familiar; the dining table and four blond maple chairs new within the month. The vase on the mantel had come from a weekend upstate, three years before—an estate sale, like the matched set of coffee mugs on her top shelf.

Familiar things—things she'd grown up with, things she'd found and loved and wanted enough to have. She looked at them now as if she had never seen them before. A stranger had come into this room, moving silently across her darkened living room, touching her couch, running his hand along her wall, taking off his watch to set there before he skirted the dining table— she couldn't think about it anymore, it really would make her ill.

She had never realized before how truly people spoke, when they said a robbery made them feel violated. This—this was worse. He'd been through her clothing, touching her garments . . .

"Stop it," she ordered herself aloud, and forced herself to move from the false security of the door against her back. She went through the living room, into the kitchen and resolutely got down a large mug and a tin of Earl Grey tea.

Vincent stayed where he was, on the next roof over. There had been one uniformed policeman with a businesslike flashlight; he'd gone over the roof of Catherine's building thoroughly but quickly, as though he didn't expect to find anything or anyone, barely glanced at the other buildings, gauged the distances between them, shook his head and left.

She was alone, down there. He could feel her restlessness, knew the fear she tried to stifle. He shifted, let his weight sink back onto his heels. He could cross to her roof once more, go down the ladder—but he had promised her he would stay away. He clutched at his head. The man who watched could not know who he was or where he came from—but he dared not risk that was a certainty. She would be the first one to say so.

And others watched her also tonight, whether she wanted it or not. Police; the man Joe. He let out a held breath with a sigh, and suddenly felt terribly tired, unbearably depressed. How long could this continue? How much longer could he bear to leave her in her own misery and terror before he must go to her, no matter what the cost?

Her small gold watch lay next to the telephone; she'd been suddenly unable to bear the feel of cool metal against her skin, as though she were feverish. She'd last looked at it at eleven forty-five; she thought perhaps half an hour had gone by. Hard to tell from where she sat—in the dark, the balcony doors closed, the drapes pulled tight across them. She'd tugged them away from the glass, down near the handle—enough to press her high-resolution bird-watching binoculars up against the window. The scissors lay under her chair, the heavy brass poker propped in the angle between the chair seat and the back.

She'd been staring through the binoculars for what felt like hours; it was dark out there, those few windows she could see into showed nothing, except once a very overweight young woman in a bright yellow leotard dancing by herself. She'd jerked sharply, pulling the lenses away, and it had taken her several minutes to bring them back up to her face—to a face flushed with the shame of having spied on a fellow human being, a woman who thought herself safe from such watchers.

He was out there; he must be out there where she

could see his windows, if only she knew where to look! She could still hear him, that whispery, resonant voice: "I can see you. Hi."

The binoculars fell from nerveless fingers, rapping hard against her shin, and she swore feelingly. It was just the elevator. This time of night, she could hear it groaning up the shaft. But she sat frozen in place, hand reaching for bruised skin, listening with every pore of her body. The elevator went on to the top floor, stopped there briefly; she heard the doors clomp shut, heard the machine easing its slow way down to the main floor. It did not stop, as she'd almost expected it would.

She picked up the binoculars by the strap, pulled them onto her lap, and sat, eyes closed, quietly breathing, until her fingers were steady enough to hold them again.

Across the park, in an equally darkened apartment, the man moved away from his brother's telescope, lips set in a hard, thin line. She was there, she must be there. He'd seen the French door curtains shift not long ago. Nothing since. Dark apartment, dark windows, drapes pulled back into place. She had not taken his hint, had she? Why did she think he'd left the curtains to her terrace and bedroom flung wide? Stubborn—women could be so stubborn, he must cure her of that. She must learn to pay attention when he showed her what he wanted.

He walked into the living room, glanced down at the coffee table and smiled. The white camisole gleamed in the faint light coming from the half-closed bathroom door. He picked it up, held it against his face as he walked into the bathroom, set it on the counter. The little porcelain box sat next to the sink, next to a bottle of clear liquid and a thick square of white flannel. He uncapped the bottle; the cloying smell of chloroform wrinkled his nose. Ether might have been better—but the source that got him names when he wanted them, phone numbers to go with addresses—the source wasn't as good at getting pharmaceuticals. He folded the flannel into a heavy pad, drenched it with chloroform and stuffed it into a self-sealing plastic bag, the bag into his jacket pocket. Easy to get at and get free, if there was any need for it. There still might not be. He'd give her time. Some women needed time.

He recapped the bottle, left the door open to air the room, shut off the light and went back through the living room. Perhaps she'd opened her curtains. It couldn't hurt to look.

She turned her watch face-down, unwilling to keep looking over and see the hands seemingly stopped. She'd managed to get the cup of tea down and now it sat in her stomach uneasily. She had hesitated for a long time before turning on the table lamp that illuminated the end of the couch. She felt exposed, sitting under its dim light, even with the doors and windows locked. *He's out there.* The thought came back every few moments, despite her best efforts to quell it.

She'd been absolutely unable to climb into her bed; she couldn't see the doors from her bed, and it was utterly essential she be able to see the terrace doors, the locks on the front door. She'd finally dragged the comforter off the bed, brought out all her pillows and stuck them behind her back so she could see the doorknob over the back of the couch. It had taken even more courage to kick off her shoes; and now she had her feet up on the sofa, she wasn't certain she could bear to put them on the floor again. Something might be there, under the sofa, waiting, ready to touch her. . . .

"Stop that," she ordered herself. Ridiculous; a thought like that ought to be enough to break the spell and leave her giggling. She'd never felt less like laughing in her life. She sat bolt upright on the couch, listening to the furtive little sounds her apartment made at night. How had she ever slept here, the way the coolant in her refrigerator hissed after the motor shut off, the clock over the mantel ticking—how had she never realized the shower dripped, the sound magnified by the ceramic tiles? She started as the elevator started up again, as someone down in the street gunned a car, a siren howled in the distance. She fought that, fought to relax against the pillows, but her face was hot against chill percale and her stomach knotted with dread almost immediately as a helicopter clattered over her building and hovered over the park. She could see white light through the heavy curtain. "Open the drapes." She started; but the voice was in her mind.

"I like the red sweater . . ." "No!" she said aloud, and swallowed, clutching at the back of the sofa with both hands. Had that been a sound in her bedroom? She held her breath but her heart was thudding so hard, so loudly, she couldn't be certain what she'd heard. If she'd heard.

She slipped cautiously from under the quilt, slid one foot at a time silently onto the floor. Got herself upright, somehow got herself to move. She hesitated for a long time outside the bedroom, finally leaped for the light switch and threw it up.

There was no one, nothing there. She had known, really, that there would be nothing. She forced herself to look inside the bathroom, the closet, behind the dresser even though a child couldn't have fit there. Under the bed. She switched off lights behind her and stopped on the top step, gazing down into her dimly lit living room. Her fortress. "God," she whispered. Dawn must be a month away; she'd already endured a week of this night.

Tea, she decided. Not Earl Grey this time, though; one of those herb ones Jenny'd given her, that fancy assortment. One of them was supposed to have soothing things in it. If ever there was a time for such a thing, this had to be it.

She shut off the kettle before it could let out the high-pitched whistle, filled the pot. The stuff smelled a little odd, but not bad; it was full of tiny yellow flowers, leaves. *Bark and twigs*, she'd told Jenny when she'd first brought the box over. Jenny'd just laughed.

There was an unfinished paperback on the counter; the spy thriller someone had told her she simply *had* to read. At the time she'd been vaguely amused by the plot; it didn't seem to have much basis in reality and the writer didn't know a damn thing about law. But tonight she didn't want anything too realistic. She poured a cup of pale brown tea, sniffed gingerly and shrugged, picked up the book and started back to her sofa-nest.

And stopped, cold, in the doorway, fingers closing on the handle of the cup. She let the book fall unnoticing; someone was out in the hall! Someone moving across the light that normally came under her front door. ... Before she could move, she heard her neighbor's deep, husky voice murmuring, "This way, that's not my place." A woman's low, rather embarrassed-sounding laugh. Andrew from down the hall, bringing home another one, she thought, and managed a rueful grin. Some people never did learn. The smile faded as she bent to pick up her book. She'd left the living room for just a minute and someone had come along to stand outside her door; she hadn't even heard the elevator from her task in the kitchen. Hadn't heard anything. If it had been—had been *him*— Now all she could hear was Jenny's earnest voice as she sipped at Jenny's supposedly soothing chamomile tea, Jenny's whispered "You *died*, Cathy."

Vincent had moved back onto her roof and now sat with his back to the little shack that contained the elevator equipment, next to the door that opened onto the emergency stairs. He still fought the urge that wanted to send him down those stairs; to go down the fire ladder to her terrace. To go to her. She was so afraid, still; he could not bear to know her fear and know he could not ease it. But he had promised her; and she was strong. She could deal with her own fear. So she said.

Vincent let his head fall back, looked up into the night sky as a plane went over, on a downward trajectory that would bring it into Kennedy Airport. He would stay where he was; he would keep his promises. But he would not go away from her. If she needed him, he had to be there for her.

* * *

Blue-white light stabbed down through tree branches; the tan jacket would catch light, they'd see him! He fell back against a thick, moss-clad trunk and waited until the helicopter moved on. Light shone on the Reservoir, moved across still water, followed the path which came out eventually on Fifth Avenue, with occasional forays into the dark on either side of the path. He smiled crookedly as the police copter flew slowly away from him. It was an omen; things were going just the way he wanted them to. She would be waiting for him.

The tea mug was empty; the taste hadn't been bad but her mouth felt coated, and she decided against a second cup. It hadn't soothed her nerves noticeably, but that was probably a lot to ask of an over-the-counter hot beverage. At least it hadn't twisted her stomach like the regular tea had. She had the book open on her knees, the cover wrapped around her legs. She'd turned three pages since she sat back down, but she couldn't remember any of it. Words swam on the page; they were less real than the ones in her mind.

Had she heard that voice before? Was that why he'd whispered into the telephone? But he hadn't whispered that last message: "Why aren't you there? You're with him, aren't you?" She brought her eyes away from the page, stared toward her feet. It had just sounded like— like any ordinary man's voice. Except for what he said. "Of course you're with him. Why do I even ask? Whore!"

It still wanted to make her ill: in all her life, no one had ever called her that. No one had ever spoken to her like that. As though he owned her: as though she were a thing, property. Her head came up, she looked sharply at the locked and bolted door. Was that roses she smelled? Damn Jenny and her dream, flowers all over the place, she'd said, and then that bouquet. She'd let the police take the bouquet that had rested on her bed earlier, but even then she hadn't been able to smell anything where they'd rested. True hothouse ones, fortunately, barely scented. She wondered how she would have been able to handle it if they'd been fragrant like the ones at work . . .

Roses—flowers everywhere. *And I died.* She couldn't think, dammit! All she could hear was Jenny's voice, Joe telling her about people like that who killed—that man's insidious voice. She let the book fall, drove both hands through her hair. It couldn't be past two in the morning; suddenly the thought of sitting on this couch for four or more hours, just like this, pretending to read—watching the door, waiting for a shadow to cover most of the hall light, for the knob to turn—oh, God, no!

Out, she thought suddenly. "I've got to get out of here," she whispered, and the words stung her to action. She threw the cover aside so hard it slid over the back of the sofa and slithered to the carpet, carrying the paperback with it; she pulled her shoes over, jammed her feet into them and tied them, grabbed up the jeans jacket from the hook near the door, patted the pockets for her spare keys. Car keys, door keys—she hooked one of the new keys onto the ring by its metal twist, threw the other two onto the table next to the door, turned the old knobs and the stiff, new one. Eased the chain free gently, so it wouldn't rattle, and yanked the door open.

The hall was empty. She turned back and locked the door, pleased to see her hands were suddenly very steady indeed, walked down to the elevator and pressed the down button, stood back to wait. She could hear the machinery start up overhead, hear the cables groaning down the shaft. A glance at the red LED number between the up and down buttons showed it was coming slowly up from the third floor.

She moved up almost to the door, stuffed her hands in her jacket pockets, let her eyes fix blankly on the brushed metal door, waited. God, it was a slow thing! And now it was stopped on fifteen . . .

Stopped. All the fear she had left behind in her apartment fell on her, wrapping around her heart painfully; she stumbled back from the elevator door. Who was getting off—or on? *He* was there, in that car, in a moment it would stop, he'd step out and his hands would wrap around her. . . . She fell back another step, turned and fled.

Apartment—no! She couldn't go there, he'd be waiting—panic buried rational thought, left her panting for air, her vision swimming as she caught hold of the stairway door; by the time it thudded shut behind her, she was halfway down the steps, headlong, to the next floor. The elevator stopped at twenty-one, metal slamming against metal as the brakes took, as the doors opened. She would have been greatly surprised—and very irritated—to see Joe, enormous take-out coffee cup in one hand, an open magazine in the other, come out of the car and head purposefully for her apartment. Would have been rather touched and even more irked to watch him spread out on the little wrought metal table outside her door, taking over the chair next to it, settling in to watch. And wait.

Her hands hurt from catching herself on the heavy iron railings; her knees ached from the speed of her flight. The panic that had filled her above was growing by the moment, until there was only here and now, this echoing, white-walled tube, metal stairs: twelve and a landing, twelve more, a landing, a door. And on down, twenty-one floors' worth.

She had to stop outside the door marked "10" for breath; her lungs ached, her throat was raw from dragging in cold air. Her heart thudded wildly. She held onto the railing, rested her hot forehead against its cool length momentarily—but only momentarily. A furtive sound brought her upright: someone had opened a door up there—how far above her, she couldn't tell. And there were footsteps, steps that sounded like someone moving with stealth. They came down, and she found herself counting breathlessly: twelve, a pause, three more, twelve. A door opening and closing softly.

Him? A tenant? But only one floor, and at this hour? She shook her head, fought for air and kept going.

* * *

Vincent was on his feet, the open door to the roof in his hands; he stood irresolute between the landing and the roof, listening. Where was she going? And why?

Joe swore as coffee sloshed and a little spilled out the air holes and over his fingers. Damned stuff was hot. He set it aside, shifted in the little uncomfortable chair— they were made for those damned tiny fifteenth-century French nobles, not real people, he thought grumpily, and laid the magazine face-down on the table. He glared at the door not five feet away. Damned stubborn woman, he didn't care about her personal life—sure he didn't—but he was damned if she was going to sit in there and play target for some sick wacko! He sat up straighter, leaned forward to listen. Her phone was ringing. One, two—he frowned. Hadn't she set it on the machine when he left? Couldn't remember. But it was still ringing, and she wasn't answering.

Something wrong. "Dammit, woman," he muttered and jumped to his feet. Seven, eight—still ringing. Something was *very* wrong.

The stairs weren't very well lit at this hour; a bulb had burned out on the fourth-floor landing and she'd panicked again, absolutely certain *he* had taken it out so he could hide there, waiting for her. Somehow she'd managed to force the thought away, to assure herself he couldn't know what she'd done or where she had gone. "You're safe, Chandler," she whispered breathily. Her tennies made no noise down here, where the stairs were concrete instead of metal. Altogether she made little enough sound that she had no difficulty hearing the creak high above her. Door—was it a door opening? Someone there? She stopped short, held her breath and tried not to think about the pain that was a hot band around her chest, the twin agonies of her knees, the right ankle that had turned under her somewhere around the fourteenth floor.

Silence. Silence, except for her harsh breathing, and

the faint scrape of shoe against concrete when she
started down once more.

Her phone was still ringing: thirteen, fourteen. Joe
tapped against the door and shouted: "Cathy? Radcliffe?"

If she was there, she'd have heard him; fifteen, six-
teen. Only an idiot would stand where he was, was he
going to knock politely next? The new lock might be
good but the door was a joke and so was the jamb: he
backed up and brought up his right leg in the one good
karate kick he knew. The door slammed against the wall,
almost back into him as he ran into the room. The light
was on; a dim little thing with a dark shade, just enough
to let him see the room was empty. He stopped uncertainly. "Cathy? It's Joe!"

She wasn't in the bedroom; the bathroom was slightly
damp from her earlier shower, as empty as the rest of
the apartment. He bared his teeth; the damned phone
was *still* ringing. If it was that bastard, he'd be sorry he
ever . . . He came across the living room in two enormous
strides and scooped it up. "Hello?"

Silence, which he'd expected. Then: "Who is this?"
in a woman's strained voice—which he hadn't.

"Who's this?" he demanded harshly in turn.

"Jenny." If she was surprised to find him there, it
didn't show.

"Jenny, it's Joe. Do you know where Cathy is?"
Damn-fool thing to ask, he knew as soon as the words
were out.

"No!" Jenny replied tightly. "But—she's in trouble."
He held the receiver away from his ear and scowled at
it. *Lady, you are telling me,* he thought sourly. "Get over
here, she needs you," he snapped and dropped the
receiver with a clatter. He ran back into the hall then,
and found himself praying that was true: that she was
still alive to need anyone.

Down, all the way down. Cathy hesitated only briefly
at the main floor. That brightly lit lobby, the relatively

dark street beyond it—if he was waiting for her out there, he'd see her without any problem at all. Just the empty, lit lobby, just the thought of it—she couldn't step out there. She clutched her keys and ran the rest of the way down, past the door to the basement, on to the underground parking and her car. *License—I didn't bring my wallet*, she thought confusedly. It didn't matter. Thought of getting a ticket for driving without a license, to get away from that man, from certain death by her own gun—it was almost funny. Too bad she didn't have enough air left to laugh.

She'd laugh later, once she was inside her locked car, on the street, driving away from this building.

It was chilly in the garage; she pushed the stairway door open and stood in the draft, irresolute. All those cars, the dimly lit concrete cavern . . . She swallowed, caught up the tatters of her nerve in both hands and stepped into the open.

He was there, behind the door, waiting. The single footstep came up behind her to close the distance between them and his square-fingered hands came around her, catching her close, dragging her back against him.

Opposite the door marked with a large "10," Vincent halted, aware she had stopped here, still uncertain whether he was doing the right thing in following her: her terror shook him, screamed through his mind as the garage-level door closed behind her and her enemy. It brought him upright and sent him flying down the steps, cloak sailing behind him as though he were truly winged.

Eighteen

Iғ he'd remained silent, she might have stayed frozen, locked in her terror; but when she made no effort to break free of him he leaned into her and began whispering against her ear. At first, she could make no sense of the words, so strong her horror of his touch. Words sorted themselves out: he was cursing her, calling her unspeakable names, railing at her in a voice that hissed and sprayed little drops of spittle onto her ear and neck. Fury broke the paralysis; she threw her weight back into him, jabbed with first one elbow and then the other.

But he was unexpectedly strong for the size of him; he evaded her blows, sidestepped the kick she aimed at his shin and dug both hands into the nerves just above her elbows. Before she could counter, he went under her arm, caught her by the throat and slammed her into the wall, knocking the wind from her. His weight was against her, then, pinning her against the wall, his grip tightened on her throat, fingers digging hard into the hinges of her jaw. The white cloth flashed across her line of sight and clamped down hard on her nose and mouth. His voice was full strength now, his eyes blackly boring into hers. "You're going to him, aren't you? I knew you would. You'll go to him but you won't come to me!" The words bludgeoned her, they followed her down an echoing, black tunnel. "No more," he said. "No more." She heard nothing else.

High above her, Joe turned back in the apartment door to look at the room behind him: he had to make a choice, anything might help him. Cathy was gone but the couch was warm where she'd been sitting, the tea in the bottom of the mug above room temperature. She hadn't been gone long. And since he'd come up in the elevator, and not all that long ago—what, five minutes? He turned and caught at the door angled away from hers; leaving her broken door swinging behind him. The stairwell echoed with running footsteps; not all of them, he realized grimly, were his.

She didn't completely lose consciousness, but she couldn't move—not when he picked her up in a horrid travesty of a lover's embrace, not even when she felt his hands in her pockets or felt him taking her keys. He carried her a short distance; she heard keys turning a lock, felt the familiar fabric of her car seat, the faint scent that marked it as hers—a compounding of car, the cleaner her garage used, her favorite cologne. The door closed, shutting her in—*passenger door* she thought blankly. Consciousness faded, so she wasn't aware of anything for several moments: somehow, *he* was in the seat next to her, the car was running, pulling jerkily back out of her parking place, tires screeching on the smooth concrete. She heard him swear evilly, forced one eye open a slit to see a darkened expanse of garage and then the ramp that led between parked cars to the outside. And Vincent, light touching his teeth as he roared in a hellish fury, frantic to reach her. Her companion gave a low chuckle and tromped hard on the accelerator. The car leaped forward. "No!" She couldn't make any sound at all; couldn't move to grab an arm, the steering wheel, to get her foot under his leg—stop him! "Vincent." Her lips moved, agonizingly slowly; she was never certain after if she saw his body fly over the hood of the car or if she only imagined it. The impact shuddered through her; she couldn't even move enough to turn her head, to see where he was. The squeal of tires filled her ears, her mind, all her thoughts, driving her down under the impact of sound; she felt the jolt as the front tires hit the ramp and started up, then nothing else.

Vincent lay where he found himself, between two red cars, staring glassily at his reflection in a polished hubcap and trying to remember how to breathe. He had seen her, one brief glimpse of a huddled shape in the passenger seat as the car caught him and threw him into the air, sent him rolling to land with bruising force against the wall. Anything broken—he didn't think so. He couldn't let it matter, Catherine was in terrible danger, and it was already too much his fault for not acting sooner. She was gone, he must follow. He had pulled himself onto badly scraped elbows, ready to try and stand, when the door to the stairwell slammed open with enough force to hit the wall. Sound echoed, drowning out the last sound of an automobile screeching up the ramp and out into traffic. He looked up to see Joe, face ghastly white, rocking to a stop, staring toward the exit sign. He whirled, then, and threw himself back into the stairway.

Vincent set his teeth to keep the groan behind them, pushed himself upright and leaned against a car while he ran a quick check of his bones, joints. Nothing broken, except the skin on his palms; his left wrist wouldn't bend and was already swelling but that had to be only a sprain; there was blood and dirt mixed on his sleeves and his back felt raw.

He shook his head to clear it; she was that way, heading north, rapidly. That would help, a little; he settled his cloak back around his shoulders and started for the door Joe had just gone through. Back through her basement, into the tunnels, down to the northbound subway lines: it was late, but there were always trains running. He'd find one, let it take him. Perhaps by the time he had to abandon it and set out on his own two feet, they'd be ready to carry him.

He took his eyes from traffic now and again—it was absurdly light, at such an hour—to glance at her. She slept, curled into the passenger seat, one hand under her head. She slept so beautifully, he thought and smiled at her fondly. So foolish of her to have made it difficult for him—but women so seldom knew what they really wanted. Until the right man told them.

The best way—he considered this as he slowed for a blinking light. It had been a while since he'd driven in the city, and a long time since he'd gone to the lake. Mother'd always taken the George Washington Bridge, unless traffic was bad. And he could see the lights ahead, off to the left. He smiled at his companion and pressed down a little harder on the gas. It would be nice to get to the lake while it was still dark. She'd like the lake, he thought. He'd never brought another woman to the lake since Mother'd died; she'd be flattered when she found that out.

The subway train had taken him miles north; it wasn't far enough, though, and now he could tell the car carrying Cathy had turned, was heading west and gaining speed. He dropped onto darkened track as the car slowed, stepped back into the dark to sort out where he was. He didn't know the tunnels here as well as he ought to, for what he must do now. But—there should be a branch, just a little way back; he'd have to find a way down, then, in order to get under the river.

Catherine. He couldn't speak her name aloud. Could only let it fill him as he sped down steps treacherous with seeping water, as he edged through a passageway in poor repair, pipes buckling into the walking space. *Catherine, be safe. Wait for me, I'm coming!*

He'd been running for what felt like hours; it had been

a long time in fact; through the electrical tunnel under the river, through a maze of wiring tunnels and branched shortcuts that were Underground-made— back when it seemed reasonable and safe to extend their passages. Along an underground stream with muddy banks that changed gradually to gravel and then to slick concrete. He paused there for breath; one hand clinging to a crack between cinder blocks, feet slipping on the bank.

He hurt, and he was tiring; it was beginning to be an effort to breathe. But the car had stopped; she was ahead of him, miles away but at least no longer moving. He crossed the stream and entered a low-ceilinged, shortcut full of crumbling dirt and fallen stone, came out in an abandoned train tunnel, miles from any other. The denizens of Underground weren't the only ones to pull back from overambition. He descended more stairs—what felt like hundreds of them—and found himself facing a tunnel on the verge of collapse. He'd been here once, years before; there had been no purpose even then to keeping this area in good repair and apparently no one had. He looked at the overhead beams, measuringly, then shook his head and plunged on. He must get to her, nothing must stand in the way of that. This—dangerous as it was, it would hold together long enough for him to pass.

She had lost time, too much of it, and now when she let one eye open the least bit it was dark all around: dark and eerily silent. The car no longer moved, the ordinary city sounds she took for granted were missing. *Countryside*, she thought, and her courage failed her. She could be anywhere; even with a city as big as New York, there were isolated places within an hour. Places a body could be left and never found.

"No," she whispered. There was no answer; the man who had brought her here was not in the car. *Gone*, she thought, and the thought gave her momentary hope. But she couldn't move, even when she heard the rustling of footsteps around the car, heard the latch of her trunk release. When he opened the passenger door, she fell limply against him, lay helplessly against his thigh and felt his hands stroking her hair.

He straightened up, then, bringing her partly upright against him, got his arms awkwardly around her and dragged her out of the car. Every muscle protested, knotted in agony as she tried to move, to fight him. The faint odor of gasoline, oil—and incongruously, pine oil. He laid her on a hard surface—the interior of her trunk, she suddenly knew. Something soft under her cheek—a pillow? "No," she whispered faintly; the sound came as she felt his breath against her face, against her lips. She thought he intended to kiss her but after a moment she felt him straighten and pull away from her, muttering angrily to himself. Her fingers scrabbled weakly against the carpeting that lined the trunk, her eyes opened enough to let her see him standing there, outlined in starlight.

"I like it here," he said softly, soothingly. "I used to play here when I was a kid. Now you'll be here, and I'll come visit you."

Oh, God; he was utterly mad; he was going to kill her and no one would ever know where she was. No one except—*Vincent*. "No," she whispered again, and inwardly cursed herself for her fear and her weakness, for whatever he had given her that left her so helpless. She saw his outline move, felt his hand on her hair, and before she could even try to pull away from his touch, he was gone. The slam of the trunk lid reverberated through her bones, hiding the sound of his retreating footsteps.

What would he do to her? She hadn't long to wait for an answer: she heard the ratchet of a released hand brake, felt a jerk as the car lurched forward and began to roll down an incline. The splash as it entered water echoed through the trunk, settled in her stomach like ice.

But that wasn't imagination, that last; she could suddenly feel the chill of water against her hip, soaking into her sweatpants and shoes; the smell of algae and icy lake water was thick in her nostrils.

He stood on the bank, gave a little sigh as the nose of the car slid underwater and watched the vehicle slide forward. For one anxious moment, he wasn't certain it would go in far enough, but it settled, shifted sideways a little and when it stopped, only the back ridge of the trunk and the roof were above water. By midday, it would have slid further, down underwater. They'd never find her; that brute from her terrace would never know where she'd gone. He smiled and hugged himself, then turned away. Behind him as he started to walk off, he could hear a faint hammering, as though someone beat on metal with desperate fists. That was the worst of women, never knowing just what they wanted. But this was the last time she'd have to worry about changing her mind. She was here, here just for him now. She was his.

The water was cold enough to bring her back to sense: she rolled onto her back, bending her neck to keep her head out of the water, tried to bring her legs up to use against the trunk lid. No, oh, no! She couldn't die, not tonight—not like this.

There wasn't room enough to use her legs. She rolled over, gasping as ice water soaked the back of her head, momentarily making her forget everything but the pain it caused. Over—over and up onto your knees, she ordered herself. The trunk was solid, there wasn't any cardboard panel between trunk and backseat like the car she'd seen on some TV show; no escape that way. She hammered wildly on the trunk lid until the noise left her dazed. Water—it was over her legs, creeping past her waist; she slewed around to keep her face in the air pocket at the back of the car, kept her right fingers moving along the ridge where the trunk lid ran around, the left ones scrabbling wildly around her for something to use as a pry. If there was anything, she couldn't remember it—she couldn't feel it. It was utterly black in here, the only sound the gurgle of water coming into the trunk, compressing her precious air bubble. She stopped searching for a tool and began pounding on the trunk again, now beyond rational thought. Now only desperate to free herself.

There was mud all down his side; his boots squelched from the last minutes in that tunnel, where the water had risen to his knees. The walls were greasy with black mud, broken and rusted pipe lay everywhere, rats and other unclean animals ran underfoot. But that was behind him now; he came into clean night air, into utter blackness and crashed through thick brush. She was in terrible danger; he did not dare let himself think how deadly her position. He drew in a deep breath, yanked his cloak free of bushes, leaped across a narrow ravine. His boots scraped on granite; a ledge, he could see now. Below him, surrounded by tall fir trees, a lake—almost a pond, it was so small. He could hear the noises made by small night creatures that lived in such a place. So far away, though!

He skirted tall rock, leaped down to the next level, down again, passed through a tight grove of aspen and went down again, coming out finally on ground that sloped down to the lake. It was rocky here, footing treacherous and he was exhausted beyond bearing. But Catherine needed him. He drew a ragged, pained breath and began to run.

The water stopped coming in when she could feel the chill against her ears. Her face was out of it, the fingers of one hand. But the air was going bad, every breath she took draining the oxygen from it. *I'm going to die.* She could have wept with frustration, but there were no tears in her. She was so terribly, terribly tired. "Vincent," she whispered.

He stopped so suddenly the sodden hems of his cloak wrapped around his shins; exhausted as he was, it was enough to pull him off balance. There was no sound out

266

there, except for the crickets and pond frogs: much nearer now. But the inner ear, the one tuned to her . . . "Catherine." She was so weak; he could feel her breath coming in tiny pants, feel her heartbeat changing to a thin, light patter. He yanked the cloak away from his legs and staggered on.

It caught him by surprise, tearing the last of his strength away: the disorienting sense of her heartbeat pattering above his thudding heartbeat was suddenly gone—a horror of loss poured into him, blackening his vision and driving him to his knees. "No!" The scream tore from his throat; his roar silenced the night sounds.

Silence. His head snapped up as another sound, immediate, cracked across the night: someone had stepped on a branch. He knew at once who was there, who now stood before him. So ordinary-looking a man: tan chinos and a tan jacket, brown hair, a plaid shirt collar sticking out above the jacket. Both hands shoved in the jacket, pouching it out before him. But the look on his face— and the evil that filled him. He stared down at Vincent; this creature, this man who had wanted to keep her from her proper place—it was right that he be here. "Too late," he whispered. "She's *mine*."

Whatever else he intended to say no one would ever know; Vincent's hand caught him between head and shoulder, ripping through jacket, shirt and something small and white under the shirt. The left spun him around the other way, flinging him limp and dying into a tree trunk. Vincent stepped over the broken, bleeding body and into the open.

He could see the roof of her car now; starlight gleamed on the polished metal, sending it back in a shower of broken light. Or perhaps that was his tears.

Nineteen

Dead: the man who had threatened his Catherine was dead. She—he fought dread and a black horror, kept his body moving forward, toward the lake. She must not be dead, he could not face that. His head came up, his pace quickened.

She would not be dead; he would not permit it!

He was running now, down the gentle slope, across grass and smooth ground, into marshy stuff as he came to the water. The car—*her* car—was just in front of him, not that far from shore. He yanked his feet out of gluey mud at the water's edge and waded out, ankle-deep, shook his head in angry frustration and clambered onto a rock that edged into the water, gathered his last strength for one great leap. His boots came down on the roof of the car, and the clangor echoed through metal, across the lake and the silent woods surrounding them.

It had hurt, so terribly: her lungs, her head: the fingers she'd scraped, frantically digging at solid steel, trying

to fight her way from the trunk. The pain faded so gradually, she was not aware of its going, only its absence.
It had been black where she was, the only light pin-
wheels and sparks inside her eyelids, hallucination
caused by lack of oxygen and impending death.

Death. The word rang through her, made no sense,
was gone. She stood in a place neither warm nor cold,
and there was light—there. She came slowly around to
face it, to take a step and then a second. Somewhere in
the back of her mind was chill, green-scented water, a
shallow, terrified panting, cold and black terror; someone in that place whispered "Vincent" as a name, a
prayer—hope that held back the worst of the fear. Someone—she let it slip from her and took another step toward the light.

It should have hurt her eyes, it was so bright; but now
someone stood there, between her and the light—
shielding her. Protecting her. Two people. The two who
had always protected her. "Mother," she whispered,
and sighed as a deep happiness washed through her,
taking the last of the fear, the last black memories with
it.

The automobile was shifting under his feet as though
it might slide off whatever underwater rock or ledge held
it, send it plummeting to the depths; there was no time
for caution, no rational thought left in him, only a certainty that she was there. The trunk: he turned and went
cautiously down onto hands and knees, felt his way back
along the roof and down the glass. As his hands felt
their way, he was whispering, over and over, "Don't
leave me. Please—don't leave me."

It was warm here, peaceful. Utterly silent. She could
remember nothing else; there had been nothing but this
moment. Her throat was tight, her vision blurred and
she blinked tears aside. Her mother—her father waited
for her, and she could not see their faces yet but she
knew they both smiled. Her mother's arms were out-

stretched. "Mother," she whispered, and now she moved readily, eager for that embrace.

The car shifted again, settled into mud and held firm as he braced his feet on either side of the trunk lid, got a purchase under the edge with his nails. Even with his strength, it should have been nearly impossible to break the lock from such an angle, with only his nails. Terror and the blackness that threatened to overwhelm him gave him a strength beyond any he had ever felt: he tore the trunk from its hinges and threw it across the lake. It landed with a splash that echoed from the rocks he'd come down; he heard none of it. His entire attention was fixed on the slender woman curled in on herself, her face just underwater; his hands trembled as they caught her up and he held her close. He could never remember later how he reached shore.

Her own arms were extended, reaching . . . her mother's face, so near, and her father: when had she last seen such peace in her father's eyes? Another moment, and her fingers would touch them, she would be drawn into that loving embrace, forever.

The arms that caught hold of her shoulders were enormous, rough against her skin, and they trembled. They pulled her around, caught her up and close against a rough, padded shirt. She could feel the heart underneath pounding wildly; without conscious thought she closed her eyes to the light, buried her head against the thick shirt and clung to it as though her very life depended upon it.

She had lain so white and still at first; he held her desperately, already breathing life into her as he knelt on the damp grass. He felt the shock of that first convulsed movement, jolted to the core of his being as her lungs drew in air, sucking it from him. Her hands were wrapped in his shirt; he could not have worked them loose even if he had wanted to. Somehow, he managed to bring her up enough to wrap the cloak around her back and shoulders, pulled it around them both so he could warm her now shivering body with his own.

He had to fight not to hold her too tightly, not to hurt her with his own need. She sagged against him, pressed her face against his throat. "Catherine," he whispered.

She tightened her grip on his shirt, hearing what lay behind her name, and responding to it. "I love you," she said simply.

It was nearly an hour later when a frantic Joe Maxwell climbed out of Greg Hughs' car and pushed his way through the mob scene at the edge of the lake; police cars everywhere, red and blue lights flashing across trees and rock, casting weird color and shadow on the now choppy lake; floodlights shining into the woods, up onto ledges, down onto the shoreline. He stopped, staring aghast at the tow truck backed up to the water, at the car being pulled out of it, water pouring from the open doors. Cathy's car. More cars—reporters, an ambulance, another. But the chatter on Hughs' car radio had said she was alive, he reminded himself. It didn't help much; alive could mean almost anything. He caught hold of the nearest uniformed cop. "New York District Attorney's office, where's Cathy Chandler?" he demanded.

"Over there." "There" was the back of an ambulance. Joe fought his way over to it, one part of his mind taking in his surroundings, fragments of conversation: "He has a record, but he's never gone this far before. His license is a New Jersey but he's got a card in the wallet with a Fifth Avenue address; see if that's across the park from her place."

He'd driven over to the Thirty-third Precinct, afraid to take the time to call from her apartment. He'd done that right, at least, there was a call-in from out west of the city limits not long after, people complaining about prowlers at a private lake, and someone had seen a car that sounded like hers. A few minutes later, in Hughs' unmarked car, a radio message came through with a plate number—Cathy's, beyond doubt. Hughs had let

Joe take the radio then, while he slapped the portable light onto the dash and flipped it on.

He had finally put the radio down and stared out the window, willing the already speeding car to go faster.

They'd found her first, huddled wet and dazed on the shore; found the guy minutes later—or what was left of him. Enough for someone to match his face to the face on the driver's license and call him through.

They couldn't think she'd killed him, at least there was that. She couldn't have done that to anyone, no matter what. Wild dogs, someone said; this wasn't exactly a civilized end of the world. Or someone's pit bull, maybe—got loose, but who'd ever admit it?

That wasn't his concern either.

She sat on the back end of the ambulance, wrapped in several layers of dark clothing—someone's sweatshirt, some thick pants, some kind of black wool hooded blanket over all. She looked exhausted, as gray-faced as he'd ever seen her, her hair wet and sending little runnels of water down to stain the sweatshirt. Someone had given her a green plastic thermos cup full of strong coffee and she was sipping at it, eyes closed, answering questions. Or trying to.

He'd been so damned mad at her, he could have strangled her for scaring him like that. He stopped dead in his tracks, anger draining from him. There were lines running from her nose to the corners of her mouth; it drooped, her shoulders sagged and the cup trembled as her hands shook.

"You don't remember how you got out of the trunk?" someone in plain clothes asked. She shook her head. Trunk? Joe let his eyes close briefly and swallowed, hard.

"No." It was an exhausted whisper, didn't sound like her at all. Enough, he thought, and stepped forward.

"Cathy?" She opened her eyes, forced her head up and gave him a wan smile. "Are you okay?" Dumb question, he thought, but she merely nodded. "Are you sure?"

She nodded again. "Can you take me home?"

He came over to lift the empty thermos cup from her

nerveless fingers, wrapped an arm around her shoulders and helped her to her feet, ready to carry her if need be. But with his arm to balance her, she seemed able to walk. "Sure," he replied soothingly, and turned to the cop who'd been questioning her. "New York DA's office, I work with her. You can reach her through Greg Hughs at the New York Thirty-third."

He thought for half a moment the guy would object and he had the arguments ready: she was a victim, not a criminal; the man who'd done this was dead, the details could wait, dammit! But the plainclothes detective looked at Cathy, turned to a fresh page in his notebook, made a note of the address and waved them away.

Hughs was standing just outside the driver's side of his car; he'd turned off the flashing light and taken it off the dash, now stood talking to one of the other cops. Waiting to take them back to New York. Joe looked down as Cathy shivered and pulled the black heavy wool around her shoulders. Odd damned thing; it looked like some kind of cloak. "What is this?" he asked and fingered the hood. She was silent for a moment, then shrugged.

"Someone gave it to me to keep me warm," she said simply. He glanced at the people around the lake: no one he could see looked the type, but it wasn't really important. So long as she was all right. His arm tightened around her shoulders.

He rode in back with her, ear tuned to the radio Greg kept on loud. There didn't seem to be much else to learn; the apartment on Fifth Avenue was leased to a man with the same last name—a brother, perhaps. Someone was going through the steps to get a search warrant for the apartment; the brother was supposedly out of the country but they hadn't been able to get much out of the building supervisor yet.

Cathy lay curled up on the seat, her damp head resting against Joe's knee, and he thought she slept all the way to Central Park West. He woke her when the plain blue car pulled up at the curb outside her building.

She looked a little less haggard, not quite so pale. The sweatpants were too long and baggy, the shirt hung down halfway to her knees. She pulled the black wool from her shoulders once they were in the lobby and he'd called the elevator, folded it into neat thirds and laid it across her arm. She gave him a little smile that warmed her dark eyes as the elevator doors closed. He smiled back, pushed twenty-one. He was still upset with her, but this wasn't the time to berate her. Certainly not the time—if there ever was one—to say "Told you."

She felt the elevator take her up, felt Joe close by, not quite touching her, kept her eyes closed. Odd. She couldn't remember anything after the police came; had no idea how they'd found her. Something—maybe she'd remember later, something about neighbors hearing screams, about trouble at the small lake before. Not important. Vincent had left her only when they saw the lights of the first police car. There'd been lights, then: unfamiliar faces, hands prodding her, radio voices and noises all around; brilliant blue-white lights, cold vinyl against her wet shirt, a stethoscope so cold it made her gasp. Dry clothes, then, thick, oversized cotton garments and the back of the ambulance to herself so she could remove her soaked, ruined sweatpants and shirt. It had been almost more than she could manage, stripping and redressing. She'd felt visible, vulnerable; the least noise made her start, setting off pains and aches in outraged muscles. But it was done, somehow; there was hot coffee then, a pair of heavy socks to envelop blocks of ice that had once been feet.

Endless questions.

And then Joe, who'd taken her from the noise, the prying, who'd given her the dark quiet of the car, who'd asked nothing. She would thank him for that, when she was able to make the words work right, to say it so she wouldn't offend him.

The elevator ground to a stop on her floor; she stepped into the hall, patting herself for keys. There were none, she remembered with a pang; no pockets, no keys.

Gone, somewhere. She slowed at her door, unable to think what she'd do next, how she'd get in.

But the door was already open; she stopped and stared blankly as Jenny stood there, gaping slackly at her. Jenny was so white; she'd never seen Jenny that pale. "You're all right, oh, God, you're all right," she whispered. "I was so scared."

I ought to hug her, to reassure her. She simply couldn't; there wasn't enough strength in her for that. She wasn't certain she could find the energy or desire to touch anyone, just now. Cathy stopped once she was in the room, leaned against the back of her couch. Jenny was watching her, eyes shifting anxiously. "Are you all right? Tell me you're all right."

She nodded, took the easy way out. "I'm fine, fine. Just—just tired." Joe—let him think she simply needed more sleep; she willed him to go, now, take Jenny with him. It was too much of an effort to talk, couldn't they realize that? She heard Joe, thought for one moment he was talking to her; but when she glanced over her shoulder, he was looking at her friend.

"Can you stay with her?" he asked Jenny. Jenny nodded.

"No." Cathy shook her head, got the word out before Jenny could say, "Of course."

"Yes," Joe overrode her flatly and added accusingly, "You scared me, Radcliffe." As though that settled the matter. She had to let that go, too; she couldn't argue with Joe. Jenny might prove easier, particularly if she got rid of Joe first. He had turned back to Jenny again. "What about the door?"

"They're going to fix it tomorrow morning."

He nodded. "Good. I'll leave a cop downstairs."

Door—Cathy frowned. "What happened to my door?"

Joe glanced at her on his way out. "I kicked it in," he said, and pulled it closed behind him. It groaned on warped hinges, and didn't close quite right. Jenny fastened the one lock that would still turn, pulled the chain across.

He ached all over, and the return through abandoned and ruined tunnels seemed endless. He wasn't certain he could climb onto the last car of the subway train but the alternative of walking so many extra miles somehow gave him the strength to pull himself up and hold on. He had to rest a while before he came out of the tunnels under her building and began that last climb.

It took extra caution: there were police in the lobby, a man in plain clothes lounging in front of the building. He evaded them all, and rested again—longer this time—on the roof. The night was nearly gone, the air cool—overly cool where it dried sweat on his forehead.

She had returned; she was there, below him. Alive. He let his eyes close, and gave a deep sigh.

Jenny was hovering anxiously when Catherine came out of the shower, trying not to look as though she were hovering. It was hard to keep the irritation out of her face, out of her voice: it must have been terrible for Jenny, to wait and not know. But he would come soon, if he was not already here; there was no place for anyone else here tonight.

Her friend ran a hand through her curly hair and smiled nervously. "What can I get for you?"

She smiled back, and put all the warmth she had into that, into her words. "Jenny, really, I'm okay," she said gently. "You don't have to stay."

"I know," Jenny said simply. "But I am—no," she added as Cathy tried to speak, "I'm staying. Now, what can I get for you?"

Silence. Cathy finally shook her head. "Jenny. I won't be alone."

It took a moment; they didn't talk about such things, ordinarily—Cathy never did, at least, and she could feel the blood heating her face. The look on Jenny's face was almost comical, when the full meaning of the words sank in. "Oh." She blushed painfully, tried to cover it with a laugh. "Well! What am I doing here?" She came across the living room, took Cathy's shoulders in her hands.

Cathy hugged her and gave her a grateful look.

"Thanks," she said. It took a minute to get Jenny's things together, to assure her one last time she was all right, to get her out the door, get the door closed behind her. By the time the door was shut and she was alone again, Cathy was trembling so hard she found it nearly impossible to refasten the locks. She hit the light switch, plunging the room into darkness, hurried past the bedroom and shut off the light there. Cool air touched her face and she turned.

The terrace doors were open, curtains moving gently in a predawn breeze. Vincent stood there, the city behind him. Waiting for her.

She must have moved; she couldn't remember anything but seeing him and then his arms, clinging to her as desperately as she clung to him. The wool of his shirt rubbed against her cheek, his face was against her damp hair. "I felt you go," he whispered, and his voice shook. "I felt you go—"

She had to try twice before she could speak. The last moments in that trunk—she remembered now, all too clearly. *I died. I was dead.* "Hold me tighter," she said desperately, and felt his hands against her back, the strength of his arms, the slow, strong beat of his heart against her ear. Her hands caught hold of each other around his back, pulling him even closer.

The last days of April were summer-warm; she bought new candles, two new lamps, set them about the terrace. She wore silver tonight, silver with a low summer neckline and short sleeves, silver beads across the bodice that caught the light as she worked the brass match and held the flame to the votive candle before her. It caught, flared, illuminating the strong hands of the one who held it. Vincent smiled down at her, brought the candle up to begin lighting tall white candles in a polished antique silver candelabra. Little individual lights began to chase night away. She lit another votive candle, set the extinguished brass match down, lit two other candles and hesitated. He turned from his task to look at her in concern. There was a sudden tension in her, visible in her eyes as she moved away from the lights to gaze out across the city. "Someone else could be there," she said softly. "Watching."

He set the little candle down and came to stand beside her. "Perhaps."

He never lied to her; she found herself suddenly grateful for that and her smile broke the tension. "We can't be afraid, can we? We can't let that stop us."

"No. This balcony is our window, our vantage point." Another thought occurred to him and he voiced it. "And perhaps, someone behind one of those lights *is* watching. And smiling on us."

It had been exactly the right thing to say; her eyes told him that. "Perhaps they are." She came back across the terrace and picked up her candle once more, moving from surface to surface until the votive was as much a puddle of melting wax as a candle, until the terrace glimmered with firefly-like lights.

She set the little candle down close to the French doors, reached out as Vincent came to her, to wrap an arm around his waist. She leaned her face against his breast, felt his arms warm and reassuring around her. Time ceased to matter: it could have been hours, moments, a lifetime, or no time at all before he stirred and asked softly: "What are you thinking? Are you afraid?"

"No," she said at once. "Not afraid. Just very grateful."

She felt him nod. "We've endured much," he replied. She leaned back in his embrace to look into his eyes.

"Yes. We have." His face so near hers, his eyes looking deeply into hers. He was beautiful; his love made her feel beautiful in a way nothing else in her life ever had. It surrounded her, as hers did him: she never wanted to move again, unless it was to come closer to him. "Whatever happens, from now on—I know we will always endure."